EDWARD MARSTON was born and brought up in South
Wales. A full-time writer for over thirty years, he has
worked in radio, film, television and the theatre. A former
chairman of the Crime Writers' Association, Edward lives
in the Cotswolds with his wife fellow author Judith Cutler.

www.edwardmarston.com

a&b

The Trip to Jerusalem

An Elizabethan Mystery

EDWARD MARSTON

Allison & Busby Limited
13 Charlotte Mews
London W1T 4EJ
www.allisonandbusby.com

First published in Great Britain in 1990.
This paperback edition published by Allison & Busby in 2012.

A CIP catalogue record for this book is available from
the British Library.

10 9 8 7 6 5 4 3 2 1

ISBN 978-0-7490-1023-2

Typeset in 10.5/16 pt Sabon by
Allison & Busby Ltd.

The paper used for this Allison & Busby publication
has been produced from trees that have been legally sourced
from well-managed and credibly certified forests.

Printed and bound by
CPI Group (UK) Ltd, Croydon, CR0 4YY

Dot poenas laudata fides

To Lord Lucas of Ormeley

I know not how I shall offend in dedicating my unpolisht lines to your Lordship, nor how the worlde will censure mee for choosing so strong a proppe to support so weake a burthen, onelye if your Honour seeme but pleased, I account my selfe highly praised, and vowe to take advantage of all idle houres, till I have honoured you with some graver labour.

She was a worthy womman al hir lyve
Housbondes at chirche dore she hadde fyve
Withouten oother compaignye in youthe –
But thereof nedeth nat to speke as nowthe.
And thrice had she been at Jerusalem.

CHAUCER: *The Canterbury Tales*

Chapter One

Enemies surrounded them. Though theatre flourished in London as never before, bestowing vivid entertainment upon the nation's capital and earning daily ovations from large audiences, its practitioners were under constant threat. Acting was a perilous enterprise. Players had to walk a tightrope between fame and oblivion – with no net to soften their fall. They faced the official disapproval of the Lord Mayor and the civic worthies, and endured the outright hostility of religious leaders, who spied the hand of the Devil at work on the stage, and the hand of the lecher, the harlot and the pickpocket moving with licensed freedom among the spectators. Voices of protest were raised on all sides.

Nor could the acclaim of the onlookers be taken for granted. The public was a fickle master. Those who served it with their art were obliged to perform plays that were in vogue, in a manner that was acceptable to their patrons. Indifference was a menace. So indeed were the other theatrical companies. Naked competition was rife. Players could be poached and plays could be pirated. War could be waged between the different troupes in ways that ranged from the subtle to the blatant.

Those who survived all this could still be brought low by fire or by fighting. Tobacco smokers had more than once ignited the overhanging thatch in the theatres, and there was always the risk that drunken spectators would start an affray. If human intervention did not harm or hamper a performance, then bad weather might. Arenas that were open to the sky were vulnerable to each wind that blew and each drop of rain that fell. God in his wisdom washed away countless stabs at theatrical immortality.

But the silent enemy was the worst.

It came from nowhere and moved among its prey with easy familiarity. It showed no respect for age, rank or sex, and touched its victims with fond impartiality, like an infected whore passing on her disease in a warm embrace. Nothing could withstand its power and nobody could divine the secret of that power. It could climb mountains, swim across oceans, seep through walls and bring down the most well-fortified bastions. Its corruption was universal. Every man, woman and child on the face of the earth was at its mercy.

Here was the final enemy. Doom itself.

Lawrence Firethorn spoke for the whole profession.

'A plague on this plague!'

'It will rob us of our livelihood,' said Gill.

'If not of our lives,' added Hoode.

'God's blood!' said Firethorn, pounding the table with his fist. 'What a damnable trade we follow. There are daggers waiting to stab us at every turn and if we avoid their points, then here comes the sharpest axe in Christendom to chop off our heads.'

'It is a judgement,' said Hoode mournfully.

'We might yet be spared,' said Gill, trying to inject a half-hearted note of optimism. 'Plague deaths have not yet reached the required number per week.'

'They will, Barnaby,' said Firethorn grimly. 'This hot weather will soon begin to unpeople the city. We must look misfortune in the eye, gentlemen, and foreswear all false hopes. 'Tis the only sensible course. This latest visitation will close every theatre in London and put our work to sleep for the whole summer. There's but one remedy.'

'Such a bitter medicine to take,' said Hoode.

Barnaby Gill let out a sigh as deep as the Thames.

The three men were sitting over cups of sack in the taproom of the Queen's Head in Gracechurch Street, the inn which was the regular venue for performances by Lord Westfield's Men, one of the leading companies in the city. Lawrence Firethorn, Barnaby Gill and Edmund Hoode were all sharers, ranked players who were named in the royal patent for the company and who took the major roles in its wide repertoire. Westfield's Men had other sharers but company policy was effectively controlled by this trio. Such, at least, was the theory. In practice, it was the

11

ebullient and dominating figure of Lawrence Firethorn who generally held sway, allowing his two colleagues the illusion of authority when they were, in fact, simply ratifying his decisions. He bulked large.

'Gentlemen,' he announced bravely, 'we must not be crushed by fate or curbed by circumstance. Let us make virtue of necessity here.'

'Virtue, indeed!' Gill was sardonic.

'Yes, sir.'

'Show it me, Lawrence,' said the other. 'Where is the virtue in trailing ourselves around the country to spend our talents in front of ungrateful bumpkins? Poor plays for poor audiences in poor places will make our purses the poorest of all.'

'Westfield's Men never consort with poverty,' said Firethorn, wagging an admonitory finger. 'However humble our theatre, our work will be rich and fulfilling. Be the audience made up of unlettered fools, they will yet have a banquet of words set before them.' His chest swelled with pride. 'In all conscience, sir, I could never demean myself by giving a poor performance!'

'Opinion may differ on that.'

'How say you, Barnaby?'

'Let it pass.'

'Do you impugn my work, sir?'

'I would lack the voice.'

'It is not the only deficiency in your senses.'

'What's that?'

'Your sight, sir. Remember the holy book. Before you

dispraise me, first cast out the mote in your own eye.'

'Give me the meaning.'

'Put your own art in repair.'

'It is not needful,' said Gill, nostrils flaring. 'My public is all too cognisant of my genius.'

'Then why conceal it from your fellow-players?'

'Viper!'

The row blazed merrily and it took Edmund Hoode some minutes before he could calm down both parties. It was an all too familiar task for him. Professional jealousy was at the root of the relationship between Firethorn and Gill. Each had remarkable individual talents and their combined effect was quite dazzling. Most of the success enjoyed by Westfield's Men was due to the interplay of this unrivalled pair and yet they could not reach harmony offstage. They fought with different weapons. Firethorn used a verbal broadsword that whistled through the air as he swished it about while Gill favoured a poniard whose slender blade could slide in between the ribs. When argument was at its height, the former was all towering rage and bristling eyebrow where the latter opted for quivering indignation and pursed lips.

Edmund Hoode adopted a conciliatory tone.

'Gentlemen, gentlemen, you do each other a grave disservice. We are all partners in this business. As God's my witness, we have foes enough to contend with at this troublesome time. Let not headstrong words create more dissension. Desist, sirs. Be friends once more.'

The combatants took refuge in their drinks. Hoode was

13

grateful that he had checked the quarrel before it got to the point where Gill always hurled accusations of unbridled tyranny at Firethorn who, in turn, retaliated by pouring contempt on the other's predilection for young boys with pretty faces and firm bodies. An uneasy silence hovered over the three men. Hoode eventually broke it.

'I have no stomach for touring in the provinces.'

'Beggars cannot be choosers,' said Gill.

'In my case, they can. I'd as lief stay in London and risk the plague as walk at the cart's tail halfway across England. There's no profit in that.'

'And even less in the city,' argued Firethorn. 'How will you live when your occupation is gone? You may be a magician with words, Edmund, but you cannot conjure money out of thin air.'

'I will sell my verses.'

'Your penury's assured,' said Gill maliciously.

'There are those who will buy.'

'More fool them.'

Lawrence Firethorn gave an understanding chuckle.

'I see the truth of it, Edmund. There is only one reason that could make you linger here to taste the misery of certain starvation. Why, man, you are in love!'

'Leave off these jests.'

'See how his cheeks colour, Barnaby?'

'You have hit the mark, Lawrence.'

'He scorns his fellows so that he may lodge his bauble in a tundish. While we tread the road in search of custom, he would be bed-pressing like a lusty bridegroom.' Firethorn

14

gave his colleague a teasing nudge. 'Who is this fair creature, Edmund? If she can tempt you from your calling, she must have charms beyond compare. Tell us, dear heart. What is her name?'

Hoode gave a dismissive shrug. In matters of love, he had learned never to confide in Lawrence Firethorn, still less in Barnaby Gill. The one was a rampant adulterer who could seduce the purest maid while the other had nothing but contempt for the entire female sex. Edmund Hoode kept his own counsel. A tall, slim, pale, clean-shaven man in his thirties, he was an actor-playwright with the company who had somehow resisted the coarsening effects of such an unstable life. He was an irredeemable romantic for whom the pains of courtship were a higher form of pleasure and he was not deterred by the fact that his entanglements almost invariably fell short of consummation. His latest infatuation was writ large upon his face and he lowered his head before the mocking scrutiny of his companions.

Lawrence Firethorn was built of sterner stuff, a barrel-chested man of medium height who exuded power and personality, and whose wavy black hair, pointed beard and handsome features were a frontal assault on womanhood. Gill was older, shorter, stouter and attired with a more fastidious care. Morose and self-involved offstage, he was the most superb comedian upon it and his wicked grin transformed an ugly man into one with immense appeal.

Hoode was torn between his passion and his plays.

'Westfield's Men could well spare me.'

'Gladly,' said the waspish Gill.

'I might join you later in the tour.'

'Come, Edmund,' said Firethorn, clapping him on the shoulder. 'No more talk of desertion. We are dumb idiots without our poet to put words into our mouths. You'll travel with us because we love you.'

'My heart is elsewhere.'

'And because we need you, sweet friend.'

'Go forth without me.'

'And because you are contracted to us.'

Firethorn's curt reminder terminated the dispute. Being a sharer in the company imposed certain legal responsibilities upon Hoode. His freedom of action was limited. He blenched as yet another burgeoning romance withered on the stem.

Lawrence Firethorn sought to offer consolation.

'Courage, man!' he urged. 'Do not sit there like a lovesick shepherd. Consider what lies ahead. You forfeit one conquest in order to make others. Country girls were born for copulation. Unbutton at will. You can fornicate across seven counties until your pizzle turns blue and cries "Amen to that!" Hark ye, Edmund.' Firethorn clapped his other shoulder. 'Westfield's Men are not being driven out of London. We are journeying to paradise!'

'Who is to be our serpent?' said Gill.

Nicholas Bracewell stood in his accustomed place behind the stage and controlled the performance with his quiet authority. As the company's book holder, he was a key figure in its affairs, prompting and stage managing every play which was mounted as well as supervising rehearsals and helping with the dozens of other tasks that were thrown up. A tall, imposing, muscular man, he had a face of seasoned oak that was set off by long fair hair and a Viking beard. Striking to the eye, he could yet become completely invisible during a performance, an unseen presence in the shadows whose influence was decisive and who pulled all the strings like a master puppeteer.

The play which was delighting the audience at the Queen's Head that afternoon was *The Constant Lover*, a gentle comedy about the problems of fidelity. It had become a favourite piece and Westfield's Men had offered it several times already. But it had never been staged in quite this way before.

'What now, Master Bracewell?'

'The silver chalice, George.'

'Upon the table?'

'Present it to the King.'

'When is the table to be set?'

'For the next scene.'

'The silver chalice again?'

'The gold goblet.'

George Dart did not usually get quite so flustered. He was an assistant stagekeeper and occasionally got pressed into service as a non-speaking extra. His duties in *The Constant Lover* were light and undemanding yet he was flummoxed before the end of Act One. It was quite understandable. Everyone in the company knew that this might be their last appearance in London for a long time

17

and, in some cases, their last appearance upon any stage. Touring would inflict economies on the company. Its size would be reduced and its weekly wages would shrink. All the sharers would take to the road but the hired men would have to be carefully sifted. George Dart was one of them. Like his fellows, he was in a state of hysteria lest he be rejected, knowing full well that those discarded might fall by the wayside completely. He therefore played his tiny role in *The Constant Lover* with a kind of confused urgency, mystified as to what came next yet eager to give of his best.

Nicholas Bracewell at once stilled the general panic and made allowances for it. Some of the actors out there were, literally, fighting for their lives. In striving too hard to do well, they often marred their chances. Nicholas had great sympathy for them all but his first duty was to the audience and he concentrated on keeping the play running as smoothly as possible. It meant that he had to adjudicate at several running duels.

'Did you ever see such wanton cruelty, Nick?'

'Stand by for your next entrance.'

'He cut my finest speech.'

'You ruined two of his.'

'Gabriel is trying to savage my performance.'

'I believe he is only replying in kind.'

'The man has no honour.'

'Teach him some by example.'

'I think that you take his side.'

'No, Christopher. My concern is for the play itself.'

'Then why let Gabriel disfigure it?'

'You have been his able lieutenant in the business this past half-hour. It is to your mutual discredit.'

'I am the better player, Nick.'

'Your cue is at hand.'

'Speak up for me.'

'Go forth and speak for yourself.'

Christopher Millfield surged back out onstage to continue his battle with Gabriel Hawkes. Both were fine actors who could carry off a wide range of supporting roles with assurance and each was a real asset to the company. But there would not be room for the two of them in the touring party. One had to give way to the other. They had never liked each other but, in all previous plays, their personal antipathy had been subdued for the sake of a common cause. Threatened with unemployment, they fell back on a raw hostility that was totally in keeping with the characters they were playing but which made for some rather alarming departures from the text.

Nicholas watched it all with a mixture of surprise and distaste. He might have expected such behaviour from Christopher Millfield, an arrogant and impulsive young man who was quick to take offence where none was intended. Gabriel Hawkes was a very different person, an unassuming and almost shy character who was ill at ease with the ribald banter of the players and who kept himself apart from the general throng. Nicholas admired the talents of both men but had much more affection for Hawkes. On a long and arduous tour, his soft-edged presence would be much more acceptable than Millfield's brashness.

Yet he was giving the worst possible account of himself. In descending to open combat, Hawkes was doing his cause irreparable harm. To the amusement of the audience – but the detriment of the play – the two of them were grappling like wrestlers, throwing each other to the ground with blank verse before pummelling away unmercifully with rhyming couplets.

Then, suddenly, it was all over.

Gabriel Hawkes seemed to concede defeat. He sagged visibly and the spirit went out of his defiance. He let Christopher Millfield walk all over him and could not even offer a token resistance. It was painful to watch.

Most of the onlookers were unaware of the intense personal conflict which had been going on in front of them. Hawkes and Millfield did not have leading parts and they melted into the scenery whenever Lawrence Firethorn came onstage. He was a true King in every sense and his regal brilliance outshone everything else in view, including the hilarious exploits of Barnaby Gill as a decrepit suitor. Firethorn's rule was paramount.

He led out the company to bask in the applause that echoed around the inn yard where they had set up their makeshift stage. Westfield's Men were due to play at the Queen's Head the following week but nobody believed that the performance would take place. The plague was closing in remorselessly. Spectators who would be deprived of entertainment for long months showed their appreciation of players who would be exiled from the city. It was a joyous yet rather wistful occasion.

Lawrence Firethorn wept genuine tears and delivered

a farewell speech. Barnaby Gill snuffled, Edmund Hoode swallowed hard and the rest of the company were patently moved. Nicholas Bracewell was not carried away on the tide of emotion. His attention was fixed on Gabriel Hawkes who was strangely detached from it all. A man who loved the theatre with a deep and lasting commitment was now looking quite alienated by it all.

As they came off stage, Nicholas sought him out.

'What ails you, lad?'

'Nothing, Master Bracewell.'

'Can you be well?'

'I feel a sickness coming on but it is not serious.'

'What manner of sickness?'

'Do not trouble yourself about me.'

'Shall we carry you to a physician?'

'It is of no account, I promise you.'

'Have care, Gabriel.'

The young actor smiled weakly and touched his arm.

'Thank you, Master Bracewell.'

'Why so?'

'You have been a good friend to me.'

There was an air of finality in his voice that upset Nicholas. As Gabriel Hawkes went off unsteadily to change out of his costume and make his way back to his lodgings in Bankside, the book holder had the worrying premonition that he would never see the man alive again.

Having toyed with the city for a few weeks, the plague moved in for the kill. London was helpless. It suffered from pounding headaches, icy chills, agonising back pains, quickening pulse, heavy breathing, high fever and incurable restlessness. Ugly buboes began to appear in its groin and beneath its armpits. Vomiting was quite uncontrollable. As the body surrendered, the mind began to crumble as well. Delirium set in. The mortality rate climbed inexorably and people learned to pray once more.

'When will you leave, sir?'

'As soon as it is needful.'

'Is there no hope of escape?'

'Alas, no, my love. Seven deaths were reported in this parish alone and a dozen or more in Cripplegate. When all the parishes are reckoned up, the number will be well past thirty and even as high as thrice that number.'

'God save us all!'

'There's no comfort for we wretched players, who must be the first to be sacrificed to this scourge. The Privy Council has issued an edict. All theatres, bear-baiting arenas and other places of public consort must be closed forthwith. It is iniquitous!'

'It is inconsiderate, sir.'

Margery Firethorn clasped her husband to her and let him feel the warmth of her devotion. It had not been a placid marriage by any stretch of the imagination but he had never regretted it, even when the tempests were at their fiercest. Margery was a good wife, a caring mother, a thrifty housekeeper and a sound Christian. Living with such a rumbustious partner as Lawrence Firethorn would have cowed any other woman but she had met the challenge with unflinching bravery. They were destined for each other. Kindred spirits forged from the same steel.

'How long will you be gone?' she asked.

'Until the Queen's Head can welcome us again.'

'That day will be months away.'

'Michaelmas at least.'

'It will seem like an eternity.'

'My old heart is sad at the contemplation of it.'

'I will miss you sorely, Lawrence.'

Firethorn looked down at his wife as she lay beside him in bed and saw again the voluptuous young woman whom he had first courted all those years ago. Time had etched deep lines in her face and childbirth had been unkind to her figure but she was still an astonishing creature in her own way, with generous curves to her body that could entice and excite as of old. Firethorn had aroused the love of serving wenches and the lust of court beauties in his headlong flight into adultery but he always came back to the more mature charms of his wife and wondered, as he did now, feeling a rare pang of guilt, why he had bothered to go astray in the first place.

Margery gave him a joy beyond mere satisfaction and it was something to savour. Lying there in an attitude of complete welcome, she was as irresistible as she had been on their wedding night when the bed had creaked until dawn. Shafts of moonlight came in through the window to paint an even more wondrous portrait of her.

Lawrence Firethorn pulled her to him.

'Come closer, my love. We need each other.'

'One moment, sir,' said Margery, wanting to get the practicalities out of the way beforehand. 'How am I to live while my husband is away?'

'As virtuously as if he were at home.'

'I speak of household expenses, Lawrence.'

'You will be provided for, my angel.'

'In what way?' she pressed.

'The establishment will be much smaller when I am gone,' he said. 'I will take the lodgers, apprentices and all with me out of the house. There'll be but you, our children and our servants left here in Shoreditch.'

'Children and servants must eat, sir.'

'And so they shall. Every day, most regularly.'

'Will I be furnished with money, then?'

'Of course, Margery,' he said, stroking her thigh as a prelude to their shared delight. 'I will give you all that I am able. Let that content you.'

'And how if it should not be sufficient?'

'Be frugal, woman, and all will be well.'

'Even frugality must come at a price.'

'Have no fear, sweeting.'

'Then put my mind at rest.'

'I will, I will,' he said, letting his hand travel up to cup her ample breast. 'While I am away, I will send you more money. And if that be not enough, why, then, you must raise some capital from elsewhere.'

'Teach me how, sir.'

'Sell my second-best cloak.'

Margery was touched. She knew how much his apparel

meant to him and how he would sooner lose a limb than part with a yard of it. The cloak, a magnificent garment that was paned with yellow, green, blue and red sarcanet and lined with buckram, was a present from Lord Westfield himself and would not disgrace the wardrobe of any peer.

'Do you speak true, Lawrence? I may sell it?'

'Only if the need arises.'

'And you will not berate me for it?'

'Your comfort must come before my vanity.'

'This gladdens me more than I can say.'

It was the moment to secure his prize. Firethorn reached under the pillow for the ring which he had placed there earlier then slipped it symbolically on to the third finger of her left hand. The ruby mesmerised her.

'It is for me?'

'For whom else? Wear it till I return.'

'Nothing would make me take it off.'

'It is a token of my adoration,' he said, easing her thighs apart with gentle pressure. 'Let it be a perpetual reminder of the love I bear you. A precious jewel to show that you are the treasure of my existence. A lasting tribute to the fairest of her sex.' She gave him a kiss which set him aflame and which banished all common sense. His tone was ruinously casual. 'And if the worst should happen – sell the ring as well.'

A volcano erupted directly beneath him.

The bed creaked mightily but not for joy.

Bankside was kinder to its departing Thespians. Nocturnal pleasures were not squandered so readily by Nicholas

Bracewell. Because they were less frequent occurrences in his life, he had schooled himself to enjoy them when they came and to lock out all thought of the real world. It was only afterwards – as they lay side by side in lazy provocation – that he turned his mind to harsher matters.

'Will you stay in London, Anne?'

'Unless the plague should worsen.'

'All the signs point that way.'

'Then I will visit relatives in the country.'

'Your cousins in Dunstable?'

'Or my uncle in Bedford. Or even my other uncle in Nottingham. I'll go to one, or two, perchance all three of them before I stay here to catch the plague.'

'Is that what I am?' he teased.

'I grow feverish whenever you are near, Nick.'

Anne Hendrik was one of the more unusual residents of Bankside. In an area notorious for its brothels, its gambling dens, its taverns and its teeming low life, she owned a respectable house and ran a successful business. English by birth, she was the widow of Jacob Hendrik, a conscientious Dutchman who brought his skills as a hatmaker to London only to discover that the City Guilds were intent on keeping him and his compatriots out of their jealous brotherhoods. Forced to set up shop outside the city boundary, he chose Southwark as his home and Anne as his wife.

Fifteen happy years of marriage had produced no children. What Anne inherited was a fine house, a thriving business and her husband's belief in the dignity of work for its own sake. She also inherited Nicholas Bracewell.

'Which towns will you visit?' she asked.

'The details are yet to be decided upon.'

'In what direction do you travel?'

'North, Anne.'

'Haply, you may find your way to Dunstable, then?'

'Or to Bedford. Or to Nottingham. Or to anywhere else you should chance to be. If I am in the same county as you, I'll find a way to see you somehow.'

Anne kissed him fondly on the cheek than nestled into his shoulder. In the time that he had lodged at her house, Nicholas had become more than a friend. They shared a bed only occasionally but their lives were nevertheless intertwined. He was drawn to the tall, graceful, attractive woman who had such a refreshing sense of independence about her and she, in turn, was fascinated by his blend of humour, intelligence and quiet strength. She had never met anyone who could be so modest about his many attributes. Though he was only a hired man with the company, Nicholas had made himself indispensable and taken on duties that would normally be beyond the scope of a book holder.

Intrigued by the theatre, Anne Hendrik took a lively interest in the affairs of Westfield's Men and she was well-informed about its shifting population. Having sat through the last performance of *The Constant Lover*, she was curious to know which of its cast would appear in the play when it was taken on tour.

'How large will the company be, Nick?'

'But fifteen of us.'

'That calls for severe surgery.'

'Master Firethorn has made a swift incision.'

'And who has been cut out?'

'Far too many, I fear.'

'George Dart?'

'No, I saved him.'

'Thomas Skillen?'

'He was beyond rescue.'

Nicholas shook his head sadly. In choosing those who would remain with the company, Lawrence Firethorn was in close consultation with his book holder. They had spent hours in deep debate and Nicholas had fought hard to keep certain people, though not always with success. It was the actor-manager who made the final decisions and he did so with brutal efficiency, making no concessions to sentiment or to compassion. What fell to Nicholas was the gruesome task of telling good friends that their services would no longer be required and it had been a disturbing process.

Thomas Skillen was a case in point. The stagekeeper was steeped in theatre and as dependable as a rock but his old age and rheumatism told against him. Younger legs and more versatile hands were preferred. Peter Digby was another casualty. As leader of the musicians, he was a key figure in every performance but his expertise was a luxury that could not be afforded in a touring company. Actor-musicians were given priority because they had dual value. Hugh Wegges, the tireman, would see some of his fine costumes leave London while he was forced to stay behind.

His infinite skill with needle and thread was not enough to secure his passage. Nathan Curtis, master carpenter, was also set aside. Only minimal scenery and properties could be taken and his craft was now superfluous.

And so it was with many others. Nicholas had tried to break the news to them as gently as possible but it did not prevent tearful entreaties and open despair and bitter recrimination. For some of those he had grown to love and admire as colleagues, he was pronouncing a death sentence. It bruised his soul.

'What of Christopher Millfield?' said Anne.

'Ah! There was argument indeed.'

'He would get my vote over Gabriel Hawkes.'

'Only because you do not know him as well as I.'

'He was the brighter talent in *The Constant Lover.*'

'The more forceful, I grant you,' said Nicholas. 'That is Christopher's way. He knows how to get himself attention onstage and will put great passion into his playing but I believe that Gabriel is the better man. He will learn a part quicker than anyone in the company and bring a cool brain to his work.'

'Did you say as much to Master Firethorn?'

'Incessantly.'

'With what outcome?'

'He leaned towards Christopher.'

'Then was your cause lost.'

'Not so, Anne. I reminded him of something which made him consider the matter afresh.'

'Which was?'

'That Christopher may have the more dazzling charm but he also has the greater selfishness. If anyone will to steal some of Master Firethorn's lustre, it will not be Gabriel Hawkes. He is the safer man.'

'A cunning ruse,' said Anne with a smile. 'I can see why it worked on Master Firethorn. Is that how it stands? Will Christopher Millfield leave the company?'

'Not without rancour,' said Nicholas. 'When I told him of the decision, he was vexed in the extreme and made all manner of dire threats. He has taken it as a gross insult. There may yet be trouble from that quarter. It is not pleasant to be the bearer of bad tidings.'

'You had good news for some.'

'Indeed, yes. I spread delight as well as gloom.'

'Was Gabriel Hawkes overcome?'

'I have not been able to see him in person, Anne. He has been indisposed these last two days. But I have sent word to him. He knows his good fortune.'

'That will rally him from his sick bed.'

'I hope so.'

'You do not sound too confident.'

'Oh, I am,' said Nicholas, shaking off his fleeting anxieties. 'Gabriel is the sounder prospect for us and he will prove that on our travels. There is no man in the company I would sooner have beside me. I will visit him tomorrow and make sure that he understands that.'

'Why do you have such a high opinion of him?'

'That is the wonder of it. I do not know.'

* * *

Smorrall Lane was less than a hundred yards from Anne Hendrik's house but its dwellings were a world apart. The narrow, winding, fetid alley consisted of a series of dirty and decrepit buildings that leaned against each other for support with ramshackle companionship. Stews, taverns and ordinaries attracted a lower class of patron and those who tumbled along the lane at night were usually drunk or diseased from guzzling excess. Thieves lurked in dark corners and waited for easy pickings. Women offered their wares in doorways. Blood was often mixed with the urine and excrement that flowed over the cobbles. Smorrall Lane was easy to find. It could be located by its stench.

The tall, elegant young man who stalked along it that night was no typical visitor. Nose wrinkled in disgust, he moved along quickly and pushed away two revellers who brushed against him. When he came to the house that he sought, he looked up and saw a faint glimmer in the window of the front bedchamber. His quarry was at home.

He banged on the door but got no reply. Glancing down the lane to make sure that he was unobserved, he let himself into the house and coughed as its dust attacked his throat. He went swiftly to the staircase and crept silently up its crooked steps. Outside the bedchamber, he tapped on the door without response. All he could hear was stertorous breathing from within.

It suited his purpose. Opening the door softly, he slid into the room and crossed over to the prone figure under the ragged bedsheets. The smell of decay assailed his nostrils and his stomach churned but he was not to be deflected from his purpose. Straddling the sleeper, he got a firm grip on the man's neck and squeezed with all his power. There was little resistance. Weakened already, his victim had barely enough strength to flail his arms and they soon hung limp and lifeless.

The visitor left with furtive speed and came out into the lane again. He used a piece of charcoal to write something on the battered door of the house.

LORD HAVE MERCY UPON US.

Then he looked up at the window once more.

'Goodbye, Gabriel. Sleep with the other angels now.'

Chapter Two

Miles Melhuish believed totally in the power of prayer. As vicar of the parish church of St Stephen, he was in the ideal position to put his faith to the test and it had never been found wanting. Prayer had saved souls, cured diseases, softened tragedies, provided inspiration, secured guidance from above and generally eased the troubled mind of his congregation. If his ministry had taught him one thing, it was that ten minutes a day on his knees was far more effective than an hour on his feet in the pulpit. It was the first article in the Melhuish creed. By communing directly with God in true humility, he achieved infinitely more than he would have by haranguing the citizens of Nottingham with his sermons. He was a devout and pensive shepherd and his flock gained from it.

Ten years in the parish had confronted him with all sorts of problems and all manner of strange sights but none could compare with what lay in wait for him now. As he knelt at the altar rail in an attitude of blissful submission, the setting sun flooded in through the stained glass window to give his rubicund face a saintly glow and to encircle his bald head with a golden halo. When his prayers were done, he used the rail to lift himself up, then genuflected with portly solemnity.

The sound of running footsteps made him turn.

'Why, Humphrey! What means this haste?'

'I must speak with you, sir.'

'And so you shall but not by bursting in like a runaway bull. This is the Lord's house, Humphrey, and we must accord it all due respect. Hold there, man.'

'I obey you straight.'

'And catch your breath, dear fellow.'

Humphrey Budden leaned on one of the pews as he gulped in air. A big broad man of florid hue, he had run much further than his legs or lungs had desired and he was now bathed in perspiration. Miles Melhuish walked down the aisle towards the glistening parishioner and tried to guess at the crisis which had brought on this uncharacteristic lapse. Budden was a respected figure in the town, a conscientious lacemaker who helped to keep the name of Nottingham at the forefront of his trade. Since his marriage the previous year, he had been the happiest of men, honest, affable, upright, regular in his devotions and often given to charitable impulse. Yet here was this same Humphrey Budden, charging into church, panting like a dog and sweating like a roast pig.

The vicar put a consoling arm around him.

'Fear not, my son. God is with you.'

'I need him mightily, sir.'

'To what end, Humphrey?'

'I can hardly bring myself to tell you.'

'Succour awaits.'

'The sound still fills my ears.'

'What sound?'

'And the sight torments my mind.'

'You are trembling with the shock of it.'

'I came straight here, sir. God is my last resort.'

'How may he help you?'

Humphrey Budden bit his lip in embarrassment then cleared his throat. It had been far easier to carry his message to church than to deliver it. Words rebelled.

Miles Melhuish tried to prompt him gently.

'Are you in trouble, my son?'

'Not me, sir.'

'Your wife?'

'Indeed.'

'What ails the good woman?'

'Oh, sir . . .'

Humphrey Budden began to weep helplessly. The calamity which had brought him so recklessly into the church had deprived him of speech. Easing him down into a pew, the vicar sat beside him and offered up a silent prayer. Budden slowly regained some control.

'Tell me about Eleanor,' said the priest.

'I love her so much!'

'Some accident perchance?'

'Worse, sir.'

'She has fallen sick?'

'Worse still.'

'Dear Lord! Has she passed away?'

'Worse even than that.'

Melhuish coaxed the story out of him. Even in its garbled form it was enough to make the man of the cloth forget both his paunch and his place. Gathering up his belly in both hands, he led the way towards the door at a steady trot with Budden in close pursuit. They ran out into the churchyard then through the gate that opened on to Angel Row. The house was a couple of hundred yards away and the effort of reaching it took them both near exhaustion but they did not pause. Above the sound of their breathing, they heard a noise that froze their blood and put a last spurt into their legs.

It was the scream of a woman. Not the sudden yell of someone in pain nor yet the anguished cry of someone in distress. It was a weird, continuous, high-pitched howl of a wild animal, a noise so intense and unnatural that it did not seem to come from a human throat at all. Budden opened the front door and ushered the priest into a room that already had some occupants. Four terrified children were clustered around the skirts of an old servant, gazing up in horror at the bedchamber above their heads.

Humphrey Budden gave them a comforting squeeze then took his visitor up the stairs. During that short ascent, Miles Melhuish prayed more strenuously than even he had done in a long while. The sound was heart-rending. He had to force himself to follow the stricken husband into the bedchamber. What hideous sight lay within?

When his eyes beheld it, he crossed himself at once.

'Dear God in heaven!'

'Eleanor,' called Budden. 'Peace, good wife.'

But she did not even hear him. The wail continued with unabated fury and her hands clutched at her hair. Melhuish was dumbstruck. There in front of him, kneeling stark naked on the floor, swaying to and fro, staring at a crucifix on the wall, was a buxom woman in her twenties with flaxen hair trailing down her back towards a pair of round, beautiful, shuddering buttocks. It was a scene at once so frightening and erotic that Melhuish had to avert his gaze for a few seconds and call his righteousness to his aid.

Eleanor Budden was in the grip of some ineluctable passion. As her shriek soared to an even higher pitch, it spoke of pain and pleasure, of a torture suffered and a joy attained, of the misery of the damned and the joy of salvation. The mouth from which it came was twisted in a grimace but her face was luminescent with happiness.

'Eleanor,' said her husband. 'Look who is here.'

'She hears you not, Humphrey.'

'Stand forth where she may see you, sir.'

He motioned the priest forward until the latter was standing between the woman and the crucifix. The effect on her was immediate. Her howling stopped, her mouth fell shut, her hands went to her sides and her body no longer

37

shook all over. The deafening cry was replaced by an eerie stillness that was almost as unsettling.

Eleanor Budden looked up at the parish priest with a reverential smile. The fever had broken at last. Both men dared to relax slightly but their relief was premature. A fresh paroxysm seized her. Lunging forward, she grabbed the vicar around the waist and buried her head in the ample folds of his flesh, emitting a sound that began as a low wheeze of excitement then built up quickly until it was a cry of pure elation. Firm hands were clutching his buttocks, soft breasts were pressing against his thighs and urgent lips were burrowing into his groin. The noise surged on to a climax then spent itself in a sigh that filled the room with carnality and made her whole frame shudder with sheer ecstasy.

She collapsed peacefully to the floor in a coma.

Miles Melhuish was still praying furiously.

Death moved through the streets of London every day and sent loved ones to an early grave but the citizens of London were still not satisfied. Private grief afflicted new families by the hour but there was still enough ghoulish interest left over to send a large crowd to Tyburn for the execution. Distraught people who had sat around doomed beds now found a sense of release as they jostled for position around the gallows. A public death carried an element of celebration. In the crude but legalised murder of some anonymous criminal, they could take a profound satisfaction and dispatch him into the afterlife with sadistic jeers. What was intended as a brutal warning to them became a source of entertainment.

Everybody was keen to get a good view.

'Stand aside, sir, I pray.'

'By your leave, mistress.'

'I'll see nothing but your broad shoulders.'

'Come in front of me.'

'Let me through here.'

'Push hard, mistress.'

The tall young man heaved to the left to create a space for the old woman. Having fought her way through the press to its densest point, she found that her view was still blocked. The young man recoiled from the reek of her breath but her odour was soon swallowed up in the communal stink of the multitude. She was a countrywoman of sorts, with a basket on her arm and a slope to her shoulders that told of a lifetime of drudgery. Her lips were bared in a toothless grin of anticipation.

'Have you come far, mistress?' he said.

'Ten mile or more, sir.'

'All this way for an execution?'

'I'd skip twenty sooner than miss it.'

'Do you know who is to be hanged?'

'A traitor, sir.'

'But what is his name?'

'That does not matter.'

'It matters to him.'

'He is nothing in himself.'

'You walk ten miles for a total stranger?'

'Yes, sir,' she said with malicious glee. 'Death to all traitors! I want to see them cut his pizzle off!'

A loud cheer went up as the cart rumbled towards the gallows. The condemned man was sitting down with his arms pinioned behind his back and two gaolers standing over him. Even in his wretched condition, he had a tarnished dignity. Ragged, unkempt and maimed by torture, he yet had the bearing of a true nobleman. His apparent calm in the face of death only served to excite the onlookers to a louder display of rage. All their fear, hatred, anger and despair were channelled into a mounting roar of fury.

The young man remained silent but watched it all with detached pleasure. Justice was enforced without hesitation. The prisoner was hauled on to the platform and his sentence was read out. He was then offered the momentary comfort of a chaplain to fit his mind for what lay ahead. When he refused, he was handed over to the executioner and his assistant, hooded monsters with brawny arms and a gift for prolonging agony. They knew their trade and set about it without delay. The prisoner began to recite something in Latin but it was drowned out by the baying of the mob. His lips were still barely moving as the noose was slipped around his neck.

The rope was tightened, its position checked, the lever pulled then the trap door opened to give him his first glimpse of hell. His body stiffened as it took the impact then his legs jerked, his shoulders twisted, his mouth gaped, his face turned purple, and every vein and sinew about him strained to break through skin. It was a grotesque and repulsive sight but the spectators loved what they saw, laughing, cheering and waving in sadistic mockery, working themselves up into a state of malevolent hysteria, forgetting the troubles of their own lives in the mirthful contemplation of savagery.

The body seemed to twitch and sway for a long time before the executioners moved in. Eyes closed, mouth wide open, neck half-broken, the victim seemed to have expired. Howls of outrage went up as onlookers felt that they were being robbed of their full due. But the executioners had not botched their work. As he was cut down, he stirred briefly and let out a groan. The young man was close enough to see what happened next. From under leaden lids, the prisoner shot his tormentors a glance that was spiked with accusation. Evidently, he had bribed them so that they would let him die on the gallows and be spared the further horrors that were enshrined in his sentence.

The executioners had taken his money in all earnest then blithely forgotten their side of the bargain.

The traitor was himself the victim of treachery.

Stripped naked, the prisoner was castrated with a flash of steel, the loss of his manhood stirring up the crowd to even higher levels of blood-lust. The ritual disembowelling came next with the executioners slicing him open and pulling his entrails out in order to burn them before his eyes. When there was no more sport to be got from the bleeding carcass, the prisoner was beheaded and his body cut into quarters. The systematic butchery was at last over. Spectators had had their fill.

Christopher Millfield afforded himself a quiet smile.

* * *

41

London came out in a hot sweat. Foul contagion spread throughout its maze of streets and alleys. Bells rang out their jangling requiems all day long and ministers went scurrying from one house of death to another. Undertakers prospered and a worm-eaten generation of parish clerks grew rich from exploiting the miseries of the bereaved by increasing their fees. Vultures fattened themselves on the wasted corpses of their fellow-citizens.

The exodus from the capital grew apace.

'I am loath to depart the place, Nick.'

'There's no staying here.'

'Where she is, there must I be.'

'And so you are, Edmund,' said his friend. 'If she has your verses, then she holds your essence in her hand.'

'I had not thought of that.'

'Then do so now. Absence can only make her heart grow fonder and you may nurture that fondness with sweet poems and tender letters. Your pen will have to serve where your lips may not.'

'This is consolation indeed.'

'Woo her from all over England.'

'What a welcome I will get on my return!'

Edmund Hoode brightened. Discussing his private life with Nicholas Bracewell always paid dividends. The book holder was a man of the world with a keen understanding of the vagaries of love. His advice was invariably sound and his sympathy without limit. Hoode had found cause to be grateful to him on many occasions and that gratitude surged again now. Nicholas had shown him that a happy compromise was possible. Leaving the city did not have to be an act of desertion. He could continue his assaults on the heart of his beloved from a distance. It would make for some exquisite pangs of loneliness on his part and heighten the magic of consummation when that blessed moment finally came.

'I'll send her a sonnet forthwith,' he decided.

'You have only today in which to compose it.'

'Today and tonight, Nick. I cast aside all thought of sleep in the joy of her service, and my Muse helps me best in the hours of darkness.'

'Do not weary yourself entirely, Edmund. We have a long journey to make tomorrow.'

'I embark upon it in good spirits.'

'That pleases me well.'

'Would that dear Gabriel could be with us!'

'My mind was sharing that self-same hope.'

The two men were walking together through Bankside on a sultry morning. They had come on a grim errand. Flies buzzed over piles of refuse and rats sniffed their way through rotting food. As the friends entered the most squalid part of the district, they saw signs of death and decay on every side. They were shocked to think that one of their fellows had been forced to live in such a warren of mouldering humanity. Gabriel Hawkes had excelled at playing princes yet his own kingdom was that of a pauper.

They were only just in time. Turning into Smorrall Lane, they saw the cart trundling along about its doleful business, already piled high with its gruesome cargo. It stopped outside a door that was marked with a blue cross and another corpse was soon loaded up. The cart then went on to the house where Gabriel Hawkes had lodged. It was boarded up and the writing on the door confirmed that plague had also been a tenant. Wrapped in a dirty winding sheet, the body was carried out unceremoniously and hurled up on top of the pile.

Nicholas started forward to protest.

'Take more care, sirs!' he said.

'Away!' snarled the driver of the cart.

'That is our friend you handle so roughly there.'

'It is our trade.'

'Practise it with more courtesy.'

The driver let out a cackle of derision then snapped the reins over the backs of the two horses. They pulled hard and the cart bumped on down the lane. It had a full consignment now and made its melancholy way to a piece of waste land beyond the labyrinth of houses. Nicholas and his companion followed it all the way, determined to share in the funeral rites of their former colleague. Both of them had respected Gabriel Hawkes enough to argue for his inclusion in the touring party and it was painful to have their happy memories of him marred by what they were now witnessing. A fund of wit, warmth and real talent was tied up in that winding sheet.

The cart creaked to a halt beside a huge pit that was still occupied by busy gravediggers. Fresh mounds of earth showed that other pits had already been dug and filled. Plague victims needed to go deep into the earth lest their infection sprout forth. The driver and his assistant unloaded the corpses with as much concern as if they were handling sacks of vegetables. Human beings were dragged off the cart and thrown along the edge of the pit to await the drop into their final resting place.

Nicholas Bracewell and Edmund Hoode were far enough away to miss the worst of the stench but close enough to observe the creature who crept out of his hiding place under a bush. The man was short, ragged and hirsute, old by every external sign yet as nimble as a monkey. While the driver and his assistant had their backs turned, the newcomer moved between the winding sheets as if he knew what he would find inside them. Using a knife to slit open the material, he groped here and grabbed there until he had quite a haul from his bold plundering. It was when he bent over the body of Gabriel Hawkes that Nicholas moved into action.

Darting forward at speed, he chased the man back to the bushes from which the latter had emerged, diving on him to bring the fellow rolling to the ground. The knife was brandished in Nicholas's face but it did not deter him. Years at sea with bellicose sailors had taught him how to handle himself in a fight and he quickly disarmed his assailant, winding him at the same time with a punch in the stomach. Hoode came running up to join him.

The man retreated in a defensive snivel.

'Leave off, good sirs. I do no harm.'

'Robbing the dead is both sin and crime,' said Nicholas. 'You have defiled the body of our friend.'

'He is past caring.'

'We are not.'

'Judge me truly,' said the man, sitting up on his haunches. 'I only take from those that have no need. These things would only end up in a pit of lime and what's the use of that. Better that they help the living than lie beneath the ground with the dead.'

'You are a scurvy rogue,' said Hoode.

'Necessity compels me, sir.' He was almost chirpy now. 'Plague is meat and drink to me. It is the only time we poor people may be rich for a day. The bodies of the deceased sustain us. Their loss is our gain. When they become naked, we are clothed. When they are hungry, we are fed. Their sickness is our health.'

'Give me what you took,' demanded Nicholas.

'It is all mine.'

'Keep most of it. I want what was stolen from that last body. He was a good friend to us.'

'But not to me,' replied the man peevishly. 'There was nothing on him to take. A miserable wretch indeed!'

Nicholas dispensed with further wrangling. Grabbing the man by his beard, he shook him violently until the creature howled for mercy.

'Now, sir. Give me what was taken.'

The man spat in annoyance then slowly opened the palm of his left hand. Nestling in it was the tiny jewelled earring that Gabriel Hawkes used to wear. It sparkled in the grubby hand of its thief. Nicholas took the earring and stood up to examine it. Neither he nor Hoode made any move when the man gathered up the rest of his haul and scampered away like an old sheep dog.

The two friends exchanged a glance. Gabriel had at least been spared this final indignity. He owned little enough in life and did not deserve to have it snatched from him in death. They walked back towards the pit and saw that the bodies were now being heaved into it before being covered with spadefuls of lime. The stink was overpowering but they did not turn back. As they looked down into the gaping tomb, they saw dozens of tormented bodies lying across each other at angles. It was now impossible to tell them apart.

Nicholas tossed the earring into the pit then offered up a silent prayer. Edmund Hoode was horrified by the callous anonymity of the mass burial.

'Which one is Gabriel?' he asked.

'God will know,' said Nicholas.

They lingered until the busy spades hid the shameful sight with layers of earth. It was all so functional and impersonal. Both of them were deeply affected. When they finally turned and strolled away, neither was able to speak for several minutes. Edmund Hoode eventually came out of his brooding solemnity.

'Why, what a foul contagion it is!'

'A devilish pestilence,' agreed Nicholas.

'I speak not of the plague.'

'Then what?'

'That other fatal disease. It struck down Gabriel Hawkes and, in time, it will account for us as well.'

'How say you?'

'I talk of the theatre, Nick. That fever of the blood which drives us to madness all our lives and hurries us towards our graves.' Hoode gave a mirthless laugh. 'Who else would take up this profession but a sick man? We are both infected beyond cure. We have caught the germs of false hope and empty fame. The theatre will kill us all.'

'No,' said Nicholas. 'It keeps us alive.'

'Only so that we may suffer gross affliction.'

'The loss of our friend has hurt you badly.'

'He was destroyed by his profession.'

'Or by someone in it.' Nicholas stopped. 'Gabriel Hawkes did not simply die of the plague. The disease would not have carried him off that quickly without some help from another source.'

'Help?'

'He was murdered, Edmund.'

Like a true man of the theatre, Lawrence Firethorn could not resist the opportunity to deliver a speech in front of a captive audience. Westfield's Men were summoned to the Queen's Head that morning. Since the inn was their London home, it was also the most appropriate point of departure. The company gathered in the room that was used as the tiring-house during performance. A great adventure was now in the offing.

They were all there, including Barnaby Gill, Rowland Carr, Simon Dowsett, Walter Fenby, the beaming George Dart and Richard Honeydew with the other boy apprentices. Edmund Hoode sat pale and wan in the window. Christopher Millfield lounged in cavalier fashion against a beam. Nicholas Bracewell stood at the back so that he was out of range of the full blast of Firethorn's lecture and well-placed to gauge its effect on individual members of the company.

Also in the room, like a spectre at the feast, was the hollow-cheeked Alexander Marwood, the luckless landlord of the Queen's Head. Short, skinny and losing his hair by the week, Marwood had an uneasy relationship with Westfield's Men and only ever renewed their contract as an essay in self-torture. With no love for drama itself, he found the regular invasion by plays and players an ordeal that kept his nervous twitch in full employment. Westfield's Men brought danger to his property, to his reputation, to his serving wenches and to his sanity. He was better off without them. Yet now that they were going, now that they were quitting his hostelry for the open road, now that his yard would no longer be packed with thirsty patrons on most afternoons, now that he envisaged empty spaces and unsold beer and falling profits, he came round to the idea that they were the foundation of his livelihood.

'Do not leave me,' he said wistfully.

'We will return, Master Marwood,' promised Nicholas.

'The company will be much missed.'

'We do not leave of our own accord.'

'This plague is a curse upon us!'

'It may yet bestow some blessings.'

One of them was to shake off the gloomy landlord

and escape his endless litany of complaints. Nicholas had been quick to spot that compensation. As the person who dealt most often with Alexander Marwood, he bore the brunt of the other's sustained melancholy. It was just one of the duties that Firethorn had cunningly assigned to him.

The actor-manager now got to his feet and raised up a hand. Silence fell. He held it for a full minute.

'Gentlemen,' he began, 'this is an auspicious moment in the history of our company. After conquering London and having the whole city at our feet, we will now make a triumphal tour of the kingdom to distribute our bounty more widely. Westfield's Men have a sacred mission.'

'What about me?' wailed Marwood.

'You have a mission of your own, dear sir.'

'Name it.'

'To sell bad beer at good prices.'

There was general laughter in the room. Now that they were leaving the inn, they could afford to ridicule its mean-spirited landlord. He was not a popular man. Apart from the buoyant hostility he displayed towards the players, he had another besetting sin. He guarded the chastity of his nubile daughter far too assiduously.

'Our departure from here is not without regret,' said Firethorn. 'We have been welcome guests at the Queen's Head this long time and our thanks must go to Master Marwood there for his unstinting hospitality.'

Muted laughter. They would be back one day.

'It is only when we leave something behind that we

come to recognise its true value. And so it is with this fine theatre of ours.' Firethorn described the inn with a sweep of his hand. 'We shall miss it for its warmth, its magic and its several memories. By the same token, Master Marwood, I trust that you will miss Westfield's Men and hear the ghostly echoes of our work here whenever you cross the yard outside.'

Lawrence Firethorn was achieving the impossible. He was all but coaxing a tear from the landlord's eye. It was now time to put heart into his company.

'Gentlemen,' he continued, 'when we quit London, we do so as ambassadors. We take our art along the highways and byways of England, and we do so under the banner of Lord Westfield. His name is our badge of honour and we must do nothing to besmirch it.' Firethorn pointed at an invisible map in front of him. 'We ride north, sirs. We visit many towns along the way but our real destination is York. We have special business there in the name of our patron. York beckons.'

'Then let us go,' said Gill impatiently.

'Not in that mood of resignation, Barnaby.'

'My smile is not at home today.'

'It is spirit that I talk about, man. We must not set out as a band of stragglers with no firm purpose. It is there if only we will see it. This tour is a pilgrimage. We are palmers bearing our gifts towards the Holy Land. Think of York by another name and it will raise your minds to our higher calling. I spoke of the Holy Land. York is our Jerusalem.'

George Dart was so transported by the speech that he clapped in appreciation. Barnaby Gill yawned, Edmund Hoode gazed out of the window and Christopher Millfield had to suppress a grin but the majority of the company were enthused by what they had heard. All of them had grave misgivings about the tour. It was a journey into the unknown that could be fraught with perils yet Firethorn had made it sound quite inspiring. Stirred by his words and needing the balm of an illusion, they tried to view their progress to York in a new light.

As a trip to Jerusalem.

Sweet sorrow flooded the inn yard at the Queen's Head. When the company came out to begin the first stage of their travels, they were met by moist faces and yearning sighs. Some of the players were married, others had mistresses, most had made themselves known among the impressionable maidenry of Cheapside. Sweethearts were embraced, tokens exchanged, promises made and kisses scattered with wild prodigality. Barnaby Gill turned his back on it all in disgust but George Dart watched with a mixture of envy and regret. No sweetheart came to send him off, no lover hung about his neck. It was so unfair. Christopher Millfield was flirting and laughing with five young women, each one of them patently infatuated with him. George Dart might not have the same height or elegance or stunning good looks but he was personable enough in his own way. Why were the five of them entranced by the swaggering assurance of the actor?

Could not one of them be spared for him?

Nicholas Bracewell stood apart from the general throng with Anne Hendrik. Theirs was a more composed and formal parting, the real leavetaking having occurred in the privacy of her bedchamber during the night. She had come simply to wave him off before setting out on her own journey. Nicholas was touched.

'I had not expected this, Anne.'

'Do I shame you before your fellows?'

'Every one of them will be jealous.'

'You flatter me, Nicholas. There are younger and prettier ladies here, today.'

'I have not seen any.'

She touched his sleeve in gratitude. The gesture was eloquent. Nicholas was not a demonstrative man and he shunned the public display of affection, reserving his emotional commitment for more intimate moments. Anne respected that. She had just wanted to see him once more before their paths diverged.

'When will you leave?' he asked.

'At noon.'

'Take all proper care.'

'Do not be anxious for me.'

'Who minds things here in London?'

'Preben van Loew.'

'An excellent fellow.'

'He was Jacob's right hand. Business will thrive under Preben, I have no doubt. It takes all hesitation out of my own departure.'

53

Lawrence Firethorn reminded them of their purpose.

'We have a mission, gentlemen. About it straight!'

There was a last flurry of kisses and farewells then the players obeyed his command. Only three of the company had horses. Dressed in a superb doublet of red, figured velvet with matching breeches, and wearing a plumed hat of tasteful extravagance, Lawrence Firethorn sat astride a chestnut stallion. He wanted people to see him coming. Barnaby Gill, also attired for show, rode a bay mare. Edmund Hoode, mounted on a dappled grey, wore the more practical apparel for a traveller on dusty roads. The company's luggage was stacked into a large waggon that was drawn by two massive horses. Nicholas was to drive the waggon with the other sharers and the apprentices on board. The rest of the company was to follow on foot.

Firethorn removed his hat for a final wave.

'Adieu, sweet ladies! Wish us well!'

As the torrent of cries began, he urged his horse forward and led the small procession out through the main gate. Gracechurch Street was its usual whirlpool of activity on market day and they had to pick their way through the ranks of stalls and the surging throng. A few cheers went up from those who knew their faces and valued their work but, for the vast majority, buying, selling and haggling vigorously, the price of eggs was of more import.

The crush thinned as Gracechurch Street merged into Bishopsgate Street and they were able to move more freely. Ahead of them was one of the main exits from the city and they approached it in a welter of mixed emotions.

Firethorn had spoken of a pilgrimage but nobody could really guess what lay beyond those walls. The last sight which greeted them within the city itself was less than comforting.

High above Bishopsgate itself was a series of large spikes. Stuck on to them were the decomposing heads of traitors, bleached by the sun and pecked by the birds. One in particular caught their attention. It was the head of a nobleman which was battered out of shape and which had already lost an eye to some predatory beak. Walking along behind the waggon, George Dart looked up in horror and nudged Christopher Millfield.

'Do you see there, sir?'

'An example to us all, George.'

'What manner of man would he be?'

'That is Anthony Rickwood. Late of Sussex.'

'You know him, then?'

'He was executed at Tyburn but two days ago.'

Dart noticed something that made his hair stand on end. The single eye in the deformed and blood-stained face was glaring down with an anger that was frightening. It was trying to focus its evil intent on one person.

'Master Millfield . . .'

'Yes, George?'

'I believe he is looking at you.'

Humphrey Budden was in a fever of apprehension. He hardly dared to leave his wife's side in case she was seized by another fit. Neighbours had been scandalised by the sounds which had issued from her bedchamber and all kinds of wild rumours were now flying around Nottingham like so many bats flapping about in a belfry. It was distressing to someone in Budden's position and he had turned once more for advice from Miles Melhuish. Racked by his own ambiguous role in the domestic tragedy, the vicar urged daily resort to prayer for man and wife. He also came up with another suggestion for the suffering husband.

'Let us walk down by the river, Eleanor.'

'If you wish it, sir.'

'This was our favourite place not so long ago,' he reminded her. 'Have you so soon forgot?'

'Indeed, no.'

'You'll come with me, then?'

'I'll obey my husband.'

'This way . . .'

Eleanor was no longer the woman he had married. The comely young widow with such a light heart had turned into a serious introvert with her mind on higher things. That unexplained horror in the bedchamber had robbed him of his chief delight. Eleanor had recovered from her coma with no memory of what had happened. Her naked assault on the praying Miles Melhuish was unknown to her. All was lost. Gone was her warmth, her laughter and vivacity. She was subdued and preoccupied now. Humphrey Budden had been sleeping in a cold bed for nights.

He put his trust in God's bright sunlight.

'Sit down here, Eleanor.'

'Why, sir?'

'Because I wish to speak with you.'

'This grass will suit, I think.'

She lowered herself down on to the green turf and spread her dress around her. Budden was moved. For a second, he saw the woman he had loved, courted and won for his own. Happiness came flooding back. They had returned to the spot where it had all started. Water rippled only yards away from them as the River Trent snaked its way through verdant banks. Old magic might yet be rekindled if he was patient. He sank down beside her and took her hand in his.

'Eleanor . . .'

'Sir?'

'Be my wife.'

'I am such.'

'Be my wife in more than name.'

'You speak in riddles.'

He slipped a hand clumsily around her waist. His mouth went dry as he asked it for help. He was painfully aware of his blundering inexperience. Eleanor had been twice married and twice widowed before she met him. He had been well past thirty before he even dared to think of taking a wife. There was a gap between them. It had been bridged on their wedding night and for several joyous months to follow, but it had now opened up again and widened into a chasm.

He cudgelled his voice into action again. 'When we first met . . .'

'Yes, Humphrey?'

'We talked of children.'

'I had five but lost dear Harry in childbirth.'

'You wanted more. My children, Eleanor.'

'I do recall it, sir.'

'Our children, dear wife, and the fruit of our union.' He ran his tongue across his lips. 'The vicar is of the same opinion in this matter. By God's grace, a new baby will bring you back to me as I loved you best.' He was troubled by prickly heat. 'Be my wife again, Eleanor. Pay the due of marriage once more.'

She gazed down the long reaches of the river and watched a kingfisher skim and dive. When she spoke, her voice was dull but her words had awesome clarity.

'I will not share your bed again. Husband you have been, and as loyal a man as any woman could wish, but I have other work in other places. He has called me, sir. He has given me clear direction.'

'Who has?'

'Who else would I listen to but God?'

'Clear direction, you say?'

'I must go on a long journey.'

'Why?'

'Because it is ordained.'

'May I make this journey with you, Eleanor?'

'No, sir. I go alone.'

'Where?'

'To the Holy Land.'

'But that cannot be, wife.'

'He guides my steps. It must be.'

'The Holy Land!' exclaimed Budden.

'Be not amazed, sir. I have been summoned.'

'For what reason?'

'I will know when I arrive there. In Jerusalem.'

Chapter Three

Westfield's Men left the pulsing world of London for the calmer pastures of Middlesex. Pangs of regret troubled them immediately. Once outside the city gates, they headed due north for Shoreditch where they passed the Curtain and then the Theatre, two custom-built playhouses in which they had given memorable performances on a number of occasions. Constructed outside the city boundary in order to escape the jurisdiction of the Lord Mayor and his Council, the two theatres were busy, boisterous, bustling centres of entertainment and hordes flocked to them. There would be no such havens for Westfield's Men on their travels. The sophisticated facilities of a real playhouse would give way to the exigencies of an inn yard or the limitations of a room in a private house. In purely artistic terms, touring was no pilgrimage.

It was a sudden fall from grace.

They journeyed along the Great North Road, one of the four major highways in the kingdom. It took them past Islington Ponds, where they saw men shooting wild ducks for sport, then struck out into open country. Farms were dotted about on all sides, part of the huge agricultural belt that encircled London with green acres and which produced its wheat, hay, fruit and vegetables or fattened up cattle, sheep, pigs, chickens, ducks and geese for sale in the markets of the capital. Urban squalor had been left behind now. The air was cleaner, the sky brighter, the hues more vivid and the vistas seemingly endless. Lungs and noses which had become accustomed to the reek of a plague city could breathe salvation.

Nicholas Bracewell kept the two carthorses plodding along at a steady gait and drank in the sights and sounds of the countryside. Sitting alongside him was Richard Honeydew, the youngest, smallest and most talented of the apprentices. The boy had long since learned that the book holder was not only his staunchest friend in the company but an inexhaustible fund of information.

'Master Bracewell . . .'

'Yes, lad?'

'I have never been outside London before.'

'Then you will gain much from the experience, Dick.'

'Will there be great dangers ahead?'

'Do not think upon such matters.'

'The other boys talk of thieves and highwaymen.'

'They are but teasing you, lad.'

'Martin says gypsies may carry me off.'

'He mocks your innocence.'

'Shall we face no perils at all?'

'None that should fright you too much, Dick.'

'Then why do you carry swords?'

All the men were armed and most had daggers at their belts as well as rapiers at their sides. It was a very necessary precaution for any travellers. Outlaws, rogues and vagabonds lurked along the roads in search of prey. Nicholas did not want to alarm the boy by telling him this and instead assured him that the very size and strength of the company would deter any possible attack. Richard Honeydew would be as safe in the countryside as he would be when he slept in his bed at the house in Shoreditch under the formidable but affectionate guard of Margery Firethorn. The boy relaxed visibly.

Short, thin and with the bloom of youth upon his delicate features, Richard Honeydew had been carefully shaped by Nature to take on female roles. His boyish charms became even more alluring when he changed his sex and his unforced prettiness translated readily into the beauty of a young woman. A mop of blond hair that was usually hidden beneath a wig now sprouted out from under his cap. Because the boy was so unaware of his several attractions, they became even more potent.

'Would you like to ride on a horse, Dick?'

'Oh, yes, Master Gill.'

'Hop up behind me, then.'

'Will it be safe, sir?'

'If you hold on tight to my waist.'

63

Barnaby Gill had brought his horse alongside the waggon and was now offering a gloved hand to the boy. Nicholas intervened swiftly.

'I need the lad to help with me with the reins.'

'Do you so?' said Gill testily.

'He must be taught how to drive the waggon.'

'You have pupils enough for that task, man.'

'None so apt as Dick Honeydew.'

'Come, let me teach him other lessons.'

'He is not for school today, Master Gill.'

Nicholas spoke politely but firmly and the other backed off with a hostile glare. The boy was still unawakened to the more sinister implications of the friendship which Barnaby Gill showed towards him from time to time and Nicholas had to move in as protector. Understanding nothing of what had passed between the two men, Richard Honeydew was simply disappointed to have lost the chance to ride upon the bay mare.

'Must I truly know how to drive the waggon?'

'We must all take our turn at the reins.'

'Why did Master Gill anger so?'

'He was deprived of his wishes, Dick.'

'May I never ride upon a horse?'

'Master Hoode will oblige you at any time.'

The troupe rolled on its way, pausing briefly at a wayside inn for refreshment before moving on again. Had they all been mounted, they might have covered thirty miles in a day but their resources did not run to such a large stable of horses. Since they went at the rate of those walking on foot, they had to settle for much less distance. If they pushed themselves, they would have made twenty miles before nightfall but it would have wearied them and left them with neither the time nor the strength for an impromptu performance at the place where they stopped. Lawrence Firethorn and Nicholas Bracewell had discussed the itinerary in some detail. It was important to pace themselves carefully.

Richard Honeydew sought more education.

'Did you see that head, Master Bracewell?'

'Head?'

'As we left London. Upon a spike at Bishopsgate.'

'I marked it, lad.'

'The sight made me feel sick.'

'That was partly the intention.'

'Can any man deserve such a fate?'

'Anthony Rickwood was a traitor and the penalty for treason is death. Whether that death should be so cruel and barbarous is another matter.'

'Who was the man?'

'Part of a Catholic conspiracy,' said Nicholas. 'He and his fellows plotted to murder the Queen during a visit she was due to make to Sussex.'

'How was the conspiracy uncovered?'

'By Sir Francis Walsingham. He has spies everywhere. One of his informers learned of the plot in the nick of time and Master Rickwood was seized at once.'

'What of the other conspirators?'

'There will be further arrests when their names are known. Mr Secretary Walsingham will not rest until every last one of them has his head upon a spike. He has vowed that he will bring all Catholic traitors to justice.'

'Will he so do?'

'Doubt it not, Dick. His spies are well-chosen and well-trained in their work. He controls them all with great skill. It was not just our naval commanders who defeated the Armada. We owe much to Mr Secretary Walsingham as well. He it was who foretold the size and armaments of the Spanish fleet.'

'You seem to know much about him.'

'I sailed with Drake,' said Nicholas, 'and he was closely acquainted with Sir Francis Walsingham.'

'Was he?'

'The Secretary of State has always taken a special interest in the exploits of our navigators.'

'Why?'

'Because they had a darker purpose.'

'What was that, master?'

'Piracy.'

The boy's eyes widened with outrage at the idea.

'Sir Francis Drake a pirate!' he exclaimed.

'What else would you call raids on foreign vessels and towns?' said Nicholas. 'Piracy. Pure and simple. I was there, lad. I saw it.'

'But piracy is a terrible crime.'

'There is a way around that problem.'

'Is there?'

'Yes, and I suspect that Walsingham was the man who found it. He persuaded the Queen to become involved in the enterprise. In return for receiving a share in the spoils of the voyage, Her Majesty granted us letters of marque.'

'Letters of marque?'

'They turned us from pirates into privateers.'

'And this was done by our own dear Queen?'

'With the connivance of Walsingham. He urged her to encourage the lawless acts of Drake and his like. When they captured Spanish ships, they brought money into the Treasury and tweaked the nose of Roman Catholicism.'

Richard Honeydew gasped as he tried to take it all in. He was profoundly shocked by the news that a great national hero had at one time been engaged in piracy, but he did not doubt Nicholas's word. He was confused, too, by the religious aspect.

'Why do the Catholics want to kill the Queen?'

'She is the symbol of our Protestant country.'

'Is it such a crime to follow Rome?'

'Yes, lad,' said Nicholas. 'Times have changed. My father was brought up in the old religion but King Henry turned him into a Protestant, and the whole realm besides. Most people would not dare to believe what my father once believed. They are too afraid of Walsingham.'

'So am I,' said the boy.

'At all events, the Queen's life must be protected.'

'In every possible way.'

'That is why we must have so many spies.'

Richard Honeydew thought about the head upon the spike.

'I am glad that I am not a Roman Catholic,' he said.

* * *

York Minster speared the sky with its three great towers and cast a long shadow of piety over the houses and shops that clustered so eagerly around it. It was the most beautiful cathedral in England as well as being the largest medieval building in the kingdom. Work on it had begun way back in 1220 and it was over two and a half centuries before it was completed. The result was truly awe-inspiring, a Gothic masterpiece which represented the full cycle of architectural styles and which was a worthy monument to the consecutive generations of Christian love and devotion that went into its construction. Visitors to York could see the Minster from several miles away, rising majestically above the city like a beacon of light in a world of secular darkness.

Sir Clarence Marmion did not even spare it a cursory glance as he rode in through Bootham Bar on his horse. A tall, distinguished, cadaverous man in his fifties, he had the kind of noble bearing and rich apparel that made people touch their caps in deference as he passed. After riding down Petergate, he turned into The Shambles and moved along its narrow confines with bold care, ducking his head beneath the overhanging roofs, brushing the walls with his shoulders and using his horse to force a gentle passage through the crowd. High above him, the bells of the cathedral mingled with the happy clamour of the working day. He clicked his tongue in irritation.

His mount now took him left along the river until he was able to cross it at Ouse Bridge. As he rode on down Micklegate, people were still streaming into the city on their way to market. He swung in through a gateway and found himself in a cobbled yard. An ostler ran out to hold his horse while he dismounted and got no more than a grunt of acknowledgement for his pains. It was exactly what he expected. Sir Clarence was no casual visitor to the inn. It had been owned by his family for centuries.

The Trip to Jerusalem was a long, low, timber-framed building that wandered off at all sorts of improbable angles with absent-minded curiosity. It dated back to the twelfth century and was said to have been the stopping place for soldiers riding south to join the Crusade in 1189. At that time, it was the brewhouse to the castle but a sense of spiritual purpose made it change its name to the Pilgrim. Under the hand of Sir Clarence Marmion, it had acquired its fuller title, though its regular patrons referred to it simply and succinctly as Jerusalem.

Bending forward under the lintel, Sir Clarence went through the doorway and into the taproom. An aroma of beer and tobacco welcomed him. When he straightened his back, his head almost touched the undulating ceiling.

Mine Host responded quickly to his arrival and came scurrying out from behind the bar counter, wiping his hands on his apron and nodding obsequiously.

'Good day to you, Sir Clarence!'

'And to you, sir.'

'Welcome to Jerusalem.'

'Would that it were true!' said the other feelingly.

'Your room is all ready, Sir Clarence.'

'I will repair to it in a moment.'

'Ring the bell if you should need service.'

'We must not be disturbed on any account.'

'No, Sir Clarence,' said the landlord, bowing his apologies. 'Nobody will be allowed near the room, I promise you. Leave the matter in my hands.'

Those hands, large, moist and podgy, were rubbing nervously against each other. The visitor always seemed to have that effect on Lambert Pym. Even after a decade as landlord of the inn, he had not entirely shaken off his fear of the Marmion temper. Tremors went through Pym's roly-poly frame whenever his visitor called and the bluff manner which served all his other customers vanished beneath a display of exaggerated humility.

Sir Clarence looked down at him with disdain.

'I have received news from London.'

'Indeed, Sir Clarence?'

'A company of players is heading this way.'

'We have actors aplenty in York this summer.'

'Westfield's Men are not of common stock. They have been recommended to me by a friend and I will act upon that recommendation.'

'As you wish, Sir Clarence.'

'The company will be lodged here at my expense.'

'Your hospitality does you credit.'

'They will perform one play in your yard.'

'I will give order for it, Sir Clarence.'

'Their second appearance will be at Marmion Hall.'

'I hope they know their good fortune,' said the landlord, picking at his furry black horseshoe of a beard. 'When are we to expect these players?'

'Not for ten days at least. They have other venues.'

'None will offer the welcome of Jerusalem.'

'That is my request. See to it, sir.'

Lambert Pym bowed and then hurried across the room to open a door that led to a small staircase. His chubby features were lit by a smile of appeasement.

'Your guest is within, Sir Clarence.'

'I hoped for no less.'

'The room is yours for as long as you choose.'

'So is everything here.'

And with that solemn rejoinder, Sir Clarence stooped to go through another low doorway and ascended the noisy oak stairs. After walking along a passageway, he went into a room that was at the rear of the building. His guest was seated beside a small oak table and rose when he saw the tall figure enter. Sir Clarence waved him back to his chair then strode around the room to get the feel of it and to test its privacy. Only when he was satisfied on the latter score did he sit at the table himself.

Removing his glove, he slipped a hand inside his doublet to pull out the other letter which had been sent to him from London. Its contents made his jaw tighten.

'Sad tidings, sir.'

'As we feared?'

'Worse, much worse.'

He handed the letter over and his companion took it with frightened willingness. Small, intense and soberly dressed, Robert Rawlins had the appearance and air of a scholar. The pinched face, the shrewd eyes and the rounded

71

shoulders hinted at long years of study among learned tomes in dusty libraries. He read the letter in seconds and turned white with terror.

'Saints preserve us!'

It was a good omen. On their first night away from the comforts of the capital, Westfield's Men met with kindness and generosity. They stayed at the Fighting Cocks, a large and pleasant establishment that overlooked Enfield Chase. It was a hostelry that their patron frequented on his journeys to and from his estates near St Albans, and they were the benefactors of his fondness for the place. The landlord not only extended open arms to the company, he made sure that each of them slept in a soft bed, and would take no more than small recompense for this favour. It was a blessing for the actors. There would be times when some of them would have to sleep on straw in the stables and other occasions when they would spend a night under the stars. Real beds, even when shared with a few restless companions, were a luxury to be savoured.

There was further bounty that night. Other guests were staying at the Fighting Cocks, wealthy merchants who were breaking their journey on their way home to Kent and who wanted to celebrate their business successes with some entertainment. Westfield's Men obliged with an extempore recital. Lawrence Firethorn declaimed speeches from his favourite plays, Barnaby Gill danced his famous comic jigs and Richard Honeydew sang country airs to the accompaniment of a lute. Fine wine and admiration helped the merchants to part with ten shillings between them, a rich gift that went straight into the company coffers.

Fortune favoured them next morning as well. The weather was fine and the landlord gave them free beer and victuals to carry with them on their journey. They set out with a rising step. In Hertfordshire, they had every expectation of a welcome. Lord Westfield's name was known throughout the county of his birth and it was bound to purchase them special indulgence.

Nicholas Bracewell was sent on ahead to prepare the way. Borrowing the dapple grey from Edmund Hoode, he set off at a canter in the direction of Ware. It was not only because the book holder was such a fine horseman that he was given the responsibility. His ability to look after himself was also paramount. Lone travellers were easy game on some stretches of the road but even the most desperate villains would think twice about taking on someone as solid and capable as Nicholas Bracewell. He exuded a strength that was its own safeguard.

One of the smallest counties, Hertfordshire was the watershed for several rivers and Nicholas was often within earshot of running water. Beef cattle grazed on the pastures and the last of the hay was being gathered in by bending figures with swinging sickles. He rode on past a wood and a deer park until he came to a market garden that specialised in watercress beds. The county was renowned for the excellence of its watercress which was used as an antidote to the scurvy which afflicted so many Londoners. Nicholas took directions from a helpful gardener and then spurred the grey on.

He arrived in Ware to find a small, amiable community going about its daily business without undue complaint. Theatre companies could not just appear in a town and perform at will. Permission had to be sought first and a licence granted. In larger towns, the Mayor was the person to grant such a licence but Ware was too small to support such an august personage. Nicholas instead sought out one of its local council.

Tom Hawthornden was known for his bluntness.

'You may not play here, sir.'

'But we are Westfield's Men.'

'It matters not if you were the Queen's own company of actors, Master Bracewell. We have but small appetite for entertainment and it has been truly satisfied.'

'By whom, Master Hawthornden?'

'Such another troupe as yours.'

'When was this?'

'But two days since. The memory is fresh.'

'Ours will be the better offering,' argued Nicholas. 'We are no wandering band of players, sir. Master Lawrence Firethorn is the toast of his profession. Westfield's Men are the finest company in London.'

'Your rivals were so entitled as well.'

'Do but judge our work against theirs.'

'It will not suffice,' said Hawthornden, hands upon his hips. 'Move on, sir. Ware has witnessed as merry a comedy as we are ever likely to see. It will keep us in good humour for weeks. We need no further diversion.'

Nicholas stopped him as he tried to walk away.

'Hear me out, master. We offer you a play that has enough laughter, dancing, singing and swordplay to last the people of Ware for a year. It is a lively comedy that only Westfield's Men may stage.'

'Too late, sir. Far too late.'

'Do but see *Cupid's Folly* and you will not rue it.'

'What did you call the play?'

'*Cupid's Folly.*'

'Then is your journey really in vain.'

'How so?'

'We have seen this country tale, sir.'

'That cannot be, Master Hawthornden,' said Nicholas confidently. 'We hold the licence of that play. I have the book under lock and key. What you saw, perchance, was another play with the same title. Our comedy tells the story of one Rigormortis, an old man who is pierced by Cupid's arrow.'

'Aye,' said Hawthornden. 'He falls in love with every wench he sees yet spurns the one who loves him. Her name was Ursula and she did make us laugh most heartily.'

Nicholas gaped. It sounded like the same play. When Tom Hawthornden furnished more details of the action, the case was certain. Ware had definitely seen a performance of *Cupid's Folly* even though the play was the exclusive property of Westfield's Men. It was baffling.

Tom Hawthornden resorted to a rude dismissal.

'Go your way, sir. There's nothing for you here.'

Nicholas grabbed him by the shoulders and held him. 'What was the name of this other company?'

Within twenty-four hours of his departure, remorse set in. Margery Firethorn began to wish that she had given her husband a more joyful farewell. They would not then have parted in such a strained manner. Had she not repelled his advances, they could have spent their last night together in a state of married bliss that would have kept her heart warm and put her mind at ease. As it was, she now felt hurt, fractious and unsettled. Long, lonely months would pass before she saw her husband again.

The house in Shoreditch already felt cold and empty. Four apprentices and two hired men had lodged there and she had mothered them all with her brisk affection. Now she was left with only a part of her extended family. The most painful loss was that of Lawrence Firethorn. As man and actor, he was a glorious presence who left a gap in nature when he was not there. He had his faults and no one knew them as intimately as his wife. But they faded into insignificance when she thought of the life and noise and colour that he brought to the house, and when she recalled the thousand impetuous acts of love he had bestowed upon her in the fullness of his ardour.

Caught up in a mood of sadness, she tripped upstairs to the bedchamber she shared with a man she now saw as a species of paragon. What other husband could retain her interest and excite her passions for so many years? What other member of such an insecure profession could take such fond care of his wife and children? That he was loved and desired by other women was no secret to her but even that could be a source of pride. She was the object of intense envy. Where notorious beauties had failed to possess him even for a night, she had secured him for a lifetime. Their pursuit of him only served her purpose.

As she reviewed their last few hours together, she saw how unkind she had been to him. Lawrence Firethorn was unique and it was her place to respect and foster that uniqueness. He was not the callous father she accused him of being, nor yet the selfish husband or the compulsive libertine. He was a great man and, taken all in all, he deserved better from her.

Sitting on the edge of the bed, Margery used gentle fingers to stroke the garment he had so considerately left behind for her. It was his second-best cloak, worn during his performance in the title-role of *Vincentio's Revenge* and redolent with memories of that triumph. Knowing what it had cost him in emotional and spiritual terms to part with the cloak, she had slept all night with it lying across her. It was her one real memento of him.

Apart from the ruby.

Margery sat up with a start. She had chosen to forget all about the ring. It had been the cause of their bitter disputation and she had put it out of sight and out of mind. Now it took on a new significance. It was a love token from her husband, a reaffirmation of their marriage at a time when it would be put under immense strain. Scolding herself for being so ungrateful, she ran to the drawer where she had hidden the present. She would wear it proudly until he came back home again.

Burning with passion, she opened the drawer. But the ring had vanished. In its place was a tiny scroll. When she unrolled it, she saw a brief message from her husband.

'Farewell, dear love. Since the ruby is not welcome in Shoreditch, I will wear it myself in Arcadia.'

Margery Firethorn smouldered. She knew only too well the location of Arcadia. It was the setting of a play by Edmund Hoode. Instead of gracing her finger, the ring would be worn for effect in *The Lovers' Melancholy*. It was demeaning. Such was the esteem in which she was held.

Love had, literally, been snatched from her hand.

Her scream of rage was heard a hundred yards away.

The vestry of the parish church of St Stephen was dank and chill in the warmest weather but Humphrey Budden still felt as if he were roasting on a spit. Misery had brought him there and it deepened with every second. He had to make a shameful confession. The one consolation was that Miles Melhuish was patently as discomfited as he himself was. Inclined to be smug and unctuous for the most part, the vicar was now torn between reluctant interest and rising apprehension. Though he had married many of his parishioners and sent them off with wise words to the land of connubial delight, he had never dared to explore that fabled territory himself. This fact only served to cow the nervous Budden even more. How could any man understand his predicament, still less a rotund bachelor whose idea of nocturnal pleasure was to spend an hour on his knees beside the bed in a frenzy of prayer?

Miles Melhuish sat in the chair opposite his visitor and reached out to him across the table. A vague smell of incense filled the air. The weight of religiosity was oppressive. Their voices echoed as in a tomb.

'Speak to me, Humphrey,' encouraged the vicar.

'I will try, sir.'

'Is it your wife again?'

'I fear me, it is.'

'Not more weeping and wailing?'

'Thankfully, no, but there is further harm.'

'To whom?'

Humphrey Budden was a furnace of humiliation. His cheeks were positively glowing and he felt as if steam would issue from every orifice at any moment.

'Did you pray?' said Melhuish sternly.

'Without ceasing.'

'Has Eleanor prayed with you?'

'It is the only time I may get close to her.'

'How say you?'

'She has put me aside, sir.'

'Speak more plain.'

It was a difficult request to fulfil. A man who had mastered the delicate art of lacemaking was now forced to chisel words crudely out of himself like an apprentice stonemason. Each swing of the hammer made his brain reel.

'Eleanor . . . is . . . not . . . my . . . wife.'

'Indeed, she is,' said the vicar. 'I solemnised the marriage myself and preached a sermon to you on the importance of walking in truth. Have you done that, my son? Have you and your wife walked in truth?'

'Yes, sir . . . down by . . . the river.'

'Stop holding back.'

'I . . . have . . . no . . . wife.'

'Whom God hath joined let no man put asunder.'

'A woman hath done it.'

'Done what, man? We are going in small circles.'

Humphrey Budden steeled himself to blurt it all out.

'Eleanor is no longer my wife, sir. She will not share my bed or suffer my embraces. She says that the voice of God has spoken to her. It is sending her on a pilgrimage to the Holy Land.'

'Wait, wait!' said Melhuish in alarm. 'You go too fast here. Let us take it one step at a time. She will not share your bed, you tell me?'

'No, sir. She sleeps on the floor.'

'Alone?'

'She will not let me near her.'

'Have you given her just cause, Humphrey?'

'I think not.'

'Have you caused her some injury or turned her affections from you in some other way?'

Even as he asked the question, Miles Melhuish saw how cruel and inappropriate it was. Humphrey Budden was a strong man but he would never use that strength against a woman. No husband could have been more considerate. His wife must be to blame for what had happened.

The vicar tried to probe into the bedchamber.

'This problem is of recent origin?'

'Since I called you to the house, sir.'

'And what passed between you in former times?'

'We shared a bed in Christian happiness, sir.'

'And your wife was then . . . forthcoming?'

'Most truly!'

'She did not hold back from you?'

'I was the novice at first. Eleanor had to instruct me in my duties and she did so with wondrous skill.'

Miles Melhuish reddened as a vision flashed before his eyes. He saw the naked body of an impassioned woman in the bedchamber of a parishioner. He could sniff her fragrance, feel her touch, share her madness. It took a great effort of will for him to banish her from his mind.

He asked his question through gritted teeth.

'You say the marriage was happy?'

'Very happy, sir.'

'And that she instructed you willingly.'

'Two husbands had taught her much.'

'So you and your wife . . . mingled flesh?'

'Every night, sir.'

'The act of love is for procreation,' said the vicar sharply. 'It is not a source of carnal gratification.'

'We know that, sir, and acted accordingly. Our dearest wish was that our union would be blessed with a child.'

'I'm surprised you have not had several offspring,' muttered the other under his breath. 'With such regular activity, you could people an entire town!' He sat up and pulled himself together. 'But all that is now past?'

'This is what she says.'

'For what reason?'

'Divine command.'

'The woman is deranged.'

'She wishes to become a pilgrim, sir.'

'Poor creature! She needs help.'

'Eleanor is leaving soon.'

'Where will she go?'

'Jerusalem.'

'I spy madness.'

Humphrey Budden leaned forward to make his plea.

'Speak to her, sir!'

'Me?'

'You are our only hope. Eleanor will listen to you.'

'Will she so?'

'Speak to her!'

It was a cry from the heart and Miles Melhuish could not ignore it. Part of him wanted to shrug the problem off his own shoulders but another part of him wanted to take the full weight of the burden. The vision flashed through his mind again. Long fair hair. Round, trembling buttocks. Joyous breasts. Satin skin. Succulent lips. Total surrender in its most beautiful human form.

The answer to a prayer.

'Very well,' he said. 'I'll speak to her.'

Lawrence Firethorn pawed the ground like an angry bull. When he began his charge, nobody within striking distance was safe. It was a terrifying spectacle.

'What did you say, Nick?' he bellowed.

'They will not suffer us to play there.'

'Not suffer us! In Lord Westfield's own county? Where the writ of our patron runs wide? And they will not suffer us, indeed? I'll teach them what suffering is, call me rogue if I do not!'

'Another company got there first, master.'

'With our play! Stolen without compunction.'

'They would not hear *Cupid's Folly* again,' explained Nicholas. 'Nor would they countenance any other play from us. They have eaten their fill.'

'Then will I make them spew it up again!' raged Firethorn. 'By heaven, I'll make their stomachs burn, the unmannerly rogues, the scurvy, lousy, beggarly knaves, the foul, ungrateful rascals, the stinking, rotting carcasses of men that live in that God-forsaken hole! Keep me from them, Nick, or I'll carve 'em all to shreds with my sword, I will, and hang the strips on a line for kites to peck at.'

Lawrence Firethorn unsheathed his weapon and hacked at a bush to vent his spleen. The rest of the company looked on with trepidation. Nicholas had met them a mile south of Ware to break the bad news. Predictably, it had thrown the actor-manager into a fury. As he reduced the bush to a forlorn pile of twigs and leaves, they began to fear for the safety of all vegetation in the county. He was armed and dangerous.

It was Edmund Hoode who calmed him down. 'That bush is not the enemy, Lawrence.'

'Stand off, sir.'

'Sheath your sword and listen to reason.'

'Reason? What care I for reason?'

'We are all losers in this escapade.'

'Indeed we are,' said Barnaby Gill loftily from his saddle. '*Cupid's Folly* was to have been my triumph. I never play Rigormortis without I leave the audience in a state of helpless mirth.'

'It is those absurd breeches,' sneered Firethorn.

'My success does not lie in my breeches.'

'That we all can confirm!'

Laughter from the others helped to ease the tension. Gill spluttered impotently then turned his horse away in a huff. Hoode took the sword from Firethorn and put it back into its sheath.

Nicholas Bracewell addressed the real problem.

'How did they get hold of the play?'

'It was taken from you privily,' said Firethorn.

'That is not possible, master. The books of all our plays are locked in a chest that I keep hidden away from prying eyes. Nobody is allowed near it, least of all our rivals. *Cupid's Revenge* was not stolen.'

'It was pirated in some way,' said Hoode grimly. 'And if it can be done with one play, it can be done again with others. Who can assure the safety of my own plays?'

'There's but one answer for it,' said Nicholas.

'Revenge!' declared Firethorn.

'Only after we learn the truth, master.'

'We know it full well, Nick. This is the work of Banbury's

84

Men, those shambling caterpillars that call themselves a company of players. They mean to spike our guns but we will turn our cannon round and give them such a broadside as will blow them back to London.'

'But how was it done?' insisted Nicholas.

'Marry, that's the important point,' agreed Hoode.

'Not to me,' said Firethorn, striking a heroic pose with one arm outstretched towards the sky. 'Only one thing serves us here. Swift and bloody revenge! If those liveried lice belonging to the Earl of Banbury will dare to take on the might of Westfield's Men, so be it! Let them beware the consequences.'

He ranted on in fine style for several minutes. Banbury's Men were their arch-rivals, a talented company that strove to equal them but always fell short of their stature. Led by the wily Giles Randolph, they had made attempts to damage the reputation of Westfield's Men before but they had never stooped to this device. In London, they would not have dared to be so bold but the anonymity of the provinces gave them a useful shield. Banbury's Men had struck the first telling blow.

Firethorn intended to strike the last.

'Let us pursue them with all speed, gentlemen. They deserve no quarter. Banbury's Men have shown how low they will sink into the mire of self-advancement. There's no room in our profession for such dishonourable wags. We must expel them once and for all.' The sword came out to make a graphic gesture. 'Onwards to battle, my lads! Let us fight for our lives and our good names.'

With a practised flick of the wrist, he sent the point of his rapier some inches into the ground so that the blade rocked to and fro with mesmeric power. They were still watching the weapon vibrate as he growled his final, fatal words.

'Gentlemen – this is war!'

Giles Randolph reclined in a wooden armchair in the corner of the tavern and toyed with his glass of Canary wine. Tall, slim and dark, he had a Mediterranean cast of feature which set him apart from the average man and which made him irresistible to the feminine sections of his audiences. He had a satanic quality that excited. Randolph was the acknowledged star of Banbury's Men and he was a shrewd businessman as well as a superb actor. Trapped in the vanity of his profession, he could not accept that any man could strut a stage with more assurance or squeeze the life-blood out of any role with more devastating effect. His feud with Lawrence Firethorn, therefore, went fathoms deeper than mere professional jealousy. It was a vendetta, at once reinforced and given more dimension by the fact that the Earl of Banbury and Lord Westfield were sworn enemies. In mortifying his rival, Giles Randolph could please his patron.

He smiled complacently at his companion.

'We have made good speed.'

'Banbury's Men are ahead in every sense.'

'It must remain that way. I like not these wearisome tours but at least we can have some sport for our pains.'

'They will have reached Ware by now.'

'And found the coldest welcome.'

Randolph sipped his wine then toyed with his glass. As befitted a leading actor, he was attired with all due ostentation in a doublet of blue satin with elaborate gold patterning down the front and green hose. His hat swept down over one eye to give him a conspiratorial air and its ostrich feather trembled as he spoke.

'Firethorn must be wounded to the quick.'

'We have drawn blood enough already.'

'I want to hack off his limbs,' said Randolph with sudden intensity. 'I want to leave his gore all over the stage. If he dares to compete against my sovereignty, I will bring him down once and for all.'

'By what means?'

'Attacking his pride.'

'I'll wager it is smarting back in Ware just now.'

'Wait until he reaches Grantham. I'll pull a trick will make him wish he had stayed at home in Shoreditch with that termagant wife of his and listened to her scolding.' He put his glass down. 'Now, sir, what is his finest role?'

'Vincentio?' suggested the other.

'A scurvy play with but three speeches of note.'

'Hector, then. Master Firethorn is always boasting of his prowess in *Hector of Troy*. The part becomes him.'

'He has not played it this last year.'

'Then must we go to his favourite character.'

'What's that? You know his mind.'

'Pompey!'

'The very man!'

'The play was called for time and again.'

'By Edmund Hoode, I think.'

'Yes, sir. It is called *Pompey the Great*.'

'Then will it feel the imprint of my greatness.'

'We'll play the piece in Grantham.'

'To the hilt, sir. Lawrence Firethorn will have his reputation cut from beneath him. I'll make the role my own and throw Westfield's Men aside into the mire. This tour will yet repay me in full amount.'

Giles Randolph called for more wine from the cask.

It tasted sweeter than ever.

Chapter Four

Marmion Hall was an optical illusion. Because it nestled in a hollow and was fringed by a semi-circle of trees, it looked far smaller than it really was. Behind the modest façade, it was remarkably spacious with the main part of the house thrusting deep and with a sizeable wing that was hidden behind the outcrop of sycamores. A fire had caused extensive damage to the rear of the property some ten years earlier and there had been lengthy repair work. Sir Clarence Marmion took advantage of the rebuilding to add some new features to his home though they were not all apparent to the naked eye. Like its owner, Marmion Hall preserved an air of secrecy.

Sunday afternoon found Sir Clarence in the dining room, sitting alone at the head of the shining oak table as he studied his Bible. Dressed in subdued colours and wearing an expression of rapt concentration, he tended to his spiritual needs then closed his eyes in thought.

There was a knock on the door. A servant entered.

'Well?'

'The guests have arrived, Sir Clarence.'

'All of them?'

'Yes, Sir Clarence.'

'What o'clock is it?'

'Upon the stroke of four.'

'Thank you.'

A dismissive flick of the hand sent the servant backing out of the room. Sir Clarence lifted his lids and read the passage that he had been studying. Closing the book gently, he put it under his arm and made his way out. He now felt fully prepared for what lay ahead.

The hall was a large rectangle with oak panelling along three walls and a series of high windows along the other wall with leaded panes. Gilt-framed mirrors and family portraits broke up the monotony. A moulded ceiling gave a sense of grandeur. Furniture was all of prime oak and tastefully arranged. In the vast stone fireplace at the far end of the hall was an iron fireback bearing the Marmion coat-of-arms. Iron firedogs stood beside an iron basket piled high with logs.

When Sir Clarence entered, they were all waiting and their murmured conversations stopped at once. He looked at them all with an amalgam of pride and sorrow and then opened his arms in welcome. The whole family came across to greet him and he exchanged pleasantries with them all. Then came the moment when the baby was placed into his arms. It was a boy, barely three months old, yet strong and lusty, waving his tiny fists at the world with Marmion defiance, wriggling in his white lace robe as if anxious to be about more important business.

Sir Clarence raised the child up to plant a kiss on its forehead and almost got a box on the ear for his temerity. With a soft half-smile, he handed his first grandchild back to his daughter-in-law then led the way across to the most recent of the portraits on display. It was a painting of his father, hanging above them with a look of stern purpose and showing all the qualities of character associated with dynasty. It was a source of the utmost regret that he was no longer alive to share in family celebrations.

'Give us your blessing, Father,' said Sir Clarence.

Then he reached forward and felt behind the lower edge of the frame. There was a click and a small door opened in the panelling on oiled hinges. A narrow passage was revealed. Stone steps led downwards.

Sir Clarence indicated his tiny grandson.

'Let him lead the way.'

Carried by his mother, the child went through the entrance and down the steps. Candles provided light all the way. The rest of the family followed with the head of the house bringing up the rear. As he stepped through the door, Sir Clarence pulled it shut and it clicked tight behind him. The odour of frankincense drifted up towards him. He was drawn down the staircase and along a dank subterranean passage until he came to the room in which all the others had now gathered.

It was a chapel. Sir Clarence had commissioned the building of it and the place never ceased to give him comfort and joy. Small, cold and necessarily secret though it might be, it was as inspiring as York Minster to him and he let its wonder work on him once more. The others took up their places in the pews, then they knelt to pay homage to their maker. Sir Clarence joined them, kneeling between his wife and his grandson, crossing himself as he did so.

The altar was ablaze with candles. Standing on its centre was a large gold crucifix that reflected the fierce light and glowed as if on fire. As the little congregation looked up, their eyes were transfixed by the sight. A steel door opened beside the altar and a figure entered in the vestments of a Catholic priest. Everyone stood up at once to show their respect. The priest moved quietly into position beside the stone font and glanced benignly at the child. From his calm and assured manner, nobody would guess that the man was about to commit a heinous crime.

Robert Rawlins began the service of baptism.

'Truly, you do him wrong to put such sayings upon him.'

'I must obey the word of God.'

'But it was God who joined you in holy matrimony.'

'He has other work for me now, sir.'

'Your husband is wounded most grievously.'

'We must all suffer in the service of the Lord.'

Miles Melhuish shook his head in frustration. He was standing in the vestry beside Eleanor Budden, deeming it wise to remain on his feet so that he had the option of flight in the event of some emergency. He could not be too careful. The woman was quiescent now but he had not forgotten the overwhelming passion of which she was capable and he was anxious not to touch it off while they were alone together on consecrated ground.

He moved behind the chair on which she sat.

'I will put a question to you, mistress.'

'I listen in all humility.'

'You tell me that you have been chaste since the voice of God whispered in your ear.'

'That is so, sir.'

'Then here is my question . . .'

Melhuish groped for the words. It was not a matter he had ever raised with a woman before and it tested his resolve. When he spoke with other female parishioners in the privacy of his vestry, it was usually to scold them for not attending church or to advise them on the proper Christian upbringing of their children. Duty was now compelling him to climb into bed with a married couple and effect their union. It was a foreign country to him and he did not know the language.

'Here is my question, Eleanor,' he said nervously. 'If there came a man with a sword who would strike off your husband's head if you did not take that worthy fellow back into your bed, tell me, in all conscience, for you say you will not lie, what would you do?'

'I will answer you true, sir.'

'Would you let Humphrey Budden commit the act of love with you – or have his head cut off?'

'I would rather see him being killed.'

'That is cruelty itself, woman!'

'I cannot help it, sir,' said Eleanor calmly. 'We must turn our back on all uncleanness.'

'God has ordained love between man and wife.'

'I've submitted to His purpose three times.'

'Is that all?' said the vicar in surprise. 'Yet Humphrey spoke of daily indulgence.'

'I mean that I have shared my bed with three husbands, sir. They did not find me wanting in love.'

'Until now, sister.'

'Times have changed.'

Miles Melhuish was losing control. The aim of his examination was to put sufficient pressure on Eleanor Budden to make her see the error of her ways but she was blithely unconcerned when he chastised her. What she always came back to was the word of God and it was on that subject that he must confound her. Countless years of unremitting prayer had given him his own privileged access to divine command and he felt that he knew the timbre of the Lord's voice more intimately than any lacemaker's wife, however much she might protest her devotion.

'When did God first talk with you?' he said.

'This se'nnight since.'

'And where were you at this time?'

'Buying fish at the market, sir.'

Miles Melhuish started. 'The Lord spoke to you amid the smell of mackerel?'

'I heard Him as clear as day.'

'And what words did He use in that marketplace?'

'He said: "Put aside your husband and follow me." God called me by name and I obeyed Him straight.'

'What did you then do?'

'Return to my house and go up to the bedchamber. We have a crucifix on the wall so that Jesus may watch over us. I then proclaimed my mission.'

'How was that done, good lady?'

'That is the wonder of it,' she said with a shrug of her shoulders that made her breasts bob invitingly. 'I do not know what befell me next. But when I opened my eyes, I was lying on the floor and you were standing over me with my husband and all was blissful peace.'

'You recall nothing of a great noise you made?'

'Noise, sir?'

'A most dolorous cry came from you.'

'I was weeping for the death of Christ in torment.'

Miles Melhuish threw caution to the winds and sat opposite her. Wayward housewives had always responded to a stern reproof before. It was time to stop encouraging the woman in her fancy and to put her firmly back on the straight and narrow path of wifely duty. He knitted his brows and reached for his homiletic strain.

'Cast out these false notions!' he warned. 'If you would serve God then do so by showing proper respect for one of His ministers. It is within the four walls of this parish church that you will hear His true voice and not at the fish stall in Nottingham market.' She looked duly crushed and it spurred him on. 'Go back to Humphrey Budden.

He is a good husband and deserves better from his chosen companion in life. Let me hear no more about this chastity in your bedchamber. Cleave to your spouse. Give him the children he desires. Add some little parishioners to our congregation at St Stephen's. That only is your bounden duty and purpose here upon this earth.'

He had won. Eleanor Budden sat with bowed head and hunched shoulders, meek, mild and submitting to his firm instruction. It was a small victory for him and it gave him a flabby self-importance. He sat up straight in his chair to project his full ecclesiastical authority.

And all the while, she was in abject surrender.

Then she began to laugh. It began as a snigger, half-suppressed with the back of her hand. Then it became a giggle, almost girlish in its flippancy, increasing in volume every second until it was a full-throated laugh that set her whole body shaking, then it became a roar of mirth that made the vestry reverberate with sound, and, finally and inexplicably, it was a strange and uncontrollable cachinnation that built up into a crescendo and stopped dead.

Eyes that had sparkled with humour now ran with tears of remorse. Hands that had flapped about wildly now closed in prayer. Miles Melhuish writhed beneath the intensity of her gaze and vowed to refer the case to the diocesan synod. It was way beyond his competence. He was in the presence of witchcraft. The Dean alone was fit to pronounce on such a weighty matter.

The tears ceased but the wild stare remained. He endured its obsessional glow until he realised that she was not looking at him at all but at some object directly behind him. Turning around, he saw what had transfixed and transfigured her. It was a small lancet window into which some zealous craftsman had set the most affecting picture in stained glass. Christ was nailed to the cross with the crown of thorns upon His head. The round face was framed by long fair hair and a full beard, which took on a golden hue as light streamed in through the window. There was martyrdom and majesty in the image.

Eleanor Budden let out a sigh of pure enchantment.

She was in love.

Nicholas Bracewell ran wet hands through his hair and tossed back his mane as he completed his ablutions at the pump in the courtyard. He was up not long after dawn and the sun was taking its first peep at the day. There was much to do before departure. Nicholas had to supervise the feeding and harnessing of the horses, the loading up of the waggon, the checking of valuables to make sure that nothing was missing, the payment of the landlord and the pacification of his wife, whom Lawrence Firethorn, in a moment of drunken zeal, had mistaken for a serving wench and seized in an amorous embrace. There would also be some lessons in swordplay he had promised the boys and the purchase of some provisions for the journey. The work of the book holder was never done.

'Welcome to the day, Master Bracewell!'

'The same to you, Christopher.'

'Let us hope it bears sweeter fruit than yesterday.'

'I am sure it must.'

'Where do we stop today?'

'At Royston. God willing.'

'Royston . . .'

The name triggered off a thought. Two long days of walking on foot had taken none of the swagger out of Christopher Millfield. He looked neat and trim in his doublet and hose. Nicholas, wearing an old shirt and a buff jerkin, felt dishevelled by comparison. He had never really taken to the young actor and put it down to the latter's forced affability.

Christopher Millfield produced his annoying grin.

'May I be so bold as to make a suggestion?'

'Please do, sir.'

'If we should fail to find an audience in Royston, as we did in Ware, there may yet be employment for us.'

'From what source?'

'Pomeroy Manor.'

'You know the place?'

'Only by repute,' said Millfield airily. 'It lies on the estates of one Neville Pomeroy, a man of true breeding and culture, not unfriendly to the theatre and like to give us a kinder word than the folk at Ware.'

Nicholas nodded his thanks. The name of Pomeroy was vaguely familiar to him. He had heard it mentioned by Lord Westfield, and in terms of praise, which was unusual for their patron. A local landowner with a liking for entertainment might be able to fill his largest room with some spectators for them.

'Where is the house?' he said.

'Towards Meldreth. Not far out of our way.'

'In which direction?'

'Cambridge.'

It was worth considering. If Banbury's Men were intent on queering their pitch, then Royston might well be closed to their art. Giles Randolph would not have ruined their chances at Pomeroy Manor. He might yet be thwarted.

Christopher Millfield stood with arms akimbo.

'Why do you not like me, Master Bracewell?'

'Have I said as much?'

'I read it in your manner.'

'You are deceived. I like you well enough.'

'But not as much as Gabriel Hawkes.'

'I gave the matter no thought.'

'That is not what Master Gill believes. He tells me that you urged the name of Gabriel over mine.'

'I will not deny it.'

'May I know your reason?'

'I took him to be the finer actor.'

Millfield winced. 'You are mistaken there, sir.'

'I can only give you my true opinion.'

'It may be changed ere long,' said the other with a flash of pride. 'But was that the only cause of your preference for Gabriel? That you rated him more highly?'

'No, Christopher.'

'What else?'

'I found him more honest company.'

Nicholas gave a straightforward answer that was not to

Millfield's taste at all. After shooting a hostile glare at the book holder, he invented a nonchalant smile.

'It is of no moment,' he said.

'How so?'

'Gabriel is gone to Heaven. I am here in his place.'

'Can you spare the dead no respect?'

'He was my rival. I do not mourn him.'

'Even though he was murdered?'

Christopher Millfield was taken aback for a second but he retrieved his composure very quickly. Unable to determine if the man's reaction arose from guilt or surprise, Nicholas tried to probe.

'Did his death not strike you as sudden?'

'He was afflicted by the plague.'

'It does not usually kill its victims so fast.'

'I have seen men snuffed out in a single day.'

'The old or the weak,' said Nicholas. 'The young and the fit are able to put up some sort of struggle.'

'What are you saying, Master Bracewell?'

'Until the day when fever broke out, Gabriel was a healthy young man in the prime of life. He should have not have been carried off so speedily.'

'Your conclusion?'

'Someone helped him on his way.'

'You have proof of this?'

'I have a strong feeling.'

'Is that all?' said Millfield with a smirk. 'You will need more than that to make your case. Besides, what does it matter now? Gabriel was marked for death. If someone did kill him, then he rendered the man a service by sparing him the agonies of a lingering end.'

'You take this too lightly, Christopher.'

'It is idle contemplation.'

'When a good man is murdered?'

'By whom?' challenged the other.

'Someone who stood to gain from his early demise.'

Millfield met his searching gaze without a tremor.

Royston was no more than a glorified village with a bevy of thatched cottages huddled around the church like anxious children clutching at their mother's skirts. Westfield's Men had once more come too late. Their rivals had performed in the yard of the Barley Mow to an audience drawn from all the villages in the area. What enraged Lawrence Firethorn to bursting point was the fact that Banbury's Men had again filched a play from his own repertoire, *The Two Maids of Milchester*, another rustic comedy that was suitable for the lower sort. They were poisoning the very water from which Westfield's Men drank.

After abusing everyone in sight in the roundest terms, the actor-manager withdrew his company to a field nearby to consider their next move. Nicholas Bracewell put forward the idea mooted by Christopher Millfield and it found ready acceptance. Rather than struggle on to the next possible playing location, they elected to look for somewhere nearer. Pomeroy Manor sounded an interesting possibility and Firethorn warmed to the notion.

'Master Pomeroy is not unknown to me,' he said with

casual arrogance. 'Lord Westfield presented him after one of my performances at the Rose. He knows my worth.'

'As who does not?' asked Nicholas.

'Ware does not! Royston – be damned – does not!'

'To their eternal shame, master.'

'I would not play before these dolts if they offered me a king's ransom. Palates that have been jaded by a taste of Giles Randolph would choke on the rich food of my talent. There is a world elsewhere!'

'Shall I ride on to Pomeroy Manor?'

'With all haste, Nick,' said Firethorn, scenting the chance of a performance at last. 'Take Master Millfield with you. He knows the way and will ease your solitude.'

Nicholas could have wished for another companion but he had no choice in the matter. Edmund Hoode was quick to offer the loan of his horse to the book holder and – what was more astonishing – Barnaby Gill handed over the bay mare to Millfield with something approaching willingness. It was a gesture that Nicholas was to remember later.

The two riders set off on their expedition. Though Millfield had never been to the house before, he seemed to have a mental map as to its whereabouts. Four miles of cantering along rutted tracks brought them to the crest of a hill which presented them with a perfect view of Pomeroy Manor and they reined in their mounts to enjoy the prospect. It was truly impressive.

The property was built on the site of an ancient moated manor house which had belonged to the Church. On the dissolution of the monasteries under Henry VIII, it had been acquired by the Pomeroy family who rebuilt it in Tudor bricks, with eight octagonal chimneys having star tops, rising from crow-stepped gable-ends. The windows were low-mullioned and transomed, formed from moulded bricks that were rendered in a smooth grey clay that had been dredged from a river estuary. A porch added to the overall symmetry and acted as a trellis for an explosion of roses. Ivy had got a finger-hold on the front walls.

'It is just as I imagined,' said Millfield.

'A rare sight in this county,' observed Nicholas.

'What's that, sir?'

'Brick-built houses of this type are only found in East Anglia as a rule. Does Master Neville Pomeroy have connections with that part of the country.'

'So I am led to believe.'

'Where did you glean all your information?'

'From listening in the right places.'

Millfield chuckled and urged his horse on.

After the disappointments in Ware and Royston, they gained adequate recompense. Hearing of their arrival, the master of the house had them brought into the room where he had been going through his accounts with his steward.

Neville Pomeroy was a stout, solid man of middle years with curling grey hair and slow movements. He gave them a cordial welcome, heard their business then nodded with enthusiasm. They were in luck.

'You come at a timely hour, gentlemen,' he said. 'I am only returned from London myself today and thought to have missed you as you passed through Royston.'

'You knew of our presence here?' said Nicholas.

'From Lord Westfield himself. We have mutual friends in the city. I have seen his company tread the boards and warrant they have no equal. Master Firethorn will honour me if he plays inside my house.'

'Then we may draw up a contract?'

'Indeed so, Master Bracewell. I will need a day to send out word and gather in an audience but, if you can bide your time, then I can offer you warm applause on the morrow. How large is the company?'

'But fifteen souls, sir.'

'Then must you lodge at the inn nearby. The Pomeroy Arms will give you free board at my request. It is but a small place, I fear, but it should serve your purpose.'

'We thank you heartily, sir.'

'The gratitude is all mine. I love the theatre.'

'What would you have us play?'

'*Tarquin of Rome*.'

It was an unexpected choice but Nicholas did not question it. The play was a tragedy on the theme of tyranny and betrayal. It was strange fare for a hot summer evening in the privacy of one's house yet it revealed a serious student of the drama. *Tarquin of Rome* was an exceptional piece of writing. It furnished its title-role with speeches that could ring the withers and fire the soul. Pomeroy had chosen shrewdly.

Nicholas and Millfield rode back to their fellows. Their news was passed around with glee. Firethorn made decisions at once. *Tarquin of Rome* was not a play they had

104

planned on staging during the tour, and they had brought neither the costumes nor properties for it, but the actor-manager was in no way discomfited.

'They shall have it, Nick.'

'So I told Master Pomeroy.'

'We have a day to prepare. It is sufficient. Give me twenty-four hours and I'll be Tarquin to the life!'

He launched into the speech at the culmination of the death scene and the verse came out in a torrent. Lawrence Firethorn had the prodigious memory of a real actor who never forgets lines once learned. He carried some fifty parts in his head, each one a leading role of great complexity, yet he could produce them on demand. Swept away on a tide of emotion, he declaimed some more of Tarquin's soliloquies and filled the air with wonder.

Nicholas Bracewell became pensive then he clicked his fingers and nodded to himself. Edmund Hoode was close enough to mark his behaviour.

'Why do you nod so, Nick?'

'I think I have their secret, Edmund.'

'Who?'

'Banbury's Men.'

'Scurvy knaves! They have stolen our plays.'

'I believe I know how.'

Grantham gave them an ovation that lasted for some minutes and Giles Randolph luxuriated in it. There was a sizeable audience, culled both from the town and from the surrounding area of Lincolnshire, and they had never witnessed anything like *Pompey the Great*. Having come to watch the sort of pastoral romp that touring companies usually brought to them, the spectators were at first a trifle uneasy when they were confronted with a tale of military splendour and political intrigue, but they soon rallied as the drama unfolded with compelling skill. It was one of Edmund Hoode's most stirring achievements and Banbury's Men played it for all it was worth.

Giles Randolph gave them an intelligent and moving account of the central role but he did not have Lawrence Firethorn's martial presence or swelling power. The defects in his performance, however, were happily concealed from both himself and his audience. He was convinced that he had touched heights far beyond the reach of his hated rival, and that he had demonstrated his superiority in the most signal and humiliating way. Rippling applause fed his narcissism. In the theatre of his mind, he had left Firethorn dead and buried.

Celebrations were in order. Pompey the Great dined in style at a local inn with his company fawning avidly around him. After years in the shadow of Westfield's Men, it was heartening to sweep them aside and step out into the full glare of the sun.

Seated beside Giles Randolph was a thoughtful young man with an expression of quiet self-congratulation. The leading actor sought even more applause.

'Was I not inspired upon that stage, sir?'

'You were the very ghost of Pompey.'

'Did I not catch his greatness?'

'In every line and gesture, Master Randolph.'

'The audience loved me.'

'How could they not?'

'I walked in Elysium!'

Mark Scruton gave a smile of agreement. His whole future was vested in the success of Banbury's Men and he yielded to nobody in his appreciation of the talent of its star. All that Giles Randolph lacked was material of the highest calibre. In most of the plays from his own repertoire, he was never less than hypnotic but never more than brilliant. He was held back by the limitations of the work in which he appeared. Given a drama of true merit, handed a part into which he could pour himself body and soul, he could indeed approach magnificence.

Giles Randolph was not unaware of this himself.

'It is a well-wrought piece,' he said grudgingly.

'Master Hoode is a fine poet.'

'That final speech would ring tears from a stone.'

'He has no equal in such scenes.'

'You speak true, sir,' said Randolph. 'Away with the scribbling of apprentice playwrights! Give me men who can write a rolling line. We have good plays but none to live with the magic of this Pompey. The confession is painful to me, but I would dearly love this Master Hoode to pen his work for Banbury's Men.'

'He does, master. He does.'

Giles Randolph laughed in keen appreciation.

'When he reaches Grantham, he'll be most perplexed.'

'And cry out like the victim of a robbery.'

'With Master Firethorn howling "Murder!" in his wake.' He became businesslike. 'We must keep a distance ahead of them. It will not serve if Westfield's Men overtake us. We'll come to blows in that event.'

'I have a device to slow them down completely.'

'Tell me what it is, Master Scruton.'

'Lend me an ear.'

Giles Randolph leaned close so that he could catch the other's whisper. A smirk lit up his dark features. He liked the notion so much that he slipped his companion a few coins by way of gratitude. It was but small payment to a man who was proving such a friend to Banbury's Men. Mark Scruton was their saviour.

Night wrapped its black cloak around the Pomeroy Arms. Secure in the knowledge that an audience awaited them on the morrow, Westfield's Men rehearsed until evening then roistered until midnight. They fell into their beds and were soon asleep, dreaming sweetly in their contentment. Nicholas Bracewell shared a room with four others at the rear of the premises. Fond thoughts of Anne Hendrik flitted their way through his slumber and he might have enjoyed them all night had not something disturbed him. He was awake at once and looking around with bleary eyes. There was nothing to be seen in the darkness but he heard the others snoring in peaceful fellowship beside him. He listened carefully then realised what was wrong. Someone was missing.

The distant clack of shoes on paved stone made him slip

out of bed and cross to the window. He could just make out the tall figure of a man who was loping away from the inn. Nicholas shook his head to bring himself fully awake then strained his eyes against the gloom. The man reached higher ground and was silhouetted for a few seconds against the sky. It was enough. The book holder recognised him by his profile and his gait.

Christopher Millfield ran off into the night.

Westfield's Men improvised with characteristic skill on their journey to Ancient Rome. Sheets became togas, long daggers became short swords, bushes were pillaged for laurel wreaths and a high-backed chair was borrowed from the inn itself to do duty as a throne. Under the guidance of the book holder, actors turned carpenters to build a few simple scenic devices. Edmund Hoode's woodwork was directed at the play itself and he laboured hard with his chisel, saw and plane. *Tarquin of Rome* was a long drama with a large cast. Had they been performing it in a town the size of Bristol or Newcastle or Exeter, they could easily have recruited journeymen to make up the numbers but that option was denied to them here. The play had to be trimmed to fit their modest company, though, even in its attenuated version, it was still a powerful drama. Only a full-blooded performance and frantic doubling could bring it off. It was the kind of challenge that they liked.

Lawrence Firethorn gave them heart and hope.

'Let's make the old house ring with exultation!'

Pomeroy Manor became a magnet for the local gentry.

They came in droves to see the unlikely sight of Lucius Tarquinius Superbus, seventh and last king of Rome, in the banqueting hall of a house in Hertfordshire. It was a revelation to them. On their makeshift stage, and with minimal scenery and costumes, Westfield's Men transported their spectators back some two thousand years or more.

Lawrence Firethorn thrilled them to the marrow with his portrayal of Tarquin, drunk with power and steeped in wickedness, enhancing the power and prosperity of Rome in order to exploit it for his own selfish ends.

It fell to Christopher Millfield to end the play.

> Our soldiers brave subdue your coward band,
> Restoring peace unto our bloodied land.
> Beshrew your heart, foul tyrant, fade away.
> Honour rules upon this glorious day.
> Though cruel kings vile cruelties will send,
> Freedom's banner flutters at the end.

Neville Pomeroy leapt to his feet to lead the sustained applause for a play that had moved as much as it had entertained. Westfield's Men were feted. It made amends for all their setbacks. As they were leaving Pomeroy Manor, they had money in their purse and a triumph under their belt. It was invigorating.

Their host showered them with fresh thanks.

'You do not know what joy you have brought.'

'We are deeply gratified,' said Firethorn, still using his Tarquin voice. 'We humble wights live on the indulgence of our patrons. Pomeroy Manor has been our joy as well. We hope for like acceptance everywhere.'

'You will find it for sure, sir.'

'Not in Ware or Royston, I fear.'

'Go further north towards certain victory.'

'That is our intention.'

'I have done my share,' said Pomeroy. 'Hearing of your plans, I wrote from London to my closest friend to warn him of your coming. Westfield's Men are assured of a hearty welcome there.'

'We thank you, kind sir. Where is this place?'

'Marmion Hall.'

'In what town?'

'Close by the city of York.'

Lawrence Firethorn played the crusader again.

'York, you say? We know it by another name.'

'What might that be?'

'Jerusalem!'

The cellar was deep beneath the house. No natural light penetrated and the thick stone walls were covered with seeping damp. There was a smell of despair. The man was naked to the waist. Spread-eagled on a wooden table, he was tied in such a way as to increase his torment. Rope bit into his wrists and ankles, stretching him until he was on the point of splitting asunder. Huge gobs of sweat were wrung out of him to mingle with the streaked blood across his chest and arms. His face was a pulp. As he lay in his own excrement, he barely had the strength to groan any

111

more and did not even feel the impudent legs of the spider that ran across his forehead.

Marmion Hall was the ancestral home of one of the most respected families in Yorkshire. Nobody would have believed that it housed such a guest beneath its roof.

The cellar door was unlocked and unbolted from the outside and a candle brought light. A short, stocky man in the livery of a servant went across to the prisoner and held the flame where it illumined his battered features. Sir Clarence Marmion was impassive as he saw the tortured body.

'Has he said no more?'

'Nothing beyond cries of pain, Sir Clarence.'

'Have you tested him to the full?'

'With steel and fire. He's bled half to death.'

'Would not whipping loosen his tongue?'

'Only to let him beg for mercy.'

'They get none that give none,' said the other coldly. 'Walsingham's men are ruthless. So must we be.'

Grabbing the prisoner by the hair, the servant banged his head on the table then leered right into his face.

'Speak up, sir! We cannot hear you!'

A long moan came from between parched lips.

'Who was he?' hissed Sir Clarence. 'I want the name of the spy who informed on Master Rickwood!'

The prisoner twitched in agony but said nothing.

'Tell me!' insisted the master of the house. 'Which of Walsingham's creatures sent him to his death?'

'I cannot cut the information out of him.'

'His name!'

As his control faltered, Sir Clarence hit the man across the face with vicious blows until the blood was spurting all over his glove. He withdrew his hand and moved back to the door, his composure now returned.

'What now, Sir Clarence?' asked the servant.

'Kill him.'

Though the house in Shoreditch was now half-empty, with far fewer mouths to feed at table, Margery Firethorn still had plenty of domestic chores to keep her occupied. One of these was to make regular visits to market to buy the food and berate any stallholder who tried to overcharge her. Servants could not be trusted to get the choicest items at the best prices and so she reserved the task of filling the larder for herself. It got her out of the house and stopped her from brooding on her loneliness.

She entered the city by Bishopsgate and was caught up in a small commotion. Armed soldiers were bustling about, pushing people out of the way and dealing roughly with any complainants. Margery rid herself of a few barbed remarks at them before sauntering on towards the market in Gracechurch Street. She was soon deep in dispute with a hapless vendor about the quality of his fruit. When she had beaten him down to the price she was prepared to pay, she took her belligerence along to the next stall and set it to work.

Her footsteps eventually took her close to the Queen's Head and it prompted wistful thoughts of Westfield's Men.

Ambivalent feelings pulled at her. Still angry with her husband, she yet missed him keenly. Anxious to upbraid him severely, she would have mixed some kisses with the scolding. Margery Firethorn could not blame her spouse for everything. In marrying him, she had married the theatre and that brought special tribulation.

She was given further evidence of the fact. Sitting outside the inn on a low stool was a thin, ascetic man with a viol between his legs, coaxing plaintive notes out of his instrument in the hopes of earning a few coins from the passers-by. Margery was saddened. It was Peter Digby. Ten days before, he had been the proud leader of the consort of musicians employed by Westfield's Men. Now he was scratching for pennies in the street. The theatre was indeed a cruel master.

'How now, Master Digby!' she said.

'Mistress!'

'Have you no other work but this, sir?'

'None that pays me.'

She took a coin from a purse and pressed it into his hand. He thanked her for a kindness then enquired about the company. She had yet no news to give him but talked in general terms. Shouts from the distance made them look towards Bishopsgate. More soldiers milled about.

'What means this commotion?' she said.

'Have you not heard?'

'No, Master Digby.'

'One of the heads has vanished from its spike.'

'There's grisly work indeed!'

'Taken down in the night,' he said. 'And this was not in jest. When the culprit is caught, this is a hanging offence. They search for him in earnest.'

'Whose head was taken down?' she asked.

'That of a traitor freshly executed.'

'What was his name?'

'Anthony Rickwood.'

Chapter Five

Westfield's Men set out with high hopes but they were soon blighted by circumstance. Heavy overnight rain had mired a road that was already in a bad state of repair.

Local parishes were responsible for the maintenance of any road that ran within their boundaries but in the case of a highway like the Great North Road, an intolerable burden was placed upon them. There was no way that they could find the resources for the upkeep of such a major artery and Westfield's Men suffered as a result.

'Use the whip, man!'

'It is no use!'

'Drive them on, drive them on!'

'We are stuck fast, Master Firethorn.'

'I'll get you out if I have to drag the cart with my own bare hands, so I will!'

But Firethorn was thwarted. Though he took hold of

the harness of one of the carthorses and pulled with all his might, neither animal moved forward. The front wheel of the waggon was sunk to its axle and the whole vehicle slanted over at an angle.

Barnaby Gill was quick to apportion blame.

'This is your doing, Master Bracewell.'

'I could not drive around the hole, sir.'

'The waggon is too heavy since you brought the whole company aboard. Their weight is your downfall.'

'I could not ask them to walk in such mud, Master Gill. It would ruin their shoes and spatter their hose.'

'That would be better than this calamity.'

'Do something, Nick!' ordered Firethorn.

'I will, sir.'

'And with all speed.'

Nicholas jumped down from the driving seat and waved everyone else off the waggon. It was then laboriously unloaded. He used an axe to cut a stout length of timber then wedged it under the side of the waggon where the wheel was encumbered. With the help of three others, he used his lever to lift the vehicle up. There was a loud sucking noise as the wheel came out of its prison. The horses were slapped, they strained between the shafts and the waggon rolled clear of its problem. As it was loaded up again, Lawrence Firethorn reached for the law.

'The parishioners should be indicted!'

'They cannot mend every hole in the road,' said Hoode reasonably. 'We must travel with more care.'

'I'll have them at assizes and quarter sessions.'

'And what will Westfield's Men do while you ride off to start this litigation? Must we simply wait here?'

'Do not mock me, Edmund.'

'Then do not set yourself up for mockery, Lawrence.'

'They should be clapped in irons, every one of them.'

'How could they repair the roads, thus bound?'

They were ready to depart and trundled on with a few of the hired men now walking gingerly at the rear to avoid the worst of the mud. When they crossed the border into Huntingdonshire, they found the worst stretch of all along the Great North Road. Skirting the edge of the Fen Country, it supported more traffic than anywhere other than the immediate approaches to London, and the surface was badly broken up. Extra caution had to be exercised and progress was painfully slow. They were relieved when Huntingdon itself finally came in sight.

Richard Honeydew was bubbling with questions.

'Have you been to the town before, Master Bracewell?'

'Once or twice, lad.'

'What sort of place is it?'

'There are two things of note, Dick.'

'What might they be?'

'A bowling green and a gallows.'

'Shall we see a hanged man, sir?'

'Several, if Master Firethorn has his way.'

'And will they let us play there?'

'I am certain of it.'

But the book holder's assurance was too optimistic. When they rolled past St Bennet's Church to the Shire Hall, they met no official welcome. Banbury's Men had sucked the town dry with a performance of *Double Deceit*.

It was another play stolen from Westfield's Men and it sent Firethorn into a tigerish rage. There was worse to come. One of the Town Council had lately returned from Lincolnshire. He told them of a performance by Banbury's Men at Stamford of *Marriage and Mischief* – also purloined from their rivals – and of the staging of *Pompey the Great* at Grantham before an enthusiastic audience that included his own august self. When he went on to praise the acting of Giles Randolph in the title role, Firethorn had to be held down lest he do the man a mischief.

Foaming at the mouth, the actor-manager was borne off to the nearest inn and given a pint of sack to sweeten his disposition. Barnaby Gill, Edmund Hoode and Nicholas Bracewell were with him. Firethorn was vengeful.

'By heaven, I'll slit him from head to toe for this!'

'We have to find him first,' reminded Nicholas.

'To filch my part in my play before my adoring audience! Ha! The man has the instincts of a jackal and the talent of a three-legged donkey with the staggers.'

Gill could not resist a thrust at his pride.

'That fellow spoke well of Master Randolph.'

'A polecat in human form!'

'Yet he carried the day with his Pompey.'

'My Pompey! My, my, my Pompey!'

'And mine,' said Hoode soulfully. 'Much work and worry went into the making of that play. It grieves me to hear that Banbury's Men play it free of charge.'

Nicholas had sympathy with the author. His work was protected by no laws. Once he had been paid five pounds for its delivery, the work went out of his hands and into the repertoire of Westfield's Men. He had little influence over its staging and even less over its casting. The one consolation was that he had written a cameo role for himself as an ambitious young tribune.

'Who played Sicinius?' he mused.

'All that matters is who played Pompey!' howled Firethorn, banging the table until their tankards bounced up and down. 'Randolph should be hanged from the nearest tree for his impertinence!'

'How have Banbury's Men done it?' asked Gill.

'I have the way,' said Nicholas.

'Well, sir.'

'They have enlisted our players against us.'

'Monstrous!' exclaimed Firethorn.

'There is only one complete copy of each play,' said Nicholas, 'and I keep that closely guarded. But I cannot shield it during rehearsal or performance. If some of our fellows memorised a work between them, they could put the meat of it down with the aid of a scrivener. And it is off that meat that Master Randolph has been feeding.'

'Who are these rogues, Nick?' said Hoode.

'How many of them are there?' added Gill.

'I have neither names nor numbers,' admitted the book holder. 'But I have been going through an inventory of the hired men we have employed this year. Several left disgruntled with good cause to harm us. If enough money was put in enough pockets, they would have turned their coat and helped out Banbury's Men.'

'Aye,' said Firethorn, 'and been given a place in that vile company by way of reward. If we but overtake them, we shall find out who these varlets are.'

'They are too far ahead,' argued Nicholas, 'and we will meet but further outrage if we visit towns where they have been before us. Stay your anger, Master Firethorn, until the occasion serves. We must change our route and find fresh fields.'

'This advice makes much sense,' said Hoode. 'Where should we go, Nick?'

'To Nottingham. We stay on this road for a while yet then head north-west through Oakham and Melton Mowbray. Haply, those towns may like some entertainment.'

Firethorn and Hoode gave their approval. Gill was the only dissenter, pointing out that the minor roads would be even worse than the one on which they had just travelled, and throwing up his usual obstruction to any idea that emanated from the book holder. He was outvoted by the others and shared his pique with his drink.

Still thirsting for blood, Firethorn accepted that he might have to wait before he could collect it by the pint from Banbury's Men. Nicholas's idea grew on him. Their new destination made its own choice of play.

'Nottingham, sirs! We'll give 'em *Robin Hood*!'

It was all decided.

* * *

In referring the matter to a higher authority, Miles Melhuish knew that he was doing the correct thing. Not only was he relieving himself of a problem that caused him intense personal anxiety, but he was handing it over to a man who could solve it with peremptory speed. The Dean was feared throughout Nottingham. One glance of his eye from a pulpit could quell any congregation. One taste of his displeasure could bring the most wilful apostate back into the fold. He was far older than Melhuish, with more weight, more wisdom, more conviction and more skill. He also had more relish for the joys of coercion, for the destruction of any opponent with the full might of the Church at his back. He would cure Mistress Eleanor Budden of her delusions. Five minutes with the Dean would send her racing back to her bedchamber to fornicate with her husband in God's name and to make amends for her neglect of his most sacred right of possession.

But there was an unforeseen snag. She was closeted with the Dean for over two hours. And when she emerged, it was not in any spirit of repentance. She had the same air of unassailable confidence and the same seraphic smile. It is not known in what precise state of collapse she left the learned man who had tried to bully her out of her mission. Her certitude had been adamantine proof.

Humphrey Budden was waiting outside for her. 'Well?'

'My examination is over,' she said.

'What passed between you?'

'Much talk of the Bible.'

'Did the Dean instruct you in your duty?'

'God has already done that, sir.'

'He made no headway?' said Budden in disbelief.

'He came to accept my decision.'

'Madness, more like!'

'Do you find your wife mad, Humphrey?'

'In this frame of mind.'

'Then must you truly despise me.'

They were standing among the gravestones in the churchyard. The sky was dark, the clouds swollen. The wind carried the first hints of rain. Eleanor Budden usually dressed in the fashion of burghers' wives with a bodice and full skirt of muted colour, a cap to hide her plaited hair and a lace ruff of surpassing delicacy, this last a source of professional pride to her husband who wanted her to display her demureness to the town and thereby advertise his trade, his happiness and his manhood. She had now cast off any sartorial niceties. A simple grey shift and a mob-cap were all that she wore. Her long hair hung loose down her back.

Ironically, he wanted her even more. In that dress, in that place, in that unpromising weather, he yet found his desire swelling and his sense of assertion stiffening. Mad or misguided, she was beautiful. Immune to the vicar and impervious even to the Dean, she was still the wife of Humphrey Budden and could be brought to heel.

'You will remain chaste no longer!' he said.

'How now, sir!'

'Return home with me this instant!'

'I like not your tone.'

'Had you heard it sooner, with a hand to back it up, we might not now be in this predicament.'

'Do you threaten me, sir?'

She was calm and unafraid and he was halted for a moment, but those round blue eyes and smooth skin worked him back into resolution. He grabbed her arm.

'Leave off, sir. You hurt me.'

'Come back home and settle this argument in our bedchamber. You will not be the loser by it.'

'Unhand me, Humphrey. Mingling flesh is sinful.'

'Not in marriage.'

'We are no longer man and wife.'

He grabbed her other arm as she tried to pull free and wrestled with her. The feel of her body against his drove him on beyond the bounds of reason.

'Submit to my embraces!'

'I will not, sir.'

'It is my right and title.'

'No further.'

Her struggling only increased his frenzy the more.

'By this hand, and you will not obey, I'll take you here on the spot among the dead of Nottingham.'

'You dare not do so.'

'Do I not?' he wailed.

'God will stop you.'

Roused to breaking point, he laid rude hands on the front of her shift and tore it down to expose one smooth shoulder and the top of one smooth breast, but even as the material ripped, it was joined by another sound. The

125

door of the church opened and Miles Melhuish emerged in a state of frank bewilderment. He could not understand how Eleanor Budden had vanquished the Dean. When he saw the scene before him, however, he understood all too well and trembled at the sacrilege of it.

'Here upon consecrated ground!' he boomed.

'I was driven to it, sir,' bleated the lacemaker.

'To use force against the gentler sex!'

'You counselled strength of purpose.'

'Not of this foul nature.'

'Forgive him, sir,' said Eleanor. 'He knows not what he does. I looked for no less. God warned me to expect much tribulation. And yet He saved me here, as you did see. He brought you from that church to be my rescue.'

Eleanor fell to her knees in earnest prayer and Melhuish took the defeated and detumescent husband aside to scold him among the chiselled inscriptions. When she was finished, the vicar helped her to her feet and nudged her spouse forward with a glance.

'Forgive me for my wickedness, Eleanor.'

'You acted but as a man.'

'I sinned against you grievously.'

'Then must you wash yourself clean. Call on God to make you a pure heart and to put out all your misdeeds.'

Humphrey Budden was desolate. Abandoned by his wife and now censured by the Church, his case was beyond hope. Instead of taking home a dutiful partner in marriage, he had lost her for ever to a voice he had never even heard.

'May I know your will, wife?'

'I follow the path of righteousness.'

'She must answer the Dean's command,' said Melhuish.

'I go to Jerusalem,' she said.

'To York,' he corrected. 'Only the holy Archbishop himself can pronounce on this. You must bear a letter to him from the Dean and seek an audience.'

'York!' Budden was distraught. 'May I come there?'

'I travel alone,' she said firmly.

'What will you do for food and shelter?'

'God will provide.'

'The roads are not safe for any man, let alone for a woman such as you. Be mindful of your life!'

'There is no danger for me.'

'For you and for every other traveller.'

'I have the Lord's protection on my way.'

It began to rain.

Oliver Quilley cursed the downpour and spurred his horse into a canter. There was a clump of trees in the middle distance with promise of shelter for him and his young companion. Quilley was a short, slight creature in his thirties with an appealing frailty about him. Dressed in the apparel of a courtier, he was an incongruous sight beside the sturdy man in fustian who rode as his chosen bodyguard on the road from Leicester. The trees swished and swayed in the rain but their thick foliage and overhanging branches promised cover from the worst of the storm. As Quilley rode along, one hand clutched at his breast as if trying to hold in his heart.

'Swing to the right!' he urged.

'Aye, master.'

'We shall be shielded from the wind there.'

'Aye, master.'

The young man had little conversation but a strength of sinew that was reassuring company. Quilley forgave him for his ignorance and raced him to the trees. They were drenched when they arrived and so relieved to be out of the bad weather at last that they dispensed with caution. It was to be their downfall.

'Ho, there, sirs!'

'Hey! Hey! Hey!'

'Fate has delivered you unto us.'

'Dismount!'

Four rogues in rough attire leapt from their hiding place with such suddenness that the riders were taken totally by surprise. Two of the robbers had swords, the third a dagger and the last a clump of wood that looked the most dangerous weapon of them all. The young man did not even manage to unsheath his rapier. Terrified by the noise and intensity of the assault, his horse reared its front legs so high that he was unsaddled in a flash. He fell backwards through the air with no control and landed awkwardly on his neck. There was a sickly crack and his body went limp. It was a death of great simplicity.

The others turned their attention to Quilley.

'Away, you murderers!' he yelled.

'Come, sir, we would speak with you.'

'Leave go of that rein!'

But Quilley's puny efforts were of no avail. He punched and kicked at them but only provoked their ridicule. The biggest ruffian reached up a hand and yanked him from his perch as if he were picking a flower from a garden. Oliver Quilley was thrown to the ground.

'They'll hang each one of you for this!'

He tried to get up but they tired of his presence. The clump of wood struck him behind his ear and he pitched forward into oblivion. Pleased with the day's handiwork, the four men assessed their takings. They were soon riding off hell for leather.

Quilley was unconscious for a long time but the rain finally licked him awake. The first thing he saw was the dead body of the young man he had paid to protect him. It made him retch. Then he remembered something else and felt the front of his doublet. Tearful with relief, he unhooked the garment and took out the large leather pouch that he had carried there for safekeeping. They had stolen his horse, his saddlebags and his purse but that did not matter. The pouch was still there.

Quilley opened it carefully to inspect its contents. A murder and a robbery on the road to Nottingham. He had been lucky. The loss of his companion was a real inconvenience but the young man was expendable. The loss of his pouch would have been a catastrophe. His art was intact.

He began the long walk towards the next village.

The rain lashed Westfield's Men unmercifully. Caught in the open as they struggled through the northern part of

Leicestershire, they could not prevent themselves getting thoroughly drenched. Nicholas Bracewell's main concern was for the costumes and he pulled a tarpaulin over the large wicker hamper at the rear of the waggon but he could do nothing for his fellows, who became increasingly sodden, bedraggled and sorry for themselves. Thick mud slowed them to a crawl. High wind buffeted them and troubled the horses. It was their worst ordeal so far and it made them think fondly of the Queen's Head and the comforts of London.

Almost as quickly as it started, the storm suddenly stopped. Grey clouds took on a silver lining then the sun came blazing through to paint everything with a liquid sparkle. Lawrence Firethorn ordered a halt so that they could take a rest and dry out their clothes somewhat.

Doublets, jerkins, shirts, hose and caps were hung out on bushes in profusion. Half-naked men capered about. The carthorses were unhitched and allowed to crop the grass.

Nicholas kept one eye on Christopher Millfield. Ever since that first night at the Pomeroy Arms, the book holder had wondered where the actor had been going at the dead of night. It seemed unlikely to have been a tryst as there were wenches enough at the inn and they had singled him out for their boldest glances and loudest giggles. He had toyed with them all expertly but taken advantage of none. His nocturnal adventure had some other cause and Nicholas knew he would never divine it by asking the man straight out. Millfield always had a ready smile and a plausible excuse.

Unable to watch the man all the time, Nicholas used the services of a friend even though the latter had no idea that he was being pumped for information.

'What else did he say, George?'

'He talked of other companies that hired him.'

'I believe he was with the Admiral's Men.'

'They went out of London a month or two ago to play in Arundel, Chichester, Rye and I know not where.'

'And were they well received?'

'Very well, Master Bracewell. They played in some of the finest houses in the county, and lacked not for work at any time. They fared better than we poor souls.'

George Dart looked sad at the best of times. In his wet shirt and muddied hose, he was utterly woebegone. His delight at being included in the touring company had now evanesced into gibbering regret. As the tiniest of the assistant stage-keepers, he had always been given the biggest share of the work. Touring added even more chores to his already endless list. In addition to his duties during performance, he was ostler, porter, seamstress and general whipping boy. At Pomeroy Manor, he was forced to take on a number of non-speaking roles and was killed no less than four times – in four guises and four especially disagreeable ways – by the ruthless Tarquin. So much was thrust upon his small shoulders, that his legs buckled.

It never occurred to him he now had another job.

'One thing more, George.'

'Yes, sir?'

'Has he made mention of Gabriel Hawkes?'

'Many times, master.'

'What does he say?'

'That he is the better player of the two.'

'I did not think him so.'

'Nor I, but I dared not tell him.'

'Has he shown regret about Gabriel?'

'None, master.'

'No tribute of a passing sigh?'

'Not once in my hearing.'

'Thank you,' said Nicholas kindly. 'Should he say anything else of interest, let me know forthwith.'

'I will, sir.'

Having answered so many questions himself, George Dart now found one himself. It had been rolling around in his mind for days and Nicholas was the only person likely to give him a civil hearing. Dart's face puckered.

'When we left London . . .'

'Yes, George?'

'We came through Bishopsgate.'

'Aye, sir.'

'There was a head upon a spike there.'

'Several, if memory serves.'

'This was the most recent.'

'Ah, yes. Master Anthony Rickwood.'

'What was his offence?'

'Plotting against the life of Queen Elizabeth.'

'Was he alone in his crime?'

'No, lad. He was part of a Catholic conspiracy.'

'Why were the others not brought to justice?'

'Because they have not been apprehended yet.'

'Will they be so?'

'Sir Francis Walsingham will see to that.'

'How?'

'His men will scour the kingdom.'

Before George could frame another question, there was a scream from nearby which sent Nicholas haring off with his sword in his hand. Richard Honeydew had yelled out in fear from behind the bushes where he had slipped off to relieve himself. Nicholas got to him in seconds to find him open-mouthed in horror and pointing to something that was coming over the brow of the hill.

It was as weird and exotic a sight as any they had seen thus far on their travels. A band of some twenty or more had appeared in bizarre costumes that were made up of embroidered turbans and brightly-coloured scarves worn over shreds and patches. Their swarthy faces were painted red or yellow and bells tinkled about their feet as they rode along on their horses. They were at once frightening and fascinating. Richard Honeydew was transfixed.

Nicholas laughed and patted him on the back.

'They will not harm you, lad.'

'Who are they, master?'

'Egyptians.'

'Who?'

'Minions of the moon.'

'Are they real?'

'As real as you or me.'

'Why do they look so strange?'

'They're gypsies.'

Anne Hendrik had travelled by way of Watling Street to visit her cousins in Dunstable. She soon moved on to Bedford to stay with an uncle and was pleased when he invited her to accompany him on a visit to his brother in Nottingham. Though the town had not been part of the itinerary of Westfield's Men, it took her much closer to them and that brought some comfort. It was only now that she was parted from Nicholas Bracewell that she realised how important he was in her life. They had shared the same house for almost three years now and she had grown to appreciate his unusual qualities.

She missed his soft West Country accent and his sense of humour and his endless consideration. Many men would have been brutalised by some of the experiences he had been through, but Nicholas remained true to himself and sensitive to the needs of others. He had faults but even those produced a nostalgic smile now. As Anne wandered through the market stalls of Nottingham, her hands were busy fingering lace and leather and cambric but her mind was on her dearest friend.

She sensed that he might not be too far away.

'Do not buy that here, Anne.'

'What?'

'The finest leather is in Leicester.'

'Oh . . . yes.'

She put down the purse she had been absent-mindedly examining and took her uncle's arm. He was an old man now and there would not be many journeys left to his brother. It gave him pleasure to be able to indulge his niece along the way. She had always been his favourite.

'What may I buy you, Anne?'

'It is I who should give you a present, uncle.'

'Your visit is present enough,' he said then waved his walking stick at the stalls. 'Choose what you wish.'

'There is nothing that I need.'

'I must give you some treat.'

'You have done that by bringing me here.'

He looked around and scratched his head in thought. When the idea came forth, it brought an elderly chuckle.

'Haply, you would like some entertainment.'

'Of what kind, uncle?'

'I'll take you to a play.'

'Do they have a company here?'

'Had your head not been in the clouds, you would have seen for yourself. Playbills are up on every post.'

'Indeed?'

Excitement stirred. Could Westfield's Men be there?

'Let me but show you, niece.'

'I follow you in earnest.'

He pushed a way through the crowd until they came to Ye Old Salutation Inn, one of the taverns that nestled close to Nottingham Castle and which had quenched the thirst of needy travellers for untold generations. Nailed to a beam outside the inn was a playbill written out with a flourish. Anne Hendrik felt her pulse quicken when she saw the name of the play.

Pompey the Great. Edmund Hoode's famed tragedy.

A triumph for Westfield's Men.

Her joy turned sour on the instant. The audience would not see Lawrence Firethorn in his most celebrated role. They were being offered the more shallow talents of Giles Randolph and his company.

'Shall you see this play with me, Anne?'

'Not I, uncle. I have no stomach for the piece.'

She turned away in outrage.

They knew that they were in Nottinghamshire as soon as they saw the woodland. Leicestershire had few forests and even fewer deer parks, the land being given over largely to agriculture. The growing of barley, pulses and wheat were familiar sights as were the fields of cattle and sheep. Once across the border, however, Westfield's Men encountered very different terrain. They were in 'the shire with the wood' since Sherwood Forest accounted for over a quarter of its area.

Their morale had lifted since the sun came out. The decision to leave the Great North Road had been a mixed blessing. It gave them performances in Oakham and Melton Mowbray in front of small but committed audiences but it also acquainted them with the misery of traversing bad roads in inclement weather. Resting for the night some five miles south of Nottingham, they hoped they had put the worst of their troubles behind them.

When Lawrence Firethorn insisted that they stay at

the Smith and Anvil, the others thought that it was a rare instance of sentimentality in him. The son of a village blacksmith himself, he had the build of those who followed that trade along with the bearing of a true gentleman. The original forge was a building of napped flints with a deep thatch but the inn which had grown up around it was largely timber-framed. When they entered the taproom, they realised why the actor-manager had been so insistent that they spent the night there.

'Master Firethorn!'

'Come, let me embrace you, Susan!'

'Oh, sir! This is unlooked-for joy!'

'And all the sweeter for it.'

The hostess was an attractive woman of ample girth and vivacious manner. Susan Becket was spilling out of her dress with welcome. The plump face was one round smile and the red tresses were tossed in delight. She came bouncing across the taproom to bestow a kiss like a clap of thunder on the lips of Lawrence Firethorn.

'What brings you to my inn, sir?'

'What else but your dear self?'

'You flatter me, you rascal.'

'I am like to do more than that ere I leave.'

'Away, you saucy varlet!' she said with a giggle.

'Do you have good beds at your hostelry?'

'No man has complained, sir.'

'Then neither will I,' said Firethorn enfolding her in his arms again. 'Hold me tight, Mistress Susan Becket. Though you have the name of a saint, I like you best for being a sinner.'

Her laughter set the huge breasts bobbing merrily.

Nicholas Bracewell, as usual, organised the sleeping arrangements. The best rooms went to the sharers and the hired men had to make do with what was left. Since it was a small establishment, some of them had to bed down on straw in an outhouse. Nicholas volunteered to spend the night with a few others so that the apprentices could have the last small room. All four of them were packed into the same lumpy bed. George Dart slept at their feet.

The book holder finished his supper in the taproom with Barnaby Gill and Edmund Hoode. Carrying a large candle, the hostess guided Lawrence Firethorn up to his chamber. Gill gave a sardonic snort.

'She'll burn his candle for him till he be all wax.'

'They are old friends, I think,' said Hoode.

'Lawrence has friends in every tavern and trugging-house in England,' said Gill. 'I wonder they do not name one of their diseases after him. I know a dozen or more doxies who have caught a dose of Firethorn before now.'

'He has always been popular with the ladies,' said Nicholas diplomatically.

'Ladies!' Gill hooted. 'There is nothing ladylike about them, Master Bracewell. As long as they give him a gallop, that is sufficient, and Mistress Becket will prove a willing mount. He'll not have to ride side-saddle with her, I warrant.'

'Leave off this carping, Barnaby,' said Hoode.

'I do it but in memory of his wife.'

'Margery knows the man she married.'

138

'And so do half the women in London.'

'We all have passions, sir.'

'Not of that kind!' Gill rose from the table with an air of magisterial disdain. 'Some of us can discern where true satisfaction lies and it is not in the arms of some whore. There is a love that surpasses that of women.'

'Love of self, sir?' said Nicholas artlessly.

'Good night, gentlemen!'

Barnaby Gill banged out of the room in disgust.

Richard Honeydew had some difficulty getting off to sleep because of the high spirits of the other apprentices. They fought, laughed, teased and played tricks upon one another until they tired themselves out. George Dart was quite unable to control them and was usually the butt of their jokes. When they finally drifted off, it was into a deep and noisy sleep. Dart's snore was the loudest.

None of them yielded more readily to slumber than Richard Honeydew. Wedged into one end of the bed beside John Tallis, he did not even feel the kicks from the restless feet of his two companions who slept at the other end of the bed. Nor did he hear the latch of the door lift. Two figures entered silently and looked around in the gloom. One held a sword at the ready to ward off any interruption and the other carried a sack. When their quarry was located, the sack was slipped over his head and a hand pressed firmly over his mouth. The boy was pulled from the bed with careful speed and the interlopers made off with their prize.

* * *

Nicholas Bracewell was curled up in the straw in the outhouse when his shoulder was grabbed by someone. He came awake at once and saw George Dart beside him.

'Master Bracewell! Master Bracewell!'

'What ails you, George?'

'We have been robbed, sir.'

'Of what?' said Nicholas, sitting up.

'I did not hear a thing. Nor did the others.'

'The theft was from your chamber?'

'Yes, master. We have lost our biggest jewel.'

'How say you?'

'Dick Honeydew has gone.'

'Are you sure?'

'Beyond all doubt.'

'This is not some jest of the others?'

'They are as shocked as I am.'

'Where can Dick be?'

'I know the answer, sir.'

'Do you?'

'Stolen by the gypsies.'

Oliver Quilley sat impatiently on the chair as the physician attended to him. His brush with the highway robbers had left him bruised and battered and he felt it wise to have himself patched up by a medical man before he continued his journey. The physician helped him back on with his doublet men asked for his fee. Quilley had no money left to pay him. Instead he reached into his leather pouch and took something out.

'This is worth ten times your fee, sir.'

'What is it, master?'

'A work of genius.'

Quilley opened his hand to reveal the most exquisite miniature. The face of a young woman had been painted with such skill that she was almost lifelike. The detail which had been packed into the tiny area was astounding. Quilley offered it to the physician.

'I cannot take it, sir.'

'Why not? I'd sell it for three pounds or more.'

'Then do so, Master Quilley, and pay me what you owe. It is too rich a reward for my purse, sir, and I have a wife to consider besides.'

'A wife?'

'Women are jealous creatures whether they have cause or no,' said the physician. 'If my wife saw me harbouring such beauty, she would think I loved the lady more than her, and bring her action accordingly. Keep it, sir. I will not take more than I have earned.'

'I'll sell it in Nottingham and fetch you your fee.'

'There's no hurry, master, and you need the rest.'

'What rest?'

'To recover from your injuries.'

'They are of no account.'

'A few days in bed would see them gone for good.'

'I have no time to tarry,' said Quilley fussily. 'I am needed elsewhere. There are those who seek the magic of my art. I've lost good time already in telling the magistrate what befell me and watching my companion buried in the ground. I must go in haste for they expect me there.'

'Where, Master Quilley?'

'In York.'

Foul weather, bad roads and hilly country could force a lethargic pace upon a troupe of travelling players but there were faster ways to cover distance. A messenger who had fresh relays of horses at staging posts some twenty or thirty miles apart could eat up the ground. Word sent from London could reach any part of the kingdom within a few days. Urgency could shrink the length of any road.

Sir Clarence Marmion received the message at his home then called for his own horse to be saddled. He was soon galloping towards the city. Ouse Bridge was the only one that crossed the river in York. Hump-backed and made of wood, it had six arches. Hooves pounded it. Spurring his horse on past the fifty houses on the bridge, Sir Clarence did not check the animal until he turned into the yard of the Trip to Jerusalem. An ostler raced out to perform his usual duty and the newcomer dismounted.

Marching into the taproom, Sir Clarence ignored the fawning welcome of Lambert Pym and went straight to the staircase. He was soon tapping on the door of an upstairs room and letting himself in.

Robert Rawlins sat up in alarm.

'I did not expect you at this early hour.'

'Necessity brought me hither.'

'Is something amiss?'

'I fear me it is. More news from London.'

'What has happened, Sir Clarence?'

'Information was laid against a certain person.'

'Master Neville Pomeroy?'

'He has been arrested and taken to the Tower.'

'Dear God!'

'Walsingham's men are closing in.'

'Can any of us now be safe?' said Rawlins.

'We have the security of our religion and that is proof against all assault. Master Pomeroy will give them no names, whatever ordeals they put him through. We must keep our nerve and pray that we survive.'

'Amen!'

Chapter Six

Lawrence Firethorn roared like a dragon when George Dart banged on the door of his bedchamber at the Smith and Anvil. Reverting to the trade of his father, the actor-manager was playing the sturdy blacksmith to Mistress Susan Becket's willing anvil. He was filling the air with sparks of joy at the very moment that the rude knuckles of his caller dared to interrupt him. Plucked untimely from the womb, he flung open the door and breathed such crackling flames of anger that the little stagekeeper was charred for life. Facing his employer was a daunting task at any time but to be at the mercy of Firethorn when he was naked, roused and deprived of consummation was like taking a stroll in the seventh circle of Hell. George Dart was sacked three times before he was even allowed to open his mouth. It was a lifetime before the message was actually delivered.

'Dick Honeydew has been taken, sir.'

'By whom, you idiot? By what, you dolt?'

'The gypsies.'

'Away with your lunacy!'

'I fear 'tis true, Master Firethorn.'

Corroboration came in the form of Nicholas Bracewell and the other apprentices, who were conducting a thorough search of the premises. They had checked every nook and cranny in the building, including attics and cellars, but there was no sign of Richard Honeydew. The boy had either run away of his own free will – which seemed unlikely – or he had been kidnapped. The second option was accepted at once by Firethorn who turned it into a personal attack upon himself and his career.

'They have stolen my Maid Marion!'

'We will find him,' said Nicholas determinedly.

'How can Robin Hood play love scenes on his own?'

'You will have to use one of the other boys.'

'I like not that idea, Nick.'

'Sherwood Forest must have another maid.'

'Not John Tallis!' said Firethorn. 'He has a face more fit for comedy than kissing. Maid Marion cannot have a lantern jaw, sir.'

'Stephen Judd or Martin Yeo will take the part.'

'Neither is suitable.'

'Then choose another play, Master Firethorn.'

'Be thwarted out of my purpose! Never!' He stamped his foot on the bare boards and collected a few sharp splinters. 'This villainy is directed at me, Nick. They do know my

Robin Hood is quite beyond compare and seek to pluck me down out of base envy.'

'We must track the boy down at once, sir.'

'Do so, Nick.'

'I will need a horse.'

'Take mine, dear heart!'

Nicholas was not at all convinced that gypsies had abducted Richard Honeydew even though the band had been seen in the vicinity, but his opinion was swept aside by a man who would brook no argument. Simultaneously robbed of his orgasm and his Maid Marion, the actor-manager was in a mood of vengeful urgency.

'To horse! To horse, Nick!'

'I will meet you in Nottingham.'

'Come not empty-handed.'

'If the boy be with the gypsies, I will get him.'

'Have a care, sir! Gypsies are slippery.'

'Adieu!'

Nicholas rushed off and missed an affecting moment. Throughout the conversation between actor-manager and book holder, George Dart stood meekly by, wondering whether he still had a job or not, and whether his little body would be needed to swell the ranks in the forthcoming performance at Nottingham. Firethorn saw him there and raised a quizzical eyebrow. Dart's face was a study in uncertainty and apprehension.

'Shall I still be one of the Merry Men, sir?'

Nicholas saddled up and rode out of the stables just before dawn. Sword and dagger were at his side. He was an excellent horseman. The son of a prosperous merchant from Devon, he had, from an early age, accompanied his father on his travels and learned how to ride and to take care of a horse. When Nicholas grew older, his father's business commitments obliged the son to travel to Europe and he developed his great love for the sea, a passion that was to culminate in three years with Drake on the famous circumnavigation of the globe. Notwithstanding this, he had lost none of his feel in the saddle. Pacing his mount carefully, he went off at a steady canter.

It was four hours before he caught their scent and another two before he finally rode them to earth. They had stopped at a hamlet in Leicestershire to peddle their wares and to offer entertainment to the simple souls of the parish. While the gypsy women sold scarves or read the palms of the gullible, their menfolk turned acrobat to divert the locals. Nicholas tethered his horse and made his way to the little green where everyone had gathered. From behind the cover of a chestnut tree, he observed a scene that was lit with animation and colour. In spite of the circumstances, he was consumed with interest.

Nicholas always felt some sympathy for gypsies. They were vagabonds with an air of freedom about them. At the same time, they suffered far more severe punishment than any indigenous vagrants. In addition to being regularly fined, whipped, imprisoned or chased from a locality with sticks, stones and a posse of dogs, they were under legal threat of deportation. Throughout the reign of Henry VIII and down through that of his daughter, Elizabeth, Queen of England, the official attitude towards the so-called 'sons of Ptolemy' was consistently hostile. Bands of gypsies were shipped off to Europe and there were occasional calls for a complete extirpation of the breed.

In view of all this, their very survival was a minor miracle. Nicholas had some fellow-feeling for them. His own profession had close affinities with the lifestyle of the gypsies. Actors were also outlaws if they were not employed in the service of a noble patron such as Lord Westfield. Shorn of such livery, they could be hunted and hounded almost as ruthlessly as the gypsies and, like the latter, could often become the scapegoats for any crimes that were committed while they were passing through an area. Gypsies were far from honest and law-abiding but Nicholas always believed that tales of their inherent wickedness and sorcery were wildly overstated.

Such thoughts were still flitting through his mind when the acrobatic display came to an end. Rough palms clapped in applause and a few small coins were spared when a small child ran around the spectators holding out a large cap. Musicians now struck up and there was a display of dancing. Lithe and graceful, the men went through steps that had rarely been seen upon the green before. Nicholas admired their skill and was entranced by the elements of the fantastic. Then the boy appeared. It was evident from the first that he was not as confident as the others, going through a routine as if he were under compulsion rather than as if he were enjoying the dance.

Nicholas Bracewell had seen the jig. It was one that Barnaby Gill had taught to the apprentices and which had been mastered by one of them straight away. As the book holder studied the willowy youth in the tattered rags and the painted face, he came rapidly to one conclusion. It was Richard Honeydew. Kidnapped at night, the boy was being made to work his passage with the gypsies. He was one of them now and had to dance for his keep, however reluctant he might be. As Nicholas ambled forward to get a closer look, the boy did a somersault that drew a patter of applause and confirmed the book holder's suspicion. He had seen the apprentices practising that somersault only days earlier. Here was firm proof.

Reason would be useless with the gypsies and the parish constable would stand no chance against a band of muscular men who could fight like fury. Nicholas had to take the lad by force while surprise was still on his side. Waiting until the dance came to an end, he let the apprentice take his applause then leapt at him from behind and threw an arm around him. In his other hand was his sword, brandished with enough purpose to keep them all at bay as he backed away towards his horse.

'Come, Dick, we'll be gone from here!'

But the boy did not seem too eager to leave. Sinking his teeth into Nicholas's arm, he prised himself free then turned on his captor to abuse him in a torrent of Romany.

The book holder was totally nonplussed.

It was not Richard Honeydew at all.

Westfield's Men were in despondent mood as they set out for Nottingham. Having been battered by Fate enough times already on tour, they were now knocked flat by one vicious punch. The disappearance of Richard Honeydew was a real disaster. He was a crucial figure in every performance. Though there was still some vestigial resentment on their part, the other apprentices had come to accept that the youngest of their number was also the cleverest. He took all the juvenile female leads and relegated them to the less attractive roles of ageing Countesses and comic serving wenches, of daunting Amazons and vapid lovers. Honeydew had another string to his bow. He was the most melodious boy soprano and songs were now written for him in almost every play. Without him, discord followed.

'Rest on my shoulder, mistress.'

'It is my dearest wish, sir.'

'We'll travel side by side.'

'Like two oxen yoked together.'

'We'll pull in the same direction, I warrant.'

Mistress Susan Becket laughed at his sexual quibble then swung herself up into the saddle of her horse, using the solid shoulder of Lawrence Firethorn as a lever. He had been delighted when she offered to accompany them to Nottingham to watch their performance, not least because she brought a horse of her own and a second for his personal use from her stable. Leaving the tavern in the capable hands of her employees, Susan Becket rode off with the company and was an eye-catching figure on her white mare, a woman of substance in every sense, gracious yet sensual, lifting the morale of the players by her very presence and allowing Firethorn himself to indulge his fantasies at will.

151

She was not, however, welcomed by all the company.

'You wonder that the horse can carry her, sir!'

'She is indeed plump, Master Gill, but well-favoured.'

'And she were courteous into the bargain, Mistress Becket would put on the saddle and carry the horse.'

'That is unkind, sir.'

'Only to the white mare.'

'Has Master Firethorn known her for long?'

'An hour at a time.'

'They are old bedfellows, then?'

'Bedfellowship was their invention.'

Barnaby Gill was riding beside the waggon which was now being driven by Christopher Millfield. The other sharers and the apprentices were seated among the baggage but the hired men were forced to trudge in the rear. It was a hot day with no wind to cool the fevered brow. Gill used the occasion to unleash some tart misogyny.

'She is the very epitome of her sex, is she not?'

'Mistress Becket?'

'She'll prove a shrewd archbishop to his majesty there beside her. Though we ride to York, she'll take him on a pilgrimage to Canterbury this night and show him all her sacred relics. When Master Firethorn plunges into her baptismal font, he'll sink to his armpits in the swill of her passion and will have to pray to the holy blissful martyr to haul him out again!'

'You do not like the lady,' said Millfield drily.

'Not this, nor any other of her kind.'

'Your reasoning, Master Gill?'

'Women have no place beside players.'

'Not even underneath them?'

'They are vile distractions, sir.'

'Would you not keep them for ornament?'

'Only in a privy for that's their natural region.'

'You are harsh, master.'

'Can any sane man truly love women?'

Christopher Millfield laughed by way of reply. He liked Barnaby Gill and had learned much from watching the comedian in action on the stage, but he could not share his disgust with womanhood. Millfield aroused feminine interest wherever he went and he basked in it, viewing it as one of the few legitimate spoils of war for an actor.

Gill looked across at the handsome profile.

'May I put a question to you, sir?'

'Do not hesitate.'

'How came it that you knew Pomeroy Manor?'

'I knew but of it, Master Gill.'

'By what means?'

'The Admiral's Men.'

'Untalented rascals!'

'They had not your quality, 'tis true,' said the other tactfully, 'but they were able enough. And they knew where to earn the next meal when we were in the country. One of their number kept a list in his mind of every house in England where players were welcome.'

'That list was not too long to memorise,' said Gill ruefully. 'Far more doors are slammed in our faces than ever open to our entertainment.'

'Even so, sir. That is why I took some pains to con the list myself. Master Neville Pomeroy was on it along with others in the county of Hertfordshire.'

'And this friend of his in York?'

'Sir Clarence Marmion was also on that list. I think the Admiral's Men did play there during the last outbreak of the pestilence. But there are other houses where we may look for friendship, both here in this county and in Yorkshire itself.'

'We'll try your list some more.'

Gill's attention was diverted by a sight which made his nose wrinkle with distaste. Lawrence Firethorn burst into ribald laughter and leaned over to squeeze the shoulders of the mirthful Susan Becket. Their joviality set them apart from Westfield's Men who were still worrying about the kidnap of Richard Honeydew and the effect it would have on the standard of their work.

'Look at them!' snorted Gill.

'Like turtle doves,' said Millfield tolerantly.

'Pigs in a trough, sir! When they have finished gobbling their own discourse, they will roll together in the slime and he will tickle the teats of that old sow.'

'Mistress Becket is neither so low nor beastly.'

'She is a monster. Put her on the stage and you would need three boys to play her, stuffed together in the one dress like rabbits in a sack. While Martin Yeo would personate her, John Tallis would serve in the office of one buttock and Stephen Judd t'other. It is a pity that Dick Honeydew is not here or he could take on the role of her left breast and wear that gross beauty spot.'

154

'For shame, Master Gill!'

'I speak but as I feel.'

'Her tavern gave us good food and rest.'

'So would any other where we paid.'

'I like the lady.'

'I took you for a man of finer taste.'

Millfield looked at Firethorn and his companion.

'She keeps him much amused.'

'Any woman can do that.'

'Does his wife raise no objection?'

'A hundred by the minute, sir, but she is back in Shoreditch and he is here. Were Margery to view this scene before us, she would pluck off his stones and wear them as earrings to ward off any other women. Alas, she is not here. She defends his castle in London.'

'Stoutly?'

'As any army under siege. I pity the man who tries to take her fortress, Master Millfield. Though he bring the biggest battering ram in Christendom, it will not suffice. Margery will drown him in boiling oil.'

'Out, you rogue! Away, you rascal, you hedge-bird, you pannier-man's whelp! Do not wave your paltry reckoning at me, you pimp, you dog's-head, you trendle-tail! Marry, look off, sir! Go, snuff after some other prey! Poxed already you are, I can tell by that sheep-biting face, and I hope to see you plagued one day, you snotty nose!'

'I come but for my due, good madam.'

'Hold forth thy mangy head and I will give it thee with

this broom! Or bend over, and I will sink a foot of my handle where'll you'll feel it most and remember me as a tidy housewife.'

'Calm down, Mistress Firethorn.'

'Only when your greasy face has gone!'

The tailor was a small, sweating, diffident man who was no match for Margery Firethorn. When he came to present his bill to her, he walked into the same hurricane as his predecessors. Backing away from the threshold of the house in Shoreditch, he summoned up enough courage to issue a threat of legal action.

'I have the law upon my side, mistress.'

'And you stay, I'll gum your silks with water!'

'Pay up now to stave off a worser fate.'

'Do you want that pate split open with my broom?'

'I'd bring an action of battery against you.'

'Your widow might, for you'd not live to do so.'

'I am not married,' he confessed.

'What woman would take you?' she jeered. 'I can see it in your visage, you insolent slave! You're a miserable tailor's remnant of a man, a pair of breeches without a codpiece, a dunghill cock with no cause to crow or fright any hen from her modesty. Away, you gelding!'

'Leave off, you shrew!'

'Then go before I snip with your scissors!'

''Tis a cucking-stool you need,' he said. 'That's what they use for ducking scolds.'

'Yaaaaaaaa!'

Margery ran at him with her broom at the ready and he

156

took to his heels and ran for his life. As he raced off down the road, she yelled some more abuse at him to spur him on then relaxed and went back into the house. The tailor was the fifth creditor in the last two days and he came on the heels of a draper, a hat-maker, a cobbler and a goldsmith. All presented her with reckonings that she simply could not meet, large bills recklessly run up by Lawrence Firethorn in the knowledge that he would be leaving London soon and therefore able to outrun his debts. Margery was left in the line of fire. Five had been dispatched but all five would return again with the law to strengthen their arm. And there would be more. Her husband was nothing if not extravagant. On the eve of his departure, he had run up debts all over London.

Pulsating with fury, she stormed upstairs to their bedchamber and grabbed the cloak. It was the answer to all her problems. Not only would its sale bring in enough money to pay off all outstanding accounts, it would be a severe blow to Firethorn. The second-best cloak was much more than a mere garment. It was a due reward for his artistic endeavour, a seal of approval from his patron. The actor had worn it onstage several times and it was a glittering storehouse of theatrical memories. Though he had left it for her to sell, he had banked on her keeping it for reasons of pride and nostalgia. Those reasons now battled with feelings of outrage.

Margery was betrayed. Struggling along without him was a trial enough but he had made her predicament much more awkward. It was typical of him and she cursed herself for not foreseeing this eventuality. No word had yet come from Firethorn and, when it did, she was sure that no money would accompany it. She was on her own with mouths to feed and tradesmen to stave off.

She fingered the cloak with swirling anger. It would serve him right if he came back to find it gone. Margery crossed to the door with the garment over her arm then stopped in her tracks. Conscience troubled her. She would be meeting one betrayal with a far greater one. Whatever vices her husband had, there was one overriding virtue that drew her to him. He loved the theatre. With a passion that amounted to an obsession, he adored every aspect of his chosen profession and savoured every prize and memento that had come his way. Even at the height of her rage, she did not have the heart to stab Firethorn in the back through the silk of his second-best cloak.

Shaking with frustration, she threw it aside.

'Doll!' she yelled.

'Yes, mistress?' called a girlish voice.

'Come here at once!'

'In haste!'

The servant girl knew better than to keep Margery waiting. She had watched through a window as each of the five creditors had been sent packing with their ears on fire. Doll lived in the house and had nowhere else to go. Total obedience was the only way to appease her mistress.

She stumbled breathlessly into the bedchamber.

'Hurry, girl!'

'I am here, mistress.'

'Then go from me again.'

'How now?'

'Fetch me pen and ink.'

'It shall be done directly.'

'And something I may write upon.'

'I fly.'

'Faster, girl!'

Margery Firethorn would grasp another possibility. She would write a letter.

Nicholas Bracewell was in no position to parley. Greatly outnumbered and clearly in the wrong, his only hope lay in a swift escape. Half-a-dozen brawny gypsies were closing in on him, their scowls hidden by the paint on their faces but their gestures eloquent. The boy himself continued to shout at Nicholas then grabbed a handful of dust to throw up into his face. Blinded for a second, the book holder swung his sword in a wide arc to fend off the gypsies who moved in quickly upon him. As his eyes cleared, he saw another man running towards them with a branding iron in his hand, patently intent on murder. Nicholas rightly identified him as the boy's father and did not linger to discuss the youth's skill as a dancer.

Swishing his sword again to create more space, he then spun around and sprinted off. One of the gypsies had sneaked up behind him and tried to block his way but Nicholas knocked him out of the way with his shoulder. Pursuit was immediate and it was accompanied by all kinds of wild cries. A few dogs joined in the fun of the chase.

Nicholas was running at full pelt but found an extra yard of pace when a long knife embedded itself in a tree only inches from his face. When he reached his horse, he had no time for a leisurely mount with the stirrup. Vaulting into the saddle, he tugged the rein free of its branch and let the horse feel his urgency.

He galloped away with howls of anguish ringing in his ears. Three of them followed him and kept him within sight for a mile or more but he finally managed to shake them off and gain the cover of a wood. With time at last to catch his breath, he measured the cost of his journey. It was expensive. He had wasted valuable time, created a band of dangerous enemies and collected an aching bruise on his shoulder. Irony ruled. Believing that the gypsies had stolen a young boy from him, he finished up by doing the same to them. Guilt lay exclusively with him and he had no excuse. Nicholas knew that he had deserved the bite that was still smarting on his arm. He was lucky to have escaped with his life.

Catching up with the company was now his prime concern and he did not spare his mount on the return journey. When he reached the Smith and Anvil, he watered the horse and checked to see what time the others had left, then he was back in the saddle and riding off once more. It was now mid-afternoon and the sun was at its height, compensating for the torrential rain earlier in the week by baking the land dry. Both Nicholas and the horse were dripping with perspiration. As the River Trent came into sight, he slowed his mount to a rising trot. The cool water shimmered ahead of him. Its appeal was quite irresistible to the exhausted traveller.

He reined in his horse when the water was lapping at its fetlocks then dismounted. After tethering the animal to the branch of an overhanging tree, he slipped behind a bush and peeled off his sticky clothes. Nobody was about as he ran naked to the edge of the bank and plunged straight into the river. It was a wonderful feeling, both relaxing and invigorating, easing his pain and restoring his vitality. He swam powerfully towards the middle of the river then rolled over on his back and floated on the surface of the water. His arms were outstretched and the sun gilded his hair and body. He let time stand still.

Eleanor Budden emerged from the bushes on the other side of the river and watched the apparition that was floating slowly towards her. She had been sitting beside the Trent in deep contemplation when she first heard the splash. Her mind had been on her mission and she had been waiting for another sign from above.

That sign had now come. What she saw on the water was no fatigued book holder washing off the dirt of a long journey. She witnessed a miracle. Eyes closed, arms nailed to some invisible cross, body limp yet beautiful. Fair hair combed by the sunlight. Here was no stranger but her closest friend in the world. She had last seen him in the lancet window at the church of St Stephen.

Eleanor Budden waded happily into the water.

'Lord Jesus,' she cried. 'Take me to Jerusalem!'

* * *

Nottingham was the first sizeable town they had been in since they had left and it gave them an immediate sense of reassurance. It was tiny by comparison with London but that did not worry them. The place was a vast improvement on villages that turned them away and hamlets which could not raise an audience worth the bother. Nottingham was civilization. They were back in business.

Lodging his company at the Saracen's Head near the centre of the town, Lawrence Firethorn put on his best apparel and went to call on the Mayor. Permission to play was readily granted and the Town Hall was the designated venue. The Mayor was a keen playgoer himself and he was delighted that Westfield's Men were gracing the town with a visit. Money was discussed and Firethorn left in much higher spirits. The performance of *Robin Hood* was set for the morrow which gave them ample time to rehearse the piece, to recruit journeymen as extras and – in the event of Richard Honeydew's continued absence – recast the role of Maid Marion. All seemed to be well.

The actor-manager then returned to the inn and his world caved in around him.

'Again! This is a double insult!'

'I saw the playbill myself, Master Firethorn.'

'Did you witness the performance?'

'I could not bear to, sir. My loyalty is to you.'

'It does you credit, Mistress Hendrik.' He thumped the settle on which he was perched. 'By heavens, I'll not bear it! Giles Randolph is as arrant a knave as ever walked the face of the earth. Sure, he cannot have come from any lawful issue but was engendered by two toads on a hot day in some slimy place or other.' He jumped to his feet. 'And did he really play *Pompey the Great*?'

'But two days ago.'

'Treachery in the highest degree!'

Anne Hendrik had tracked the company down to the inn and reported her news. The long-faced Edmund Hoode sat in on the debate along with Barnaby Gill. All three of them waited until Firethorn had ranted his full and described fifteen different ways in which he would put his rival to death. Having departed from their original route in order to shake off Banbury's Men, it was dispiriting to find that they had come in their wake after all. Firethorn's beloved role had been purloined, Hoode's play had been misappropriated and all the kudos that should have gone to Westfield's Men had been diverted to lesser mortals.

The actor-manager would have raved for an hour or more had he not been interrupted by the landlord who told him that another guest wished to have private audience with him. Firethorn stalked off like Pompey on his way to clear the Mediterranean of pirates.

Anne Hendrik was able to ask after Nicholas.

'Is he not with you here?'

'Not yet, mistress,' said Hoode. 'Dick Honeydew was taken by the gypsies and Nicholas went to rescue him.'

'Alone?'

'He would not hear of company,' said Gill.

'But there are such perils.'

'Nicholas will make light of those,' assured Hoode,

then turned to the question that really vexed him. 'Tell me now, for this is like a dagger in my heart, what player with Banbury's Men did dare to take my part?'

'Your part, sir? In *Pompey the Great*?'

'Sicinius.'

'I cannot say, Master Hoode.'

'It matters not,' said Gill dismissively. 'The role is of no account and hardly noticed in performance.'

'That is not true, Barnaby!'

'Take it away and who would miss it?'

'I would, man! I would!'

'Sicinius is a mean part for any man.'

'It is mine!' wailed Hoode. 'I wrote it and I play it. Sicinius is me. I would not have myself stolen like this. So tell me – who took the part?'

Mark Scruton lifted his dagger and stabbed his victim in the back with cruel deliberation. The man fell on to his face, twitched for a few horrifying seconds, then lay motionless. Wiping the blood from his weapon, the murderer gave a malevolent smile then strode calmly away.

Another rehearsal came to an end.

Kynaston Hall was the largest private house at which Banbury's Men had performed since the tour began and it offered them the best facilities. They had free use of the hall for rehearsal, the assistance of four liveried servants and regular maids from the kitchen. It was all very gratifying and no member of the company savoured it more than Mark Scruton. He was being given his first chance to take an important role. The play was one of their own this time, *The Renegade*, a dark and blood-soaked tragedy on a revenge theme. It enabled Giles Randolph to shine in a title role that really suited his talents and it brought Scruton forward into the light.

'Excellent work, sir.'

'Thank you, Master Randolph.'

'You prosper in the role.'

'I hope the audience shares your view.'

'Trust it well.'

'Have you no criticism?'

'None,' said Randolph languidly. 'Except that you stayed too long upon the stage once you had stabbed me. The murder of the Duke is of more dramatic significance than the reaction of his killer. Once you have dispatched me with your dagger, quit the stage.'

'I will, sir.'

'My corpse will be a soliloquy in itself.'

They were in the Great Hall and the stagekeepers were scampering around moving the scenery and props. Giles Randolph was very satisfied with the way that everything was going. On and off the stage, revenge was proving to be his best suit. He was about to move away when Scruton detained him by plucking at his sleeve.

'A word, sir.'

'It is not a convenient time.'

'This will take but a second.'

'Very well.' Randolph shrugged. 'What is it?'

'I am bold to put you in mind of my contract.'

'It has not been forgot.'

'When may I view it, sir?'

'When I have drawn it up.'

'And when will that be?'

'The other sharers have to be persuaded first.'

Scruton frowned. 'My understanding was that you could carry the business alone.'

'Well, yes, indeed. No question but that I can.'

'Why then the delay?'

'I am no lawyer, Mark. The terms must be drawn up properly and the Earl himself must take note of them. It is a big translation for you.'

'You know that I have earned it, Master Randolph.'

'No man more so.'

'Give me then a date. It was your promise.'

Giles Randolph gave him the enigmatic smile that was part of his stock-in-trade then walked slowly around him in a circle. Scruton did not like being kept waiting. His willing smile took on a forced look. Randolph faced him again and came to a decision.

'York.'

'What say you?'

'That is when the articles will be signed.'

'I have that for certain?'

'My hand upon it!' They exchanged a handshake. 'You will become a sharer with Banbury's Men and taste the sweeter fruit of our profession.'

'Thank you!' said Scruton with feeling. 'I did not doubt you for a moment. This gives me true happiness.'

166

'Wait but for York.'

'It will be my place of pilgrimage.'

'Bear your cross until then.'

Mark Scruton grinned. He was almost there.

It took Nicholas Bracewell fifteen minutes to convince her that he was not Jesus Christ and even then she had lingering reservations. When he saw her wading out to meet him in mid-river, he immediately lowered his body so that he could tread water. He had never been accosted by such a strange yet beautiful woman before, especially one who kept calling on him to baptise her in the Jordan. He took an age to persuade her to return to her bank then he swam back to where he had left his clothes and dried himself off as best he could before dressing. Restored and refreshed, he rode over the bridge and back along the bank to Eleanor Budden. Her wet shift was clinging to her body like a doting lover and he noticed that it had been repaired near the shoulder. Nicholas dismounted out of politeness and touched his cap.

'May I see you safe home, mistress?'

'All the way to Jerusalem.'

'I have told you. I am with Westfield's Men.'

'Our meeting today was foretold.'

'Not to me.'

'We were destined to cross paths, Master Bracewell.'

'In the middle of the River Trent?'

'Tax not divine appointment.'

'Let me escort you to your house.'

'I have resolved to leave it for ever.'

'Yet you spoke of a husband and of children.'

'They will have to make shift without me.'

'Does duty not prompt you?' he said.

'Aye, sir. To follow the voice of God.'

Nicholas had met religious maniacs before. More than one of his fellow-sailors on the voyage with Drake had found the privations too hard to bear. They had taken refuge in a kind of relentless Christianity that shaped their lives anew and consisted in a display of good deeds and profuse quotations from the Bible. Eleanor Budden was not of this mould. Her obsession had a quieter and more rational base. That increased its danger.

'The Lord has brought us together,' she said.

'Has he?'

'Do you not feel it?'

'Honesty compels me to deny it.'

'Where you lead, I will follow.'

'That is out of the question,' he said in alarm.

'You have been sent as my guide.'

'But we are not going to Jerusalem, I fear.'

'What, then, is your destination?'

'York.'

'I knew it!'

Eleanor flung herself to her knees and bent down to kiss his shoes. Nicholas backed away in embarrassment as she tried to clutch at him. Facing up to a band of angry gypsies had been nothing to this. Eleanor was a model of persistence, a burr that stuck firmly to his clothing.

'I must come with you, Master Bracewell.'

'Where?'

'To York. I must see the Archbishop.'

'Travel to the city by some other means.'

'You are my appointed guardian.'

'Mistress, I am part of a company.'

'Then I will go with you and your fellows.'

'That is not possible.'

'Why, sir?'

'For a dozen reasons,' he said, wishing he could call some of them to mind. 'Chiefly, for that we are all men who ride together. No woman may join our train.'

'That is a rule which God can change.'

'Master Firethorn will not permit it.'

'Let me but talk with him.'

'It will be of no avail.'

Eleanor Budden got to her feet and turned her blue eyes on him with undisguised ardour. She stepped in close and her long wet strands of hair brushed his cheek.

'You have to take me to York,' she insisted.

'For what reason?'

'I love you.'

Nicholas Bracewell quailed. He foresaw trouble.

Lawrence Firethorn was slowly enthralled. More to the point, he smelled money. Oliver Quilley had invited him up to his room to put a proposition to him, and, after rejecting it out of hand, the actor-manager was slowly being won over.

The artist expatiated on his work. Strutting about the

room in his finery like a turkey-cock, the dwarfish dandy explained why he had become a miniaturist.

'Limning is a thing apart from all other painting and drawing, and it excelleth all other art whatsoever in sundry points.'

'Discover more to me.'

'The technique of painting portrait miniatures comes from manuscript illumination. Hence the term "limning". Yet Master Holbein, the first of our breed, painted in the tradition of full-size portraits that were scaled down.'

'And you, Master Quilley?'

'My style is unique, sir.'

'Do you acknowledge no mentors?'

'I take a little from Holbein and a little more from Hilliard but Oliver Quilley is a man apart from all other limners. This you shall judge for yourself.'

He opened his leather pouch and took out four tiny miniatures that were wrapped in pieces of velvet. He removed the material and set them out on the table. Firethorn was overwhelmed by their brilliance. Three were portraits of women and the fourth of a man. All were executed with stunning confidence in colours that were uncannily lifelike. Quilley read his mind and had an explanation to hand.

'The principal part of drawing or painting after life consists in the truth of the line.' He pointed at his work. 'You see, sir? No shadowing is here. I believe in the sovereignty of the line and the magic of colour.'

'They are quite magnificent!'

'All paintings imitate nature or the life, but the perfection is to imitate the face of mankind.'

'And womankind,' said Firethorn, ogling the loveliest of the women. 'Who is the lady, sir?'

'A French Countess. And the other is her sister.'

'The third?'

'Lady Delahaye. I was commissioned by her husband to have it ready in time for her wedding. It is all but finished and I can deliver it when I return to London.'

Firethorn warmed to the little man, sensing that he was in the presence of a fellow-artist, one who consorted with the nobility and whose work was worn as pendants or brooches at court, and yet who had made no fortune from his wondrous talents. The actor knew that story all too well because it was his own. Exceptional ability that went unrewarded in its proper degree. That sense of living hand-to-mouth which compromised the scope of his art and silenced its true resonance.

'Marry, sir, what a case is this!' he said. 'Here we are together. Men of genius who are packed off out of London to scrabble for every penny we get.'

'Aye,' agreed Quilley. 'Then to have it taken from us by some murderous highwaymen. Had they taken these miniatures instead, I had been ruined.'

A thought took on form in Firethorn's mind.

'You wish to travel in our company, you say?'

'Only for safety's sake, as far as York.'

'We do not carry passengers in our company.'

'I'd pay my way, Master Firethorn, be assured.'

'That is what I come to, sir.' He tried to work out which was the better profile to present to the artist. 'Is it possible – I ask but in the spirit of unbiased enquiry – that you could paint such a portrait of me?'

'Of you or of any man, sir. For a fee.'

'A guarantee of your safety?'

'I'd need a horse of my own.'

'Done, sir!'

'And a bedchamber to myself at every stop we make?'

'It shall be the first article of our agreement.'

'We understand each other, sir.'

'Such a portrait would be very precious to me.'

'And to me, Master Firethorn,' said Quilley with elfin seriousness. 'The terms of the work can be talked over at a later date but I give you this as a sign of good faith.' He handed over the miniature of the man. 'It is worth much more than I will cost you. I am but small and very light to carry.'

Firethorn looked down at the exquisite oval painting that lay in his palm. It had such fire and elegance and detail. The man stared up at him with a pride that was matched by his poise. Firethorn was overcome by the generosity of the artist.

'This is for me, sir?'

'To seal our friendship and buy me safe passage.'

'It is the very perfection of art, sir.'

'My work is never less than that.'

'But will not the subject want it for himself?'

'I fear not, sir.'

'I would hate to take his personal property away.'

'The fellow has no need of it now.'

'Why?'

'Because that is Anthony Rickwood in your hand.'

'The name is familiar.'

'You have seen his portrait before, I think.'

'Have I?'

'It is the work of another famous artist.'

'What is his name?'

'Sir Francis Walsingham,' said Quilley. 'He paints his subjects upon spikes. You may have seen poor Master Rickwood on display above Bishopsgate.'

'The man was a traitor?' gulped Firethorn.

'A staunch Roman Catholic.'

'I am holding a corpse?'

'That is the essence of Walsingham's art.'

Quilley gave a mischievous smile that only caused the actor further discomfort. Firethorn had now changed his mind about the gift. Instead of being a treasured object, it was burning his palm like molten metal.

Chapter Seven

Robert Rawlins shuffled quietly into York Minster through the Great West Door and walked slowly down the centre of the nave. Sunlight streamed in through the magnificent window at his back, throwing its curvilinear tracery, with its central Heart of Yorkshire, into sharper relief and freshening the colours of the stained glass. Rawlins was dwarfed by it all, a grey, inoffensive little mouse amid the huge white pillars. Almost a hundred feet above his head, the superb gold bosses in the vaulted roof portrayed critical events in the Christian story. Here was both celebration and warning, a lasting tribute to what had gone before and a clear direction as to what should come in the future.

Standing in the aisle, Rawlins looked around and took in the wonder of it all, at once inspired and abashed, as he always was, by this architectural marvel dedicated to the glory of God, and highly conscious of the number of lives that had gone into its construction. He fell to his knees on the bruising stone and offered up a prayer of supplication. Anxious and beset by danger, he came in to search for sanctuary and was soon deep in conversation with his Maker.

An hour passed. The rustling silence was then broken by the sweetest of sounds. Behind the choir screen with its row of kings surmounted by stucco angels, the Minster choristers had taken up their position in their gleaming stalls. Voices of sublime harmony were raised in a Mass. In his extremity, it seemed to Robert Rawlins as if the angels themselves were singing in unison. He listened transfixed to the *Kyrie, Gloria, Credo, Sanctus, Benedictus* and *Agnus Dei,* mouthing old Latin words that were sung with such beauty and expression by young throats, and sharing in the perfection of earthly worship. It was such balm to his ears and succour to his soul that tears of joy soon trickled down his face.

The choirmaster now decided to rehearse a hymn. When the voices rose again to fill the whole cathedral with a mellifluous sound, they achieved a different result.

> All people that on earth do dwell
> Sing to the Lord with cheerful voice;
> Him serve with fear, His praise forth tell,
> Come ye before him, and rejoice.

Robert Rawlins got to his feet in horror. It was not only because the singing of hymns had been introduced by the

Puritans as part of their denigration of the priests and their eagerness to involve the congregation in the divine service. What stuck in his craw was this version of Psalm 100 – *Jubilate Deo*. Rendered into the vernacular from the Latin that Rawlins loved, it was the work of one William Kethe, a hymn-writer who fled from England during Mary's reign and lived as a refugee in Geneva with such extremists as John Knox, Goodman, Whittingham and Foxe. Such names, such beliefs and such associations were quite obnoxious to Robert Rawlins and he felt it was sacrilege to sing that hymn in that place.

Spinning around, he trotted back down the nave to the Great West Door. The comfort which he sought had been denied him. God was deaf to his entreaties.

He went out once more into a hostile world.

The enormous pleasure of seeing Anne Hendrik again was tempered by the fact that he had no leisure time to spend alone with her. Nicholas Bracewell was forced to chat with her while helping to construct a makeshift tree for use in the forthcoming performance of *Robin Hood and his Merry Men*. In a corner of the inn yard, the book holder was an emergency carpenter with the dubious assistance of George Dart. Conversation with Anne Hendrik was therefore punctuated by the rasp of the saw and the banging of the hammer. It ruled out any romantic element.

'I cannot believe my luck in meeting you,' she said.

'I told you it would happen, Anne.'

'If only the circumstances were happier.'

'Indeed.'

'Is there no news at all of Dick Honeydew?'

'None, I fear.'

'Who could have taken him?'

'All sorts of people,' said Nicholas with a sigh. 'He is a comely youth and takes the eye wherever we stop. Dick would not be the first apprentice who was snatched away because someone conceived a fancy for the lad.'

'Is he in danger?'

'We must hope that he is not.'

'Where do you think he could be, Nick?'

'I have cudgelled my brain to give me an answer to that question, but it refuses. All I have is guesswork and suspicion.'

'And what do they tell you?'

'Banbury's Men.'

'Would they commit such a crime?'

'They have stolen both our plays and our audiences,' he argued. 'Why should they stop there? In stealing young Dick as well, they deal us a far harder blow.'

'You think the boy is with them?'

'Master Randolph is too clever for that. If he has ordered the abduction – and every instinct about me says that he did – then he would have assigned the task to some underling and told the man to keep Dick well away from the company for fear of detection.'

Anne's maternalism was thoroughly roused by now. She knew all the apprentices well, none more so than Richard Honeydew, and she felt a mother's distress at his untimely disappearance. Imagination only increased her fright.

'Will they harm the boy?'

'They have no need to do so,' he said, trying to reassure himself as well as her. 'Their sole aim is to harm Westfield's Men and they do that by taking from us one of our leading players.'

'What will happen to the lad, then?'

'I believe he will be released in time.'

'And when will that be?'

'When they have thoroughly discomfited us.'

Nicholas hammered in a few more nails then stood the small tree up on the square base he had just provided. It rocked slightly on the cobbles. Anne was sympathetic.

'This is no work for a book holder.'

'It is a case of all hands to the pumps.'

'Can you not assign these chores to others?'

Her reply was a yell of pain. George Dart had missed the nail he was hitting and found his thumb instead. He danced around in anguish, wringing his hand as if it were a bell then plunging it into a bucket of cold water that a groom was carrying out of the stables. Nicholas looked on with rueful amusement.

'That is why I must supervise it all, Anne,' he said. 'Our fellows are willing but unskilled. Were I not here to help and control, there'd scarce be three fingers left between the whole lot of them.'

Nicholas took over the job that Dart had abandoned. As church bells rang out nearby, Anne Hendrik turned her mind to another topic. The faintest hint of jealousy sounded in her voice.

'Tell me more of Mistress Eleanor Budden.'

'There is nothing more to tell.'

'She accosted you in the river, you say?'

'Only because she took me for my betters.'

'You are no Lord Jesus to me.'

'I am pleased to hear it.' They laughed fondly. 'Do not pay any heed to Mistress Budden. She was but a minor encumbrance in a long and busy day. I shook her free.'

'Can you be sure of that, Nick?'

'She will not travel with us.'

'Master Oliver Quilley does.'

'Only by special arrangement.'

'Will she not find the same dispensation?'

'It is outside the bounds of possibility,' he said with confidence. 'Master Firethorn will have no time for yearning missionaries. He will turn her away straight. We are a company of players who carry our tumult with us. Warm language can be spoken by headstrong spirits. Here is no place for maiden modesty, still less for any true pilgrim. Mistress Eleanor Budden wastes her breath. There is no way that she will journey with us to York.'

'It is agreed, then,' said Firethorn. 'You come with us.'

'Oh, sir!' she said effusively. 'Your kindness will win you friends in Heaven. I kiss your hand.'

'Nay, madam, I will kiss yours.'

He took the outstretched hand of Eleanor Budden with

elaborate courtesy and placed a gentlemanly kiss upon it. She curtseyed low before him and he responded with a bow. For a man who normally guarded Westfield's Men with a possessive care, he was being extraordinarily liberal. In the space of twenty-four hours, he had agreed to let an artist and now a self-proclaimed visionary accompany them on their travels. Lawrence Firethorn persuaded himself that both decisions were the right ones.

'You will not forget the money, good mistress.'

'I will bring it with me.'

'And there will be no dispute with your husband?'

'He will not stop me, sir.'

'Then I am content.'

'And I am truly bounden to you, Master Firethorn.'

She curtseyed again and allowed him another view of the delights which had finally changed his mind. Eleanor Budden was indeed a gorgeous woman and her religious fervour only served to bring out her qualities. He loved the smoothness of her skin and the roundness of her face and the appealing curves of her body. After dismissing her plea out of hand at first, he had listened to her gentle tenacity and feasted his eyes on her long hair. The combination of the two had made him think again.

Firethorn sought to clarify their relationship.

'There will be certain conditions, mistress.'

'I submit to anything that you devise, sir.'

'Would that you did!' he murmured.

'What must I do?'

'Refrain from interference with our calling. We will

be your shield on the road but we must have freedom to practise our art along the way. You must not hinder us in rehearsal or performance in any way.'

'Nor will I, sir. I'll spend my time in prayer.'

'We might find other things for you.'

'I need none.'

The simplicity of her purpose was quite moving. At the same time, he could not accept that it would sustain her all the way to York and certainly not to Jerusalem itself. Eleanor Budden had never been more than ten miles from Nottingham in the whole of her life and that had been in the company of her husband. She would find the long ride to York both irksome and perilous, causing her to turn increasingly to Firethorn for support. The idea titillated him. He had never corrupted a saint before.

'And shall I see Master Bracewell?' she asked.

'Every day. You'll ride beside him on the waggon.'

'My cup of joy runs over!'

'Haply, mine will do so as well.'

He bestowed another kiss on her hand then escorted her to the door of the inn. She waved in gratitude then flitted off over the cobbles. Firethorn chuckled to himself then went into the taproom to acquaint Barnaby Gill and Edmund Hoode with the latest development. They were antagonistic.

'This is lunacy!' yelled Gill. 'I forbid it!'

'It is less than wise, Lawrence,' said Hoode.

'The venture brings us money and companionship.'

'Who wants her companionship?' retorted Gill. 'Let her

keep her money and distribute it as alms. We are actors here, not bodyguards for hire by anyone. Our only privilege is our freedom and you throw that away by inviting some Virgin Mary to sit in judgement on us.'

'She's no Virgin Mary,' said Firethorn quickly.

'The lady is a distraction,' said Hoode. 'She has no place alongside us. Nor does Master Oliver Quilley. They should find some other means to travel north.'

Firethorn did his best to win them over but they were unconvinced. As a last resort, he knew that he could impose his will upon them but wished to avoid doing that if at all possible. Their acceptance was important. He wanted to be seen by Eleanor Budden as the leader of a company who studied to obey his every wish, and not as some petty tyrant who bullied the others into agreement.

His two colleagues left with stern warnings.

'I set my face against this, Lawrence!' said Gill.

'It will not improve your complexion.'

'I am with Barnaby,' said Hoode. 'You have made a move here that will bring us nothing but awkwardness.'

The two of them went out and Firethorn was left to mull over what they had said. He was not dismayed. They always objected to his ideas. It was simply a question of giving them time to grow accustomed to the notion. When they saw what a harmless woman Eleanor Budden was, they would alter their views. Firethorn was pleased with the new transaction. He called for a pint of sherry.

He was taking his first sip when she appeared.

'I hoped to find you here, sir.'

'Susan, my dove! Sit down and take your ease.'

'I come to inform you of my decision,' she said with a broad grin, lowering herself down into a chair. 'Your lonely nights are over, Lawrence.'

'Prove it lustily between the sheets.'

'So will I do, sir.'

'You are man's greatest comfort, Susan.'

'That is why I will not desert you now.'

'Bless you, lady!'

'Master Gill made up my mind for me.'

'Barnaby?'

'He told me even now of Mistress Budden.'

'Ah, yes,' he said dismissively. 'A holy woman who hears the voice of God. A poor, distracted creature on whom a Christian must take pity.'

'Is she young or old?'

'Ancient, I fear. And so ill-favoured that a man can scarce look fully upon her. That is the only reason I took her. Mistress Budden will be no temptation to the goatish members of my company.'

Susan Becket's eyes twinkled merrily.

'I saw the lady leave you. If she be ancient, then I am dead and buried this last ten-year. She has a bloom upon her that could seduce a bishop.'

'How came I to miss such a quality?'

'Because your mind was firmly on me, Lawrence.'

'Indeed, indeed,' he fawned.

'That is why I reached my decision. Mistress Budden is a child of nature and innocence sits upon her. I'll be a true

184

mother to her and keep those goats from grazing on her pasture. She'll thank me well for it.'

'I do not understand your meaning, Susan.'

'Your warming-pan comes with you, sir.'

'All the way?' he said anxiously.

'Every last inch.'

'I could not put you to the trouble.'

'It is my pleasure.'

Her smile of easy determination fractured all his plans for the journey. Susan Becket was an old flame he had intended to blow out in Nottingham but she had now rekindled herself. Lawrence Firethorn could not hide his chagrin. He was taking one woman too many to York.

The pint of sherry was guzzled quickly down.

Sir Clarence Marmion strolled through his garden with his soberly-clad companion by his side. Large, formal and a blaze of colour, it was a tribute to the skill and hard work of his gardeners, but their master was not interested in their craft that morning. His mind was preoccupied with something of more immediate concern.

'He would yield up no names.'

'Are you sure that he knew any?'

'No question about that, sir.'

'Did you press him on the matter?'

'As hard as any man dare.'

Robert Rawlins rubbed his hands fastidiously.

'Let me speak to the fellow, Sir Clarence.'

'It will not serve.'

'Haply, I may succeed where others have failed.'

'You have come too late for that.'

'I will lay spiritual weights upon him.'

'He would feel them not, Master Rawlins.'

'What are you telling me?'

'The man is dead.'

'Since when?'

'Since I had him killed.'

'Sir Clarence!'

Robert Rawlins put a hand to his mouth in shock and leaned upon a stone angel for support. It was not the first time that his host had taken him by surprise since he had arrived in Yorkshire but it was easily the most disconcerting. He waved his arms weakly in protest but his companion was brutally calm.

'The man was given Christian burial,' he said.

'After he was murdered.'

'Executed, sir. Like Anthony Rickwood.'

'An eye for an eye?'

'We gave him all the justice he deserved.'

'I would have sued for clemency.'

'On behalf of such a villain as that?'

'Every man has some good in him.'

'Not this black-hearted devil,' said Sir Clarence with asperity. 'One of Walsingham's jackals. He brought dozens of Catholics to their deaths and did so without compunction. Was I to let him go free, sir, to report that I was party to the conspiracy? And that Robert Rawlins is a missionary priest of the Romish persuasion?'

'I like not this business.'

'We had no choice before us.'

'You had Christian teaching to guide you.'

'So did Anthony Rickwood, and where did it land him? Upon a spike at Bishopsgate until we engineered his rescue.' His vehemence increased. 'And what of Neville Pomeroy? What guidance did his Christian teaching give him? It showed him the way directly to the Tower!'

'I did not mean to anger you so, Sir Clarence.'

'We must fight fire with fire!'

'Murder should be anathema.'

'Revenge has its own dignity.'

Robert Rawlins bit back any further comment and tried to come to terms with what had happened. Sir Clarence Marmion was a good friend and a charming host when he wished to be but a new and more callous side to his character was emerging. It was highly unsettling. Joined indissolubly by the same purpose, the two men yet had different ideas on how it could be best effected.

Sir Clarence tried to still the other's disquiet.

'He sleeps with God now, sir.'

'Will the Law not come searching for him?'

'He'll not be found six feet under my land.'

'I own I am distressed.'

'Would you rather we had been subjects for burial?'

'Indeed not, Sir Clarence.'

'Then rejoice in the death of an enemy.'

They strolled on along a gravel path that bisected the rose garden. Robert Rawlins slowly came to see some reason in what had been said. His host sounded a note of cautious optimism.

'I have prayed for help.'

'So have I, Sir Clarence. Daily.'

'Our prayers may yet meet with a response.'

'You have a sign of this?'

'Not outwardly, Master Rawlins.'

'Then how?'

'It is no more than a feeling but it grows and grows all the time. The man we seek may not need to be hunted down after all. There may be another means to find him.'

'Tell me what it is.'

'Let the villain come to us.'

'Will he do that, Sir Clarence?'

'I am certain of it. When I trust to instinct, I am seldom misled. The man is getting closer and we must be ready for him. Keep your wits about you, sir.'

'I will.'

'He is on his way to York.'

Christopher Millfield knew how to cut a dash when the opportunity presented itself. He had been cast in the part of Will Scarlet and sang the ballad which began the rehearsal of *Robin Hood and his Merry Men*. Sauntering about the stage, he let his flowing scarlet costume swish to great effect and accompanied his pleasing tenor voice with chords from a small lute. Will Scarlet truly had his moment at the Town Hall in Nottingham.

Come now and listen, gentlemen,
That be of free-born blood!
I shall tell you of a good yeoman,
His name was Robin Hood.
Robin was a proud outlaw,
Whiles he walked on ground,
So courteous a fellow as he was one,
Was never none yet found.
Robin stood in Sherwood Forest,
And leaned him to a tree.
And by him stood Little John,
The stoutest friend was he.

The rehearsal had some shaky moments. Martin Yeo, the oldest and most experienced of the apprentices, was never more than a competent replacement for Richard Honeydew in the vital role of Maid Marion. His gesture and deportment were above reproach but he had none of his colleague's radiance or supreme sense of timing. Dressed in Lincoln green, as sanctified by tradition, Lawrence Firethorn brought his usual panache to the role of Robin Hood but even he faltered slightly in the love scenes. Barnaby Gill was a droll Friar Tuck and Edmund Hoode scored in the part of Much the Miller's Son but the Merry Men were a complete shambles. Supplemented by a few journeymen brought in for the occasion, they moved about the stage like a flock of frightened sheep and scattered in utter confusion whenever Robin Hood indulged in swordplay.

Nicholas Bracewell kept the whole thing moving and minimised the effects of most errors but even he could not stop George Dart – a decidedly unmerry member of the Merry Men – from felling a tree by walking accidentally into it. Will Scarlet was one of the few to come through unscathed and he brought the proceedings to a close with another ballad sung to the music of his lute.

Then bespake good Robin,
In place whereat he stood,
'Tomorrow, I must to Kirksley,
Craftily to be let blood!'
Sir Roger of Doncaster,
By the Prioress he lay,
And there they betrayed good Robin Hood
Through their false play.
Christ have mercy on his soul!
(That died on the rood)
For Robin was a good outlaw
And did poor men much good.

Robin Hood now rounded on his Merry Men as if they had each tried to assassinate him during the performance. By the time Firethorn had finished reviling them for their incompetence and blaming them for their mere existence, their cheeks matched the colour of Will Scarlet's costume. The actor-manager spread his criticisms widely and even Barnaby Gill was made to squirm a little. Martin Yeo was totally demoralised by the attack on him. The only actor who emerged unscathed was Christopher Millfield. It put him in buoyant mood.

'How did it look to you, Master Bracewell?'

'There is much work to be done.'

'I was speaking of my own performance.'

'You sang most sweetly.'

'And my playing of Will Scarlet?'

'It was sufficient,' said Nicholas with polite evasion. 'You will not let the company down, sir.'

Millfield felt damned by faint praise. Wanting to impress the other, he had only irritated him by seeking his approval so obviously. He watched the book holder take control. Now that the rehearsal was over, Nicholas started delegating the dozens of jobs that had been thrown up in the past couple of hours. Several props had been damaged and needed repair, one of the trestles that held up the stage had to be strengthened, and two of the instruments required a new string apiece. Some of the costumes had been torn during the fight scenes and George Dart was assigned the task of mending them with needle and thread. Stephen Judd's wig was falling apart.

Nicholas was so caught up in his work that he did not see the danger that threatened. With his back to the stage, he was unaware of the fact that two of his minions were struggling to dismantle the gallows that was used in the closing scene of the play. It was far too heavy and awkward for them to handle and its weight finally got the better of them. Before they could stop it, the long spar of timber toppled over and fell towards Nicholas.

Christopher Millfield responded like lightning.

'Look out there!'

Hurling himself forward, he knocked the book holder out of the way and suffered a glancing blow from the falling prop. Nicholas picked himself up and turned to see what had happened. Millfield was now sitting on the floor and rubbing his shoulder gingerly.

'Are you hurt, Christopher?'

'It is nothing serious.'

'I owe you much thanks.'

Millfield grinned. 'I saved you from the gallows.'

'And from certain injury.'

Nicholas upbraided the two assistants who caused the accident and got them to move the timber away. Then he offered a hand to Millfield and pulled him up. The latter dusted himself off and continued to rub his shoulder.

'I will remember this,' said Nicholas.

'You would have done as much for me.'

'In your place, I might have held back.'

'Because you do not like me?'

'It is reason enough.'

'But I like you, Master Bracewell.'

It was Nicholas's turn to grin. Millfield's manner was quite disarming and it was hard to bear a grudge against him. The book holder made a concession.

'Your performance was excellent, Christopher.'

'Thank you!'

'To speak truly, I am not sure that Gabriel Hawkes could have bettered it.'

'I seek no higher praise than that.'

'You will get none.'

They shared a laugh and much of the tension between them evaporated. All actors sought approval but Millfield seemed particularly anxious to win a plaudit from the book holder. It made him quite forget the pain in his shoulder. He reached out to take Nicholas by the arms.

'I will confess something to you,' he said.

'Must I be your priest?' teased the other.

'I am in earnest, Master Bracewell.'

'Speak on.'

'Gabriel was the finer actor.'

'Only in certain respects.'

'I am honest enough to admit it,' said Millfield seriously. 'He had more range and more depth. When you chose between us, you were right to take Gabriel Hawkes.'

'No other player would allow as much.'

'Why hide the truth when the fellow is no longer with us?' His grip tightened. 'I hated him for standing in my way. I wished Gabriel dead so that I could take his place but I did not hasten his end, that I swear. If he was murdered, as you believe, then it was by another.'

Nicholas looked deep into his eyes and lost many of the suspicions and resentments he harboured against the man. Christopher Millfield had his faults but they were largely those of his profession. The book holder sealed their new-found friendship with a warm handshake that made the other wince. Concern took over.

'Let me look at that shoulder of yours.'

'It is of no account.'

'You are still in pain, I can see.'

Millfield was eventually persuaded to take off his scarlet tunic so that Nicholas could examine the injury. The shoulder was badly grazed where the timber had struck but no blood had been drawn. Nicholas used tender fingers to explore the damage then got his companion to lift his arm straight up then rotate it. He gave his diagnosis.

'You are lucky, Christopher. Nothing is broken.'

'I will get away with a few bruises.'

'And a lot of stiffness,' said Nicholas. 'Give me some time and I will prepare an ointment to put on your shoulder. It will ease the soreness.'

'Then it is most welcome. How will you make it?'

'With herbs.'

'Are you a physician as well?'

'I learned much from the ship's doctor when I was at sea. Aches and pains are part of every sailor's lot and I studied the way to soften them. The knowledge has been of use many a time.'

'No patient will be more grateful than I.'

'The gratitude is all on my side.'

'Your friendship is reward enough.'

'It comes with the ointment.'

Millfield grinned. 'Both will be cherished.'

When the actor went off to get changed, Nicholas was soon joined by another companion. Oliver Quilley had been watching the rehearsal attentively throughout. If he was to create a miniature of the actor-manager, it must contain all of his characteristics and these were most evident when he was onstage. Quilley missed nothing.

'Is Master Firethorn always so fierce?'

'You saw but a muted account of him today.'

'There's more ferocity to come?'

'He saves it for the audience.'

'I wait with interest,' said Quilley. 'When I paint a portrait, I want it to be as complete a picture as is possible. I divine the truth of a personality.'

'How long will this portrait take, sir?'

'I work from three sittings,' explained the artist with fluttering hand movements. 'At the first, I will set down the broad outline of his features, starting with the forehead and using it to calculate the other proportions of his face. At the second sitting, I will make careful note of all the colours of flesh, hair and costume, paying especial attention – for this is the crux of my art – to the expression of his eyes and the corners of his mouth.'

'What of the third sitting, Master Quilley?'

'I will finish off in fine detail.'

'You work speedily, sir.'

'Even artists have to eat.'

'How did you come to choose your career?'

'It chose me,' said Quilley. 'I was apprenticed nearly thirty years ago now to a goldsmith in Eastcheap. My master was a wealthy man and rose to be Chamberlain of the City of London and Prime warden of his Company.'

'You picked your master with care.'

'Fortune was ever at my side during the seven years I

spent at the sign of the Gilt Lion and Firebrand. I became very skilled in the making of jewellery and much taken with the notion of painting miniatures.'

'How did you begin, Master Quilley?'

'With a lady at court. She was a friend of my master's and easily flattered. It was my first work as a limner and not without flaw.'

'In what way?'

'The portrait was superb, as all my painting is, but I omitted a vital detail, Master Bracewell.'

'Oh?'

'I did not exact payment.' He rolled his eyes and tossed his hands in the air. 'Such is the life of an artist! We never get our due reward. Word of mouth pronounces me a genius and commissions roll in but do those same people actually pay me for my labours? Very rarely, sir. Very rarely.'

'You must have had some honest employers.'

'A few. Master Anthony Rickwood was one.'

'He that was executed?' said Nicholas in surprise.

'Yes, sir. He has suffered for his villainy but I can only speak of his kindness. Master Rickwood paid me twice what I asked and he recommended me to a number of his close friends, including Master Neville Pomeroy from Hertfordshire.'

'We know the gentleman.'

'Then you will be aware of his generosity. A most courteous fellow. I lacked for nothing at his home.'

'Nor did we when we performed at Pomeroy Manor.'

'He talked much of his passion for the theatre.'

'We look to visit him again on our return south.'

'Unhappily, you may not do that, sir.'

'But he invited us.'

'He is no longer there to receive you.'

'Why do you say that?'

'Because Master Pomeroy has been arrested.'

'On what charge?'

'High treason. He conspired with Anthony Rickwood.'

'Can this be true?'

'Walsingham has him locked away in the Tower.'

'What will be his fate?'

'The worst possible.' Quilley smiled wryly. 'He will die the ignominious death of a traitor. I do not think that Master Millfield will be able to save *him* from the gallows.'

Miles Melhuish blanched. He thought he could not be astounded anew by Eleanor Budden but he was mistaken. Her latest announcement made him gape. He turned to her husband who sat in the corner of the vestry but Humphrey had no opinion. Defeated by his wife in every way, he was a poor, pale relic of the man who had married her and gloried in her favours. Humphrey Budden was to be an essentially silent presence during the interview.

Melhuish summoned up some pop-eyed indignation.

'This is not wise, mistress. This is not good.'

'I believe it to be both, sir.'

'Travelling with a company of itinerant players!'

'They come from London,' she said proudly.

'That only makes it worse. You cannot conceive of

197

the minds and appetites of such creatures. Players are but friends of Hell in human disguise.'

'They have used me most properly until now.'

'Wait until you are undefended on the road.'

'That cannot be. God is with me always.'

'Yes, sister,' he said condescendingly. 'God is with us all, and at all times. But there are times when even His divine protection is not enough. You do yourself a harm by exposing yourself to such danger.'

'Of what, Master Melhuish?'

The vicar cleared his throat and plucked at his collar. He tossed a glance at Budden but there was no help from there. He plucked the nettle boldly.

'Players are notorious libertines, Eleanor.'

'I never heard it so.'

'They have the morals of the lowest beasts.'

'Why then have they been so polite to me?'

''Tis but to lure you into lowering your guard.'

'Master Firethorn is not like that,' she argued with feeling. 'Nor is Master Bracewell and he is the reason that I travel with Westfield's Men.'

'Who is Master Bracewell?'

'He hangs behind you, sir.'

Miles Melhuish turned around with a start but saw nobody there. Eleanor pointed to the stained glass window whose image of Jesus Christ looked more like the book holder than ever. The vicar was given a further shock.

'You tell me this player is . . . like Lord Jesus?'

'As like as two peas in a pod, sir,' she said. 'But he is

198

no player. Master Bracewell is the book holder with the company and a more upright man I have never met. I'd put my life and soul in his hands, so I would!'

'Take care he does not abuse your trust.'

'He would not.'

'Think of the long reaches of the night.'

'I have done with fornication,' she said chirpily.

Humphrey Budden twitched at the mention of the word and a wistful calm settled on his dull features as he let his mind play with a few robust memories. Melhuish tried further persuasion but it was futile. When her mind was made up, Eleanor would listen to nobody.

'Take another woman with you,' he advised. 'One of your servants to act as a chaperone.'

'God is my chaperone.'

'It may prove too onerous a duty for Him.'

'You question His powers?'

'No, no,' said Miles Melhuish quickly. 'I would never presume to do such a thing. It is just that . . . well, I would feel happier if you had some additional guarantee of your safety.'

'I do, sir. In Master Nicholas Bracewell.'

'That is not what I had in mind.' He looked over at the somnolent husband. 'Do you have no fears for your good lady on this journey, sir?'

'None that I know of,' he grunted.

'She will be with loose men of the theatre.'

'Good luck to them!' murmured the other.

'Rest easy, sir,' said Eleanor to the vicar. 'I will not

be the only traveller with the company. An artist makes the journey to York with us as well. And so does another woman. She will ensure my safety.'

Plague hit London with renewed force each day but Doll would have preferred to take her chances in the city all the same. Life at the house in Shoreditch was a spreading pestilence ever since the siege by creditors had begun. Margery Firethorn became more and more embattled and her servants felt the worst tremors. Doll always seemed to be in the firing line when her mistress exploded. The girl was small, young, tousled and quite unequal to the demands made on her by a ranting employer. Each day brought fresh pain and humiliation for her.

Margery Firethorn hailed her from the kitchen. 'Doll!'

'Yes, mistress?'

'Can you not hear the doorbell?'

'No, mistress.'

'Then open your ears, girl, or I'll box them!'

Doll came scuttling into the kitchen where Margery was up to her arms in flour. The girl dithered and threw a deep but raged curtsey. The doorbell rang more loudly.

'Do you hear it now, girl?'

'Yes, mistress.'

'Then answer it.'

'What am I to say?'

'If it be a creditor, that I am not at home.'

'And if it be someone else?'

'Bring me word. Now – away.'

Doll raced out and she could be heard opening the door and talking to someone for a few moments. When she came back in, the girl was wide-eyed with amazement.

'Well?' snapped Margery.

'You have a visitor, mistress.'

'Who is he?'

'There is a big coach outside the house.'

'Who is he?'

'His footman rang the bell.'

'His name, girl. What is my visitor's name?'

'Lord Westfield.'

Doll was plainly awestruck at the notion of a peer of the realm calling at a player's house in Shoreditch but Margery reacted as if it was an everyday occurrence. Wiping her floured hands on her apron, she crossed to the sink to thrust her hands into a pan of cold water. She swung her head to glare at her servant.

'Do not stand there like that, Doll.'

'What must I do, mistress?'

'Show Lord Westfield in.'

Chapter Eight

Nottingham converged on its Town Hall in large numbers. People of every degree came to see one of the legendary characters of English history in action once more. *Robin Hood and his Merry Men* was rather different from the usual fare offered by Westfield's Men in its repertoire. Classical tragedy, domestic comedy and rustic farce were their main concerns. When they dipped into their glorious heritage, they came up with stirring dramas about kings and queens and mighty battles that were fought to secure the defence of the realm. Military heroism and foreign conquest always drew an audience. Robin Hood had more in common with folk memory than historical fact but the company did not serve up the accustomed blend of romance and adventure in Sherwood Forest. Investing the story with a deeper significance, they touched on themes of loyalty, patriotism and spiritual commitment. In their portrayal of Prince John, they also drew attention to the follies of self-aggrandisement.

Packed into their Town Hall, the audience was totally mesmerised from start to finish. Lawrence Firethorn was as convincing a Robin Hood as they had ever seen. He was noble, fearless and devoted to King Richard. Powerful in the action scenes, he was yet soft and tender when alone with Maid Marion and his wooing made every woman in the house shiver with delight. Songs and swordfights moved the drama along at regular intervals and there were some clever effects, devised by Nicholas Bracewell, with bows and arrows. Dances were used cleverly throughout and the comic brilliance of Barnaby Gill was at its height when Friar Tuck lifted his skirts to dance a bare-footed jig.

Anne Hendrik sat on a bench alongside Susan Becket and joined in the applause. She had seen Westfield's Men at their peak in London and this performance fell some way below that, but it was still a fine entertainment and the people of Nottingham clearly thought they had been in the presence of a masterpiece. They stood, clapped and shouted for all they were worth. Lawrence Firethorn led the company out several times to acknowledge the ovation with deep bows. Even George Dart enjoyed it, contriving a smile that actually made him look at home among the Merry Men. After all their mishaps, Westfield's Men were back where they belonged and it was invigorating.

This was theatre.

Nicholas Bracewell was less satisfied than most. The performance had too many rough edges for his liking and there were several minor mistakes that irritated him. And while the Town Hall was a marked improvement on some of the other venues where they had played it, it was worlds away from the theatres of London and a diminution in every sense. But the chief cause of Nicholas's discontent was the absence of Richard Honeydew. Seeing the boy's role filled, albeit adequately, by someone else only brought home to him the importance of tracking the lad down. The company would never be at its best without their star apprentice and Nicholas owed it to him to begin another search with all due speed.

'Where will you go?' asked Anne.

'In pursuit of Banbury's Men.'

'Do you know where they are?'

'I will find them somehow.'

'On your own?'

'I travel faster by myself,' said Nicholas. 'In any case, Master Firethorn can spare nobody to come with me. Everyone is needed here. He would not let me go again myself until we had staged *Robin Hood*.'

'Without you there would have been no performance.'

'Even with me, it was not a source of pride.'

'The audience was entranced.'

'Their standards are not high, Anne.'

'Do not be too unkind on the company.'

The two of them were strolling through the narrow streets on their way back to the Saracen's Head. Having organised the strike party at the Town Hall, the book holder now had a brief moment alone with Anne before he set off on the trail of Richard Honeydew once more. He talked through the few solid facts he possessed.

'Master Quilley has been of some help.'

'The artist?'

'Yes,' said Nicholas. 'He was in Leicester before he came on here and encountered Banbury's Men in the town. Instead of staying on the Great North Road and going on up to Doncaster, they must have left Grantham and headed south-west.'

'Why to Leicester?'

'We might be the cause of that, Anne.'

'Westfield's Men?'

'Thinking we would be making haste to overtake them and call them to account, they sought to shake us off by changing their itinerary. But there is a stronger reason. Leicester is a welcoming port of call for many theatre companies. They have safe harbour there. Master Quilley tells me that Banbury's Men performed three times there and once in Ashby-de-la-Zouche.'

'Then on to Nottingham with *Pompey the Great*.'

'That goes hard with Master Firethorn.'

'His vanity was affronted.'

''Tis all too easily done.'

They shared a laugh then paused outside the main door of the Saracen's Head. It had been wonderful to see him again so unexpectedly but Anne knew that they would have to part again now, and without the pleasure of a long and amorous leave taking. She kissed him on the cheek and he pulled her to him for a minute.

'Take every care, Nick.'

'I shall.'

'Come safe home.'

'God willing, I'll bring Dick Honeydew with me.'

'Where can he be?'

'Waiting, Anne.'

'For what?'

'Deliverance.'

The shed was small, dark and airless. An unpleasant smell of rotting vegetation prevailed. Through the cracks in the timber walls, it was just possible to gauge the degree of sunlight. Otherwise he had no idea what time of day it was. As shadows lengthened and a deeper gloom returned to his little prison, Richard Honeydew resolved to make a greater effort to escape. What frightened him most about his kidnap was the fact that he still had no indication of who might be responsible. Whisked away from the Smith and Anvil, he had been bound hand and foot with a sack over his head. On the first stage of an indescribably uncomfortable journey, he had been strapped across a horse and taken over what felt like the most uneven terrain in the county. Bruised and breathless, he had finally been cut free and locked away.

They fed him tolerably well but gave him no freedom of movement. Still tied up, he was blindfolded whenever they came to visit him. Occasional trips to relieve himself brought further indignities because he was always under surveillance. They knew everything about him but he knew nothing about them. Except that they had not so far harmed him or threatened violence in any way. The shed was his third cell so far and he determined that it would be his last. Solitary confinement was an ordeal.

The boy got up from his stool and bounced across the floor with his ankles firmly bound together. A wooden box stood in the corner and he bent down to sweep off the pile of rhubarb leaves that covered it. His wrists were held by thick rope but his fingers were able to drag the box to the middle of the shed, directly below the central beam. Above his head was a large rusty spike that had been sunk in the timber to act as a peg. Its jagged edge was his one faint promise of release.

First of all, he had to reach the spike and that meant leaping up on to the box. It was far more difficult than he anticipated. All he had to do was to hop some eighteen inches off the ground, a paltry feat for someone with his agility and love of the dance. But his tedious incarceration had exhausted him in body and spirit, and his bonds had given him cramp in his arms and legs. The first jump was well short of the required height and the second was no better. Composing himself to make a more concerted effort, he thrust himself up from the ground only to get a partial purchase on the edge of the box. His weight tipped it off and he was thrown heavily against the side of the shed, banging his head on the rough wood and drawing a trickle of blood from his scalp.

Richard Honeydew refused to give in. He gritted his teeth and started again. Shaking himself all over like a wet dog emerging from a river, he got to his knees and righted the box before using it to lever himself up to his feet. This time he had several practise jumps before he tried to get up on to his platform. When he was fully confident, he stood beside the box, bent at the knees then shot himself upwards, bringing his feet across at just the right moment. The box rocked madly but he somehow kept his balance. Triumph was marred by disappointment. Even when he stood on his toes and stretched his arms up, he was still some six inches away from the spike.

Another, more critical jump was now needed. If he missed the spike, his fall would be even harder. If he misjudged the movement of his hands, he could easily impale himself on the rusty metal. His first instinct was to abandon the attempt altogether but then he thought about the misery of his imprisonment and the pangs of loneliness he felt away from his friends in the company. Nicholas Bracewell would never concede defeat in such a situation and nor must he. The risk had to be taken. He rehearsed it all carefully in his mind then gathered himself for the jump.

Several minutes of anxious and careful preparation were distilled into a split-second as he bent at the knees before launching himself upwards again. His hands cleared the spike, his wrists flicked forward and he was soon hanging in space with the rope bearing his weight. A new set of problems now confronted him. Fiery pain shot down his arms and settled in his shoulders. His head began to throb unbearably. His breathing was impaired. Pale, blue-veined wrists were badly chafed by the ropes. He was in agony and escape now seemed a mirage.

There was no time to waste. The longer he dangled from the beam, the more danger he was in. Putting every last ounce of his strength in the effort, he started to swing his legs, slowly at first, then with more purpose and finally with gathering momentum. The agony intensified. His slim body was awash with perspiration as he swung to and fro in the noisome shed and the rope was cutting into his wrists as if attempting to sever them completely. The first drips of blood on his face made him panic but his torment was almost over. Friction brought results. As the rope was rubbed hard against the spike, its strands broke slowly one by one. Just as he was about to lapse into unconsciousness, the last strand trembled and his own weight did the rest.

Richard Honeydew dropped from the beam, kicked over the box and thudded to the floor. He was too fatigued to move for several minutes but he was smiling in triumph. His plan had worked. When strength returned, he sat up and untied his feet, stretching his legs and wiggling his ankles. Both wrists were lathered in blood but he did not mind. He was free. The door was his last obstacle. Bolted from outside, it was firm against his push but he used guile instead of force. Banging his stool against the ground until one of its three legs snapped off, he used the amputated section as a lever to insert in the door. A gap opened up that was wide enough to admit his slender arm and he slid back the bolt.

His cell door swung open. It was late evening and all he could make out were confusing shapes in the dark. The fragrance of night-scented flowers wafted into his nostrils to refresh and delight him. A light wind helped to dry the dribbling sweat. Pain fell from him and his spirits soared. Freedom was a joyous kingdom.

He had no notion where he was but knew that he had to get away from there. Breaking into a trot, he ran across uneven ground towards the outline of a large building that stood on the edge of a field. But he did not get very far. Within a dozen yards, his way was blocked by a tall figure who stepped in front of him with such determination that the boy bounced off him and fell backwards to the ground. Dazed by the impact, he looked up at the face which was partially lit by a crescent moon.

'You're staying here, lad,' said the young man. Richard Honeydew fainted with sheer terror.

York had undeniable beauty. Set amongst the green forest of Galtres, it was encircled by three miles of white stone fortifications that were breached by four battlemented gateways. It was founded by the Romans at the confluence of the rivers Fosse and Ouse, enjoying a profitable outlet to the sea on the east coast. Ships laden with hides, wool and other goods sailed downriver to the staple port of Hull, bound for the Continent. When they returned, their holds were filled with soaps, silks, stains, perfumes, exotic spices and fine wines. York was a thriving community. It might no longer be second only to London in size but it was still so in dignity.

The streets were narrow, cobbled and overhung with gabled houses. Trades were plied noisily at every turn. Stinking midden tips added their pungent contribution to the city's distinctive atmosphere. York buzzed with life.

Robert Rawlins left his lodgings in Trinity Lane and made his way through the crowded streets to the Trip to Jerusalem. He went into the taproom and found Lambert Pym ordering his minions around with obese urgency. Mine Host gave him a smile of recognition.

'Good day to you, Master Rawlins.'

'And to you, sir.'

'These are busy days for us, I fear.'

'As I observe.'

'Whitsuntide will soon be upon us and the fair will bring in extra custom. We have to brew more beer and feed more bellies. It all needs careful preparation.'

'When will the players arrive?'

'At one and the same time,' said Pym, scratching his beard. 'We will be rushed off our feet here at Jerusalem. Every room I have will be full to bursting and my yard must serve as a playhouse.'

'I like not the drama,' said Rawlins coldly.

'Sir Clarence Marmion is a regular patron.'

'That is his choice.'

'Will you be with us long in York, sir?'

'I cannot tell, Master Pym.'

'Until your business is discharged?'

'We shall see.'

Giving nothing away, Robert Rawlins opened the door that gave access to the staircase. He was soon settling down on a chair in the private chamber above. A small black book was extracted from the folds of his coat and he began to read it in earnest. He was so absorbed by his text that it seemed a matter of minutes before he heard the familiar boots upon the oak stairs. Sir Clarence Marmion came sweeping in at such speed that Rawlins took fright and jumped to his feet.

The newcomer waved a cheerful greeting.

'I bring you glad tidings at last, sir.'

'The Queen is dead?'

'That were too great a hope,' said Sir Clarence as he pulled a letter from his sleeve. 'But we have other causes to rejoice. Our friends have not been idle.'

'It is comforting to hear that.'

'Walsingham sits in London like a great black spider at the heart of a web, waiting to catch us all. But we have our own network of spies to protect us. They have delivered up the informer.'

Rawlins took the letter that was handed to him.

'This is the man who betrayed Master Rickwood?'

'And Master Pomeroy,' said Sir Clarence. 'I knew that the trail would lead him here eventually. We shall be ready for him. He will not deliver a Marmion into the hands of Mr Secretary Walsingham.'

'Forewarned is forearmed.'

'God is sending the vile wretch to us.'

'Does he travel alone?'

'No, he comes with a theatre company from London. They are a convenient shield for his purposes but he will not be able to hide behind them here. The man's journey ends in York. For ever.'

* * *

213

Kynaston Hall was able to confirm that a performance of *The Renegade* had been given there by Banbury's Men but nobody at the house knew the company's next destination. Nicholas Bracewell thanked them for their help and went due north on the chestnut stallion he had borrowed from Lawrence Firethorn. The animal was full of running and it was given free rein. Nicholas stopped at every village, hamlet or wayside dwelling to enquire after the whereabouts of his quarry but he was given precious little help for his pains. Whichever way Banbury's Men had gone, they seemed to have covered their tracks very effectively. It was frustrating.

His luck eventually changed. He came upon an old shepherd who was sitting in the shade of a tree with his dog and munching an apple. Though he was no playgoer, the shepherd could recognise a theatre company when he saw one. His bony finger pointed down a bumpy track.

'They went that way, master.'

'Are you sure, friend?'

'I sit here every day and they passed me by.'

'How many were there?'

'Oh, I don't know. Twelve or fifteen, maybe.'

'On horse or foot?'

'Both, sir. They'd a couple of horses and a cart piled high with baskets. Most of them walked behind.'

'Can you be certain they were players?'

'They were no shepherds, that I know,' said the old man with a cackle. 'Their clothes were too bright and their noise too loud. I'd frighten away my sheep if I went around making those alarums.'

'How far away were they when you saw them?'

'Not more than a hundred yards.'

The shepherd had not been deceived. Banbury's Men had evidently gone past and he had taken due note of their passing. Nicholas pressed a coin into his gnarled hand then rode off again. It was evening now and the company would soon seek shelter before nightfall. His heels sent the horse into a full gallop. Five miles later, he caught up with them.

They had camped by the roadside and lit a fire. Since it was a clear, dry night, they were obviously going to spend it under the stars. Nicholas approached with a caution borne of his misadventures with the gypsies. He did not want to be set upon by the whole company. After tethering his horse behind some bushes, he moved in on foot, hearing the telltale banter of true actors floating on the night air. He had run Banbury's Men to ground. What he now had to establish was whether or not Richard Honeydew was with them.

Creeping in ever closer, he got his first proper look at the encampment. His heart constricted. There were about a dozen of them, as reported, and they wore the gaudy apparel of travelling players but here was no London theatre company on tour. Their clothes were threadbare and their horses were spindly nags. Whatever was being roasted over the fire had not been paid for because they were patently impoverished. Gaunt faces chewed on their food. Thin bodies lounged around the flickering blaze. They were actors but of a different sort and temper to Banbury's Men. They had never performed in a real theatre

215

in their lives or tasted the fleshpots of the capital. Lacking any noble patron, they were no better than outlaws and could be arrested for vagrancy. They scraped a bare living by keeping on the move like the gypsies.

It was sobering to reflect on how removed their world was from that of the London companies and Nicholas felt a pang of shame that Westfield's Men had come to take their audiences from them. Then he recalled the purpose of his journey and shook off such considerations. Marching boldly into the camp, he introduced himself as a fellow-actor and was given a cheerful welcome. It waned somewhat when he asked after Banbury's Men who were seen as London predators come to swoop on the provinces. They had scorn for the other company but no knowledge of its present location. Nicholas thanked them and withdrew.

Darkness was beginning to close in and he needed a bed for the night. He had passed a small inn a few miles back and now rode off again in that direction, his mind grappling with the problem of where Banbury's Men could be and his concern for Richard Honeydew rising all the time. Absorbed in his thoughts, he let his guard fall.

'Hold there, sir!'

'That is a fine horse you have.'

'Let us guess its age by its teeth.'

The three men came out of the woodland and ambled towards him with amiable grins. He was not fooled. Each of them had a hand on his sword. They had caught him on a deserted track that ran between the trees. Nicholas knew that they would not close in on him like that unless they had someone at his back. He swung his horse around in the nick of time. The fourth man was running silently towards him with a cudgel in his hand, ready to hack him down from behind while his attention was diverted.

Nicholas got his kick in before the cudgel fell and the man staggered back. When he came charging in again, he felt a sword go clean through his shoulder and yelled out in agony. His accomplices sprinted in to wreak revenge but they had chosen the wrong target. As the first of them swished his sword, it met such a forceful reply from Nicholas's rapier that it was twisted out of his hand. The book holder dismounted in a flash, pulling out his dagger as he did so and daring the two armed men to come at him. They flashed and jabbed but could get nowhere near him. Unable to recover his sword from the ground, the third man produced a dagger and raised an arm to throw it but he was far too slow. Nicholas's own dagger hurtled through the air and pierced the fellow's wrist, causing him to drop his own weapon with a cry.

The others had had enough. Now that the odds were not so heavily in their favour, they gathered up their two stricken colleagues and limped away. Nicholas gave chase and let some air into the jerkin of one of them. Three of them scrambled into their saddles but the cudgeller was too badly wounded to ride and had to be helped up behind one of his friends. Cursing their assailant, they beat a hasty retreat into the forest.

Nicholas walked across to the horse that they had left behind and patted its neck. It was far too good a mount for common highwaymen and had clearly been stolen. In the fading light, he could just see the monogrammed gold initials on the saddlebags – O.Q. When he searched inside the pouches, he found some food and some articles of apparel. What really interested him, however, was the folded parchment that was tucked away at the very bottom of one of the saddlebags. It was a list of names and addresses, written out in a fair hand. Two of the names had been ticked and they leapt up at Nicholas.

Anthony Rickwood and Neville Pomeroy.

A third name had a question mark beside it.

Sir Clarence Marmion.

From the initials on the saddlebag, Nicholas knew that he had found Oliver Quilley's stolen horse. He now had the feeling that he had found something far more important as well. The artist had told him of the arrest of Master Neville Pomeroy on a charge of high treason and how the prisoner languished in the Tower. Those events took place over a hundred and fifty miles away.

How did Oliver Quilley know about them?

Lawrence Firethorn was hoist with his own petard. After encouraging Susan Becket to accompany him to Nottingham so that she could share nights of madness with him, he could not then dismiss her when she elected to travel on with him. It was very inhibiting. At a time when he hoped to get acquainted with a new potential conquest, he was forced to ride alongside the hostess and listen to her amiable chatter. Eleanor Budden, meanwhile, was seated beside the driver of the waggon, George Dart, seeing to his spiritual needs and generally inhibiting everyone on the vehicle with her presence. Firethorn stole a glance in her direction. Eleanor and Susan were the extremes of womanhood, the respectable and the disreputable, the virtuous and the voluptuous, the sacred and the profane. If the two could blend into one, mused Firethorn, then he would finally have found perfection in human form.

The chuckling Susan Becket nudged him gently.

'She is not for you, Lawrence.'

'Such a thought never entered my mind!'

'Mistress Budden is already spoken for.'

'I met her husband when we set out.'

'It is not him I mean, sir. The lady is enamoured elsewhere. She talks of nobody but your book holder.'

'Nicholas did make an impression on her.'

'If I saw him naked in the River Trent, he would have made an impression on me,' said Susan with a giggle. 'He is a fine figure of a man with a pleasing demeanour.'

'Nick only floated on the water,' said Firethorn testily. 'She speaks as if he walked upon it!'

They were heading north through thick woodland that was redolent with memories of the famous outlaw. Lapsing back into his role in the play, Christopher Millfield began to sing snatches from the ballad. With Nicholas out of the way, he had regained all his sprightliness. The other hired men walked beside him and grumbled about the three outsiders who travelled with them. Oliver Quilley had a lordly manner as he rode near the front of the little procession,

Susan Becket reserved her favours for the actor-manager, and Eleanor Budden brought an unwanted injection of Christianity into their lives. They had lost one valuable apprentice and gained three unnecessary passengers. They were convinced that nothing good could come from it.

George Dart begged leave to differ. Embarrassed at first to have Eleanor alongside him, he soon began to take a pleasure in her company. They had a mutual hero.

'Tell me of Master Bracewell,' she said.

'He is a wonderful man and runs the company in all the ways that matter. Others may get the credit and the rewards but it is he who deserves them, yet you will not hear a boastful word on his lips.'

'His modesty becomes him.'

'He is my one true friend, mistress.'

'That cannot be,' she said. 'What of your mother? Is not she a true friend to her son?'

'Belike she was when she was alive. I do not know. She died when I was but a tiny child.'

'How came you into this profession?'

'No other would take me, mistress. It was Nicholas Bracewell's doing. He taught me all I knew and it has kept me from starvation ever since.'

'He is a Christian soul.'

'None more so in the company.'

'How long has he been in the theatre?'

'Four years or more. I cannot say.'

'Before that?'

'He was at sea,' said George proudly. 'He sailed with

Drake around the world and saw things that most of us cannot even comprehend, such is their wonder. Master Bracewell has been everywhere.'

'Except Jerusalem.'

'Why do you say that, mistress?'

'Because I would take him there with me.'

'And will he go?' said Dart in amazement.

Eleanor Budden gave him a beatific smile.

'Oh, yes. He must. He has no choice.'

Lavery Grange was in the northernmost corner of the county of Nottingham and the head of the house, Sir Duncan Lavery, was an amenable and gregarious character. Given the chance to act as host to Banbury's Men, he welcomed them with open arms and put his Great Hall at their disposal for a performance of *The Renegade*. Good fortune was tinged with bad news. Banbury's Men learned from a visitor to the Grange that their rivals had just scored a triumph in Nottingham with a play about Robin Hood.

Giles Randolph stamped a peevish foot.

'They are closer to us than we thought.'

'Yet still a day behind us,' said Mark Scruton.

'I like not such nearness, sir.'

'They will not catch up yet.'

'Find some other way to delay them.'

'I have it already in my mind.'

Randolph strutted around the Great Hall and watched the stage being erected. He tested the acoustics with a speech from the play and his voice had a poetic beauty to it. The tour had so far been a tale of continuing success that was all the more gratifying because it had involved the abject failure of Westfield's Men. Now, however, his rivals were on his heels and it made him nervous.

He snapped his fingers to beckon Scruton over.

'Yes, master.'

'You have another trick, sir?'

'It will leave them naked and ashamed.'

'About it straight.'

'What, now?' said Scruton in surprise.

'Before they close in on us.'

'But there is the performance of *The Renegade*.'

'You will have to miss it.'

'Then I miss the best role I have,' protested the other. 'Let me but act it here this evening and I'll waylay them tomorrow and cause my mischief.'

'Tomorrow is too late.'

'How will you play without me?'

'Young Harry Paget will take on the part.'

'But it is mine!' complained Scruton angrily.

'Mind your tone, sir.'

'You do me a great injustice.'

'It is but for one performance, Mark,' soothed the other. 'When we play the piece again, you will be restored to your glory. You have my word upon it.'

'And when we reach York?'

'You sign a contract that gives you larger roles in every play we stage. If I approve it, that is.'

Mark Scruton was cornered. Despite all he had done

for the company, he was still not legally a sharer. Until his elevation to that level, he was still at the mercy of Randolph's whims and commands. He fell back on the polite obsequiousness that had served him so well in the past.

'I will set off at once.'

'Cause havoc in the ranks of Westfield's Men.'

'They will not dare to play thereafter.'

'That thought contents me.'

'And my reward?'

'It waits for you in York.'

The four liveried servants rode at a gentle canter along the Great North Road. They bore their master's crest upon their sleeves and his money in their purses. His orders were to be carried out to the letter and they knew the penalty for failure to comply with his wishes. It was a strange assignment but it took them out of Hertfordshire to pastures new and there was interest in that. Their leader set the pace and they rode some five yards apart like the corners of some gigantic scarf. In the middle of that scarf was the person whom they escorted with such care and concern. It was an important mission.

They came to a crossing and saw a large white stone beside the road. Carved into its face was a number that outraged their travelling companion. She shrieked aloud.

'One hundred miles to York!'

'Yes, mistress,' said one of the men.

'We make tardy progress.'

'It is for your own comfort.'

'Mine! Ha! I'll ride the thighs off any man.'

'What is the haste, mistress?'

'I need to get there.'

Margery Firethorn kicked her horse on and it broke into a gallop that left the others behind. The four bemused servants of Lord Westfield gave chase at once and wondered what this madwoman, sitting astride a black horse and hallooing at the top of her voice, was actually doing. Her reckless conduct was unsettling to them but she did not bother herself about that.

Margery was going to York.

She had something to say to her husband.

'Hold still, Master Firethorn, you must not move about so.'

'I am flesh and blood, sir, not a piece of marble.'

'An artist needs a motionless subject.'

'Wait till I am dead and paint me then.'

'You are being perverse, sir.'

'My neck is breaking in two!'

'Take five minutes rest.'

Oliver Quilley clicked his tongue in annoyance. They were in his bedchamber at the inn where they were spending the night. The artist had suggested a first sitting to Firethorn but his subject had been less than helpful. Not only did he talk incessantly throughout, he could not keep his head in the same position for more than a couple of minutes. It was most unsatisfactory.

Firethorn came over to see the results.

'How far have we got, Master Quilley?'

'Almost nowhere.'

'Show me your work.'

'It is hardly begun.'

'But I have been sitting there for a century!'

Quilley was at a small table with his materials in front of him. The portrait was on vellum that was stretched and stuck on a playing card. Pigments were mixed in mussel shells and applied with squirrel-hair brushes made out of quills. An animal's tooth, set in the handle of the brush, could be used for burnishing at a later stage. Limning was an exact art that required the correct materials. It was not surprising that Quilley kept them in his leather pouch and hid them beneath his doublet. His livelihood travelled next to his heart.

Firethorn studied the sketched outline of his face and head, not sure whether to feel flattered or insulted. There was a definite likeness there but it was still so insubstantial as to be meaningless to him. The actor's art could be displayed to the full in two hours' traffic on the stage and he expected similar speed from the miniaturist. Quilley's was a slower genius. It grew at the pace of a rose and took much longer to flower.

'There is not much to see, sir,' said Firethorn.

'That is your own fault.'

'Can you not hurry yourself?'

'Not if you wish for a work of art.'

'I will settle for no less.'

'Then learn to sit still.'

'I am a man of action.'

'Contemplate your greatness.'

The circle of vellum on which Quilley worked was barely two inches in diameter. Lawrence Firethorn's personality had to be caught and concentrated in that tiny area and it required the utmost care and skill. When the artist tried to explain this, his subject was diverted by another thought.

'What card have you chosen?'

'Card, sir?'

'Stuck to the vellum. The playing card.'

'Oh, that. I chose the two of hearts.'

'So low a number?'

'It betokens love, Master Firethorn,' explained the other. 'Most of my subjects want their portrait to be a gift to their beloved. Hearts is the favourite suit. I did not think you would prefer the Jack of Clubs.'

'Indeed, no, sir,' said Firethorn, warming to the idea at once. 'Two hearts entwined will be ideal. It will be the badge of my sentiments when I bestow the gift.'

'Your wife will be enchanted.'

'What does she have to do here!'

Firethorn went back to his seat and struck a pose. The artist came across to adjust it slightly before he went back to his table. Quilley changed his tack. As the actor froze into a statue before him, he heaped praise upon his performance as Robin Hood and Firethorn hardly moved. Flattery succeeded where outright abuse had not. The artist actually began to take strides forward. It did not last. Firethorn was quiescent but others were not.

Someone banged plaintively on the door.

'Are you within, sir?' called George Dart.

'Go away!' bellowed his employer.

'We must not be disturbed!' added Quilley.

'But I bring important news, Master Firethorn.'

'Good or bad?'

'Disastrous.'

'How now?'

'Send him away,' urged Quilley. 'We'll hear this first, sir.'

Firethorn dived for the door and flung it open. Dart was so scared to be the bearer of bad tidings once more that he was gibbering wildly. Firethorn took him by the shoulders and shook him into coherence.

'What has happened, man?'

'We have been robbed again.'

'Another apprentice?'

'No, master. Our costumes have gone.'

'Gone where?'

'Into thin air, sir. The basket has vanished.'

Lawrence Firethorn reached for his neck to throttle him then thought better of it. Charging downstairs to the room where the costume basket had been stored, he was shocked to see that it had, in fact, been taken. Their entire stock had gone. The cost involved was enormous but the consequences of the theft were much more crippling. Without their costumes, they could not stage a single play. Someone was trying to put Westfield's Men right out of business.

Firethorn clutched at his hair in desperation.

'Oh, Nick!' he howled. 'Where are you now!'

A full day in the saddle finally brought its reward. With two horses at his disposal, he could ride much faster and much further afield, changing his mounts to keep them fresh and towing one of them behind him. Nicholas Bracewell was tireless in his pursuit. Endless questioning and riding eventually brought him to Lavery Grange. There was no mistake this time. Banbury's Men were in the act of presenting *The Renegade* to an attentive audience. Posing as a late arrival, Nicholas gained admission to the Great Hall and lurked at the rear. Giles Randolph dominated the proceedings but the book holder was much more interested in those around him, searching for people who had betrayed Westfield's Men by yielding up the secrets of their repertoire. Nicholas recognised several faces but none had ever been employed by his company. He was mystified.

Who had stolen their major plays?

He did not expect Richard Honeydew to be anywhere on the premises. Banbury's Men were far too clever to be caught red-handed. If they were holding the boy, they would do so in some other place that was not too distant. Nicholas sidled out and chatted to one of the servants. The man spoke of three inns within an easy ride. Nicholas set off at once to check them out. He drew a blank with the first two but his conviction did not waver. He was now certain that he was closing in on Richard Honeydew.

His third call bore fruit. Though there was no sign of the

boy inside the place, the landlord told him that the company would be staying there for the night. Most of them had rooms but a few would be sleeping with their luggage in the stables. Nicholas went out to inspect the alternative accommodation and could still find nothing untoward. He was about to give up and move away when he heard the noise.

It was a tapping sound, low but regular, and it seemed to come from a stone outhouse adjoining the stable block. When he got closer, he could hear it clearly enough to identify what it was. Someone was trying to kick against the heavy timber of the door. Nicholas ran forward and threw back the bolt. Opening the door, he stared into the gloom to see the sorry figure of Richard Honeydew, all trussed up and lying in the straw. With the very last of his energy, the boy had been trying to beat a tattoo on the door. Rescue was now at hand.

'Thank God I've found you, Dick!'

The gag in the boy's mouth prevented his reply but his eyes were liquid pools of eloquence. Nicholas read their dreadful message much too late. Something very hard and blunt hit him on the back of the head and he plunged forward into the straw.

Chapter Nine

It was the worst night of his life. A man who had scaled the heights of nocturnal bliss so often and with such joyous confidence now fell backwards through space into the abyss. Lawrence Firethorn was in despair. His book holder was gone, his apprentice was kidnapped, his costume basket was stolen and his company was in disarray. Susan Becket lay upstairs in his bed unsatisfied and Eleanor Budden slept between her sheets untouched. They were so near and yet so far from him. Firethorn was undone.

Barnaby Gill and Edmund Hoode shared his panic.

'They have cut off our heads, sirs,' said Firethorn.

'And our pizzles,' said Hoode.

'Mine is still in place,' insisted Gill haughtily.

'I did not think they would stoop so low.'

'Can we be sure this is their work, Lawrence?' asked Hoode. 'Some common thieves may have taken our basket.'

'Why should they take that when there were purses to be cut?' said Firethorn. 'No, Edmund. The footprints of Banbury's Men are stamped all over this enterprise. Only another company would know how best to imperil us. And that is by stealing the very clothes that we wear.'

They were in the taproom of their inn, sitting over cups of sack with collective melancholy. Barnaby Gill suddenly jumped to his feet, tossed his head, folded his arms and stood on his considerable dignity.

'I'll not play without my golden doublet,' he said huffily. 'If they find not my green velvet breeches and my yellow stockings and my shoes with the silver buckles and my hat with the three feathers in it, I'll stir not a step upon the stage!'

'We are all in this together, Barnaby,' said Hoode.

'Where is my suit of blue satin and my green cloak?'

'Be silent, sir!' snarled Firethorn.

'What of my cambric shirts and my lawn ruff?'

'Cease this whining!'

The actor-manager's roar cut short the fit of pique. Gill dropped back into his seat and stared moodily into his drink. At times of crisis, he could be relied upon to put his selfish interests before anything else. Edmund Hoode had far more compassion for his fellows.

'My thoughts are with poor Dick!' he said.

'So are mine upon occasion,' murmured Gill.

'I would surrender every shred of clothing that we own to get the lad safe back again. Where can he be?'

'Nick will find him,' said Firethorn.

'Aye,' agreed Hoode. 'Nick is our one bright hope.'

'How can you think that?' said Gill. 'If it were not for our esteemed book holder, we would not now be in such a case as this. I lay the guilt on him.' He spoke on over their protests. 'Defend him all you can, sirs, but this I declare. Nicholas Bracewell must bear the guilt. He it is who was most responsible for the safety of the apprentices yet one of them was taken from under his nose.'

'Nick cannot be everywhere,' defended Hoode.

'That is plain, Edmund. Were he not now gallivanting around the whole county, then our costumes would have been secure. He would have been here to do his duty and defend them properly.' Gill sat up sulkily. 'And I would still have my golden doublet!'

'Someone had to go after Dick Honeydew,' said Hoode.

'And the only man fit for the task was Nick,' added Firethorn. 'He may yet extract us from this morass. I'll not hear one word of carping about him.'

'Then I'll hold my tongue,' said Gill sarcastically.

Firethorn drank deep from his cup and moaned aloud.

'What a world of pain is this touring! I do not like it, sirs, and I fear it does not like me. Nothing but dire calamity has come of it. We have faced rain, robbery and ruin. And the worst of it is that I am far from home and can draw no comfort from the soft bosom of my wife.'

Gill and Hoode traded a glance of tired amusement. With one woman upstairs in his bed and another featuring prominently in his fantasies, Lawrence Firethorn could still indulge in a bout of marital sentimentality with every sign of complete sincerity. Happiness was his ability to expel Margery entirely from his thoughts. It was only at moments of stress that she reappeared in his considerations and reminded him that he was her husband.

His colleagues listened to his maudlin reminiscences with a measure of cynicism. Their situation was drastic but there was yet some humour to be drawn from it. As Firethorn reached a crescendo of uxoriousness, he was interrupted by the arrival of the tentative George Dart.

'What is it?' growled Firethorn.

'I bring you a message from the lady, sir.'

'Mistress Becket?'

'Mistress Budden.'

'Speak it forth.'

'We sat beside each other on the waggon, master, and I was bold enough to praise you in her hearing.' He finally put a smile on Firethorn's face. 'I talked about your fine voice, sir, and how you could recite the prayer book as if it were the music of Heaven.'

'So it is, George. So it is.'

'Mistress Budden was much taken with all this.'

'What is her message?'

'She sits in bed,' said Dart. 'It is her dearest wish that you should read to her from the psalms ere she closes her eyes in Christian slumber.'

Lawrence Firethorn felt the reassuring surge of his lust. An opportunity which he believed would never come had now presented itself to him. Eleanor Budden was lying in her bedchamber with complete trust in the sound of his voice. Psalms could lead to sighs of love. As temptation licked at his loins, he saw the obstacles. Susan Becket was waiting in the next bedchamber. A costume basket had to be traced. Plans had to be made. Work would keep him downstairs for several hours.

Disappointment gnawed at his entrails but there was no way out for him. Ignoring the smirks from Hoode and Gill, he turned to the messenger with lofty calm.

'Tell her I may not come tonight,' he said. 'But I will pray for Mistress Budden most heartily.'

And he left it on that ambiguous note.

The first thing he noticed was the smell. It assaulted his nostrils. The outhouse had been used to stable a donkey and its droppings were mixed freely with the straw. When he tried to move, he felt as if someone were trying to pound the back of his skull to gain entrance. Nicholas Bracewell remained absolutely still until his head began to clear. Something was tickling the end of his foot. He opened a misty eye to make out the sad figure of Richard Honeydew, stretching out a leg to make contact with him. The boy was still bound and gagged. Nicholas's first impulse was to release him and he jerked forward, only to be held by ropes of his own that were tied to an iron ring in the wall. The lump on the back of his head ached anew but the gag in his mouth muffled his groan.

Nicholas waited till the pain eased off then he took stock of the situation. He was seated upright against a rough stone wall, unable to move because of his bonds. Opposite him was Richard Honeydew, who had been secured to the iron bars across the window. His delight at seeing the boy was shadowed by the condition in which he found him. Honeydew's face was besmirched with blood and his clothes were torn and stained. He did not look as if he had eaten very much since he had been abducted. Nicholas was seized with remorse. Instead of riding to the rescue of the apprentice, he had let himself be captured as well.

He struggled hard but his bonds held firm. When he tried to speak, his words came out as faint grunts. There was so much to ask but he had no means of asking it. He looked around for help and saw the old stone walls with their flaking coat of whitewash. An idea formed. Angling himself over so that he could swing his legs up, he used his toes to scrape one big question on the wall.

WHO?

Richard Honeydew responded in kind. Pulling himself up on the bars, he swung his legs across until they just made contact with the whitewash. In the half-dark of their stinking cell, he slowly and laboriously traced a name on the wall. The letters were ragged and indistinct but their impact was still potent.

Nicholas Bracewell was absolutely stunned.

It was incredible.

Christopher Millfield remained cheerful in the midst of adversity. Long faces and short tempers surrounded him but his resilience was remarkable. Instead of being dragged down by the general mood of gloom, he was chirpy and positive. Sharing a room with George Dart and the three apprentices gave these qualities ample scope.

'It will all seem better in the morning,' he said.

'It could hardly be worse,' sighed Dart.

'There is a solution to every problem.'

'We have so many, Master Millfield.'

'Let hope into your heart, George.'

'There is no room for it.'

Christopher Millfield leaned over to pat him on the shoulder. Hearing snores from the other bed, he lowered his voice so that he did not rouse the sleepers.

'We are players,' he argued softly, 'and nothing must be allowed to smother our art. If one of our apprentices be taken, why, then we fill his role with another voice. If all our costumes be stolen, we beg, borrow or make some more. These are setbacks only and can all be overcome.'

'You forget Master Bracewell.'

'By no means, sir. I have the utmost faith in him.'

'What if he does not come back?'

'Nick Bracewell will return,' said Millfield with confidence. 'I have never met a more capable man in the theatre. This whole company revolves around him and he would never desert it in its hour of need.'

'I thought you did not like him,' said Dart.

'There is nobody in Westfield's Men I respect more and that includes Master Firethorn. I admit that I was hurt when our book holder recommended Gabriel Hawkes in place of me but that is all past now. I have come to accept the truth of it, George.'

'Truth?'

'Gabriel was the better man.'

'He was always kind to me.'

Millfield sighed. 'It pains me that we were such rivals. In other circumstances, Gabriel and I could have been close friends. He has been a great loss.' The positive note returned. 'That is why I am so grateful for the chance to travel with the company. I have prospered from Gabriel's death and that grieves me, but it also fills me with determination to make the most of my opportunity and to be undaunted by any mishap. We are fortunate men, George. We are employed. Think on that.'

The other did as he was advised and soon drifted off to sleep in a haze of consolation. Millfield was a true son of the theatre. Whatever disasters befell it, the company simply had to press on regardless. George Dart's snores joined the wheezing slumber of the other innocents.

Christopher Millfield waited half an hour before he moved. Then he got up, dressed quietly and left the room. A few minutes later, he was saddling a horse and leading it out into the yard with shreds of sacking around its hooves to muffle their clatter on the cobblestones.

He rode off happily into the darkness.

Nicholas Bracewell was still quite groggy. His head was pounding, his vision was impaired and blood was trickling down the back of his neck. The stench in the outhouse was almost overpowering and his stomach heaved. Trussed up tightly, every muscle in his body was aching away. What hurt him most, however, was the fact that Richard Honeydew should see him in this state. The boy was desperately in need of help and all that his would-be rescuer could do was to get himself into the same parlous condition. Guilt burned inside Nicholas like a raging fire. It served to concentrate his mind on their predicament.

The first priority was to be able to speak to the boy and that meant getting rid of the gag. Unable to brush it down with his knees, he looked around for a source of aid. A wooden rake was standing against the wall on his right. Though he could not reach it with his feet, he could scoop the straw towards him and that brought the implement ever closer. It also brought piles of dung and his shoes were soon covered with it, but he did not give up. Richard watched with interest as his friend got the rake within reach and then lifted both feet before jabbing them down hard on the prongs. The rake flipped up and Nicholas had to move his head aside as the handle smashed into the wall beside him. He trapped the implement with his shoulder then used the end of it to push his gag slowly upwards. It was agonising work that earned him several jabs in the face but he eventually managed to move it enough to be able to speak.

His words tumbled out through deep breaths.

'How are you, lad?'

The boy nodded bravely and his eyes showed spirit.

'Have they hurt you badly?'

Richard Honeydew shook his head and made a noise.

'Let's see if we can get your gag off now, Dick.'

Nicholas used his body and feet to propel the rake

towards the apprentice and the latter tried to copy what he had seen. It took him much longer and collected him many more painful pokes with the end of the pole but he did finally force the gag out of his mouth. He filled his lungs gratefully then coughed violently.

'They'll stink us to death in here,' said Nicholas.

'How did you find me, Master Bracewell?'

'Never mind that, Dick. The main thing is to get you out of here safely. How many of them are there?'

'Two. They kidnapped me together.'

'At the behest of Banbury's Men.'

'Is that who stole me away? I had no idea. They keep me locked up and only come when it is time to feed me.'

'You look poorly.'

'I am fine,' said the boy unconvincingly.

'They will pay for what they have done to you.'

'It is not them that I fear, master. They have tied me up but they have not ill-treated me.' He looked around with disgust. 'What makes me afeard is the dark and the damp and the smell and, most of all, the rats.'

'Rats?'

'They come snuffling around sometimes. I am afraid that they will eat me alive!' He relaxed visibly. 'But not now that you are here. I feel safe with you.'

'No rats will harm you, Dick.'

The boy smiled. 'I knew you would come for me.'

'Tell me exactly what has happened to you.'

While he listened to Honeydew's tale, his eyes roved the outhouse in search of a means of escape but none presented itself. Then he noticed some movement under the straw beside a wooden bucket of water. When the boy caught sight of it, he flew into a panic.

'A rat! A rat! Another rat!'

The creature came out of the straw and shuffled towards the terror-stricken boy. Nicholas yelled and lashed out at the animal with his feet, putting it to flight and kicking over the bucket as well. As cold water made his discomfort even greater, he began to fret and complain but he soon checked himself. The accident might yet be turned to account. He almost smiled.

'I spy some hope, Dick.'

'Do you, master?'

'There may yet be a way out.'

'How?'

'You will see. But I need your help.'

'I will do anything I can, sir.'

'Encourage me.'

Richard Honeydew soon understood what he meant. The packed earth beneath the straw had been loosened by the deluge and gave way to urgent feet. Using his shoes as a rudimentary spade, Nicholas began to scoop out a hole close to the wall. The deeper he went, the softer was the earth and he kicked it out into a heap beside him. It was a long and laborious process which brought the sweat streaming out of every pore and made his body ache as if it was ready to split asunder. Whenever he felt like giving up, however, he glanced across at the boy and was given all the exhortation he needed.

'Keep on, sir! You are working wonders! Stay there!'

Nicholas struggled on, getting bruised and filthy in the process but making definite headway. Ultimately, the hole was big enough for him to be able to lower himself into it and take the strain.

He had undermined the wall completely. When he tested his strength against it, the stone moved slightly. Richard Honeydew giggled with delight.

'We are almost there!'

'Not yet, lad.'

'I know your strength, sir. You will do it.'

Nicholas nodded wearily. The real effort now began. He pushed, felt it give some more, rested a moment then adjusted his position. Calling on all his reserves of energy, he shoved hard with his feet and let his broad shoulders attack the solidity of the wall. It was the work of several wounding minutes but his efforts were not in vain. With a low crumbling noise, the wall gave way and chunks of stone came crashing down around him. Nicholas was cut, bruised and bloodied but his hands were now free of the metal ring. He began to rub his wrists against the sharp edge of a piece of stone.

'You did it, Master Bracewell!' said the boy.

'With your help.'

'All I did was to watch you.'

'And stiffen my resolve.'

'Can you saw through the rope?'

'It is done!' said Nicholas, holding up his hands.

He cast aside his bonds and dragged himself across to

untie the boy's wrists. Before they could tackle the ropes on their ankles, however, they heard the sound of running footsteps. Nicholas pulled himself upright and bounced to the door as it was unbolted from outside. A stocky young man came rushing in with a dagger at the ready. Grabbing him by wrist and neck, Nicholas threw him hard against the remains of the wall, diving on top of him to disarm him and hold the weapon to his throat. The man was dazed and fearful.

'Do not kill me, sir!' he pleaded.

'Who are you?'

'An ostler, sir. I work here at the inn.'

'You have been our gaoler.'

'Only because I was paid. I meant no harm.'

'Do not move!'

Nicholas used the dagger to slit through the ropes that held his ankles then he cut the boy loose as well. He placed a knee on the ostler's chest and held the point of the blade just in front of the man's face.

'You struck me down from behind,' he accused.

'I was told to guard the boy.'

'What else were you told?'

'To hide the basket in the stables.'

'What basket?'

'They were costumes, sir.'

'From Westfield's Men?'

'That was the name.'

Nicholas stood up and yanked the ostler to his feet. He did not have to threaten his captive any more. Plainly terrified, the man led them immediately to the part of the stables where he had concealed the costume basket. Nicholas was pleased to see his two horses there as well and took the opportunity to repossess his own sword and dagger. He used his rapier to pin the man to the wall while he pondered.

'Has the company returned?' he said.

'Not yet, sir. They celebrate at Lavery Grange.'

'Take me to Master Randolph's room.'

'Who, sir?'

'He will have the finest bedchamber here.'

''Tis at the front of the inn, sir.'

'Teach me the way.'

'I have no place up there.'

'I do,' said Nicholas. 'Lead on or lose an ear.'

They went stealthily across the yard.

Lambert Pym stood in the brewhouse at the rear of his inn and watched another cask being filled. It would now be stored in his cellars for conditioning until it was ready to be tapped and drunk. Pym had grown up with the smell of beer and ale in his nostrils and it stayed with him wherever he went. His customers at the Trip to Jerusalem bought beer, or, if they had a little extra money, some ale. He imported some wine from Bordeaux but it was too costly for most people. Malmsey wine from Greece was even more expensive, as was sack, but Pym kept a supply of both for certain patrons. During the three days of Whitsuntide, he would need to draw deeply on all his stocks.

The landlord came back into the taproom as Robert Rawlins was about to leave. Lambert Pym raised a finger in deference and beamed ingratiatingly.

'Shall you be with us at Whitsuntide, master?'

'I hope so, sir.'

'You'll see an ocean of beer drunk in here.'

'That is not a sight which appeals.'

'Drink has its place in the affairs of men.'

'I know!' said Rawlins with frank disapproval.

'Christ Himself did sanction it, sir.'

'Do not blaspheme.'

'He turned the water into wine at the wedding feast in Cana,' said Pym. 'That was his first miracle.'

'But open to misinterpretation.'

'Wine has its place,' mused the other, 'but you will not part an Englishman from his beer. Look at the example of Fuenterrabia.'

'Where?'

'It is northern Spain.' Pym grinned oleaginously as he told his favourite story. 'The first campaign in the reign of good King Henry, who was father to our present dear Queen. He sent an army of seven thousand English soldiers to help his father-in-law, King Ferdinand, take Navarre away from the French. Do you know what those stout-hearted men found?'

'What, sir?'

'There was no beer in Spain. Only wine and cider.' He cackled happily. 'The soldiers mutinied on the spot and their commander, the Marquis of Dorset, was forced to bring them home again. They could not fight on empty bellies, sir, and beer was their one desire.'

Robert Rawlins listened to the tale with polite impatience then turned to go but his way was now blocked. Standing in the doorway were two constables. One of them held up a warrant as he moved in on him.

'You must come with us, sir.'

'On what charge?'

'I think you know that.'

Before he could say any more, Robert Rawlins was hustled unceremoniously out. Lambert Pym was mystified but instinct guided him. He summoned his boy at once.

'Take a message to Marmion Hall.'

'Sir Clarence Marmion has commissioned a portrait.'

'Of himself, Master Quilley?'

'Yes, sir.'

'A miniature?'

'I am a limner. I paint nothing else.'

'Your fame spreads ever wider.'

'Genius is its own best recommendation.'

'Do you look forward to painting Sir Clarence?'

'No, sir. I simply hope he will pay me for my work.'

Oliver Quilley brought realism to bear upon his art. Commissions had never been a problem area. That lay in the collection of his due reward. Far too many of his subjects, especially those at Court, believed that their patronage was payment enough and Quilley had collected dozens of glowing tributes in place of hard-earned fees. It

246

gave him a cynical edge that never quite left him.

He was riding beside Lawrence Firethorn as the company rolled north once more. Westfield's Men were in a state of depression. Deprived of their costumes, their apprentice and their book holder, they saw no hope of survival. It was a grim procession.

'How did you meet Anthony Rickwood?' said Firethorn.

'Through a friend.'

'Did you not take him for a traitor?'

'I saw it in his face.'

'Yet you accepted the commission?'

'His money was as good as anyone else's.'

'But tainted, Master Quilley.'

'How so?'

'Rickwood betrayed his Queen.'

'He paid me in gold,' said the artist. 'Not with thirty pieces of silver.'

'I could not work for such a man myself.'

'Your sentiments do you credit, Master Firethorn, but they are misplaced. You have played to men like Anthony Rickwood a hundred times, yea, and to worse than he.'

'I deny it hotly, sir!'

'Did you not visit Pomeroy Manor?'

'Indeed, we did. My Tarquin overwhelmed them.'

'It will not be staged there again,' said Quilley complacently. 'Master Neville Pomeroy lies in fetters in the Tower. It seems you have entertained traitors.'

'Can this be true?' said Firethorn.

'I have it on good authority.'

'God save us all!'

'He may be too late for Master Pomeroy.'

Firethorn drew apart to consider the implications of what he had just heard. It caused more than a ripple in the pool of his vanity. The visit to Pomeroy Manor was a triumph he hoped to repeat on his way back to London. It did nothing for the reputation of Westfield's Men to admit that one of their most appreciative patrons was an enemy of the state. Neville Pomeroy would not watch any more plays from a spike above Bishopsgate.

The actor-manager sought consolation in the prospect of Eleanor Budden but he found none. Though her beauty now had a ripeness that was glorious to behold, he was not given access to it. Frowning deeply, she was in the middle of a dispute with Christopher Millfield as he drove the waggon. The couple sat side by side in lively argument.

'I responded to the voice of God,' she said.

'You answered some inner desire, mistress.'

'His word is paramount.'

'If that indeed was what you heard.'

'I am certain of it, Master Millfield.'

'Certainty is everywhere,' he argued. 'The Puritans, the Presbyterians, the Roman Catholics and many others besides, all these are certain that they hear the word of God more clearly than anyone else. Why should you have any special access to divine command?'

'Because I have been chosen.'

'By God – or by yourself?'

'Fie on your impertinence, sir!'

'I ask in all politeness, Mistress Budden.'

'Do you doubt my sincerity?'

'Not in the least. A woman who would abandon a home and a family to face the hardship of travel must indeed be sincere. What I question is this voice of God.'

'I heard it plainly, sir.'

'But did it come from without or within?'

'Does that matter?'

'I believe so.'

'It is not for us to question God's mystery.'

'Nor yet to submit blindly to it.'

'That is blasphemy!'

'You have your convictions and I have mine.'

'Are you an atheist, sir?' she cried.

Before he could reply, two figures appeared ahead of them on a chestnut stallion. A second horse was dragging a litter that had been fashioned out of some long, slender boughs. Lashed to the litter was a basket that everyone recognised immediately. Nicholas Bracewell was back. He brought the missing apprentice and the stolen costumes as well as Oliver Quilley's horse. A cheer went up from the whole company as they hurried towards their hero.

The newcomers were soon enveloped by friends and bombarded with questions. Eleanor Budden gazed down on her beloved and called his name. Barnaby Gill demanded to know if his golden doublet was unharmed. Edmund Hoode asked if they knew who had played his part of Sicinius. Martin Yeo, Stephen Judd and John Tallis hailed their fellow-apprentice with an enthusiasm that bordered on hysteria. Susan Becket clucked excitedly. George Dart was able to join the Merry Men once more.

Lawrence Firethorn waved them all into silence with an imperious arm and called for full details. Though they looked tattered and travel-weary, the two companions had washed themselves off in a spring and found that their injuries were only minor. Reunion with their fellows put new strength and spirit into them.

'Who kidnapped the lad?' asked Firethorn.

'Banbury's Men,' said Nicholas.

'Scurvy knaves! We'll have them in court for this!'

'There are other ways to get even, sir.'

'And the costumes, Nick?'

'Taken by the same hands.'

'Where did you find my horse?' said Quilley.

'That was providential.'

Nicholas told him the story and gained fresh looks of adoration from Eleanor Budden. When he talked of putting four men to flight – and did so in such modest terms – Susan Becket also experienced a flutter. The female response was not lost on Firethorn who sought to divert some of their admiring glances his way.

'By heavens!' he roared, pulling out his sword and holding it in the air. 'I'll put so many holes in the hide of Giles Randolph that he'll whistle when he walks across the stage! I'll challenge him to a duel and cut the varlet down to size! I'll make him pay for every crime he has committed against us. Hang him, the rogue!'

'Worry not about Master Randolph,' said Nicholas.

'Frogspawn in human shape!'

'He has problems enough of his own.'

'Prison is too good for such a wretch!' yelled Firethorn. 'He dared to steal *Pompey the Great*!'

'My play,' said Hoode. 'My part of Sicinius.'

'They will not perform it again, Edmund.'

'How can you be so certain, Nick?'

'Because we have stopped them.' He winked at his companion. 'Show them, Dick.'

The boy ran across to the costume basket and threw back its lid to draw out a pile of plays. He read out their titles to a delighted audience.

'*Cupid's Folly. Two Maids of Milchester. Double Deceit. Marriage and Mischief. Pompey the Great.*'

'All returned where they belong,' said Nicholas. 'They cannot stage our plays without these prompt books.'

'By all, this is wonderful!' shouted Firethorn. 'Let me embrace you both, my lovely imps!'

He dismounted and put a congratulatory arm around each. The worst night of his life was being redeemed by one of the best days. Nicholas added even more joy.

'Time brings in its revenges, sir.'

'What do you mean?'

'Master Randolph will not laugh this morning.'

'Did you strike a blow for Westfield's Men?'

'I think so,' said Nicholas.

Giles Randolph stared at the empty chest with a mixture of fear and dismay. It had been stored all night beneath his fourposter and chained to one of the legs. Its lock was strong and apparently undamaged yet the treasure chest was bare. The company's most priceless possessions had gone. Randolph screeched a name and Mark Scruton came running. One glance made the newcomer turn white.

'When did you discover this, sir?'

'Even now.'

'You did not open the chest last night?'

'The journey back from Lavery Grange was too tiring and much wine had been taken. I fell into bed and slept soundly until this morning.' Randolph kicked at the empty chest. 'Had I known of this, I'd not have closed my eyes!'

Mark Scruton thought quickly then glanced towards the door. Beckoning the other to follow, he ran out of the bedchamber and down the stairs, making for the door that led to the yard. With Randolph at his heels, he hurried across to the outhouse beyond the stables and wondered why one of its walls was damaged. He unbolted the door and flung it open to reveal a sight that might have been comical in other circumstances. The stocky ostler was bound hand and foot and tied to the bars at the window. A large apple had been placed in his mouth and held in place by a strip of material that was knotted behind his head. His eyes were as red and bulbous as tomatoes.

'Where are they?' demanded Scruton.

The man shook his head and hunched his shoulders.

Giles Randolph let out a howl and kneeled down. In the middle of the straw was a pile of prompt books that were caked in manure and sodden with water. The symbolism was not lost on him. Rising up in sheer disgust, he jabbed a shaking finger at his vandalised property.

'Mark Scruton!' he hissed.

'Yes, sir?'

'This is your doing.'

'A thousand apologies.'

'Clean up your mess!'

He left the scene of the outrage in high dudgeon.

The blacksmith hammered in the last nail then lowered the hoof to the ground. He wiped his brow with a hairy arm and turned to the full-bodied woman who held the bridle.

'Take more care with the animal, mistress.'

'I have not the time, sir.'

'He was ridden too hard over rough ground,' said the blacksmith. 'That is why he cast a shoe.'

'He may cast more then before we arrive.'

'Where do you go?'

'To York.'

'It is a goodly distance yet, mistress.'

'Then do not detain us with your prattle.'

Margery Firethorn put a foot in the stirrup and hauled herself up into the saddle without asking for any assistance. An imperious snap of the fingers brought one of the liveried servants scuttling across to her.

'Pay the fellow!' she said.

Then she rode off at an even fiercer pace.

* * *

253

Westfield's Men got their first glimpse of York and paused to take in its full magnificence. Seen from that distance and that elevation, it looked like a fairytale city that was set against a painted backdrop and even those who had seen it before now marvelled afresh.

Eleanor Budden summed it all up in one word.

'Jerusalem!'

They stopped to take refreshment and gather their strength for the last few miles of a journey that had become increasingly strenuous since they crossed the county boundary. Horses were watered and refreshment taken. Nicholas Bracewell chose the moment to have word alone with Christopher Millfield. Having disliked the actor so much at first, he now found himself warming all the more to him.

'How did you fare in my absence, Christopher?'

'We never lost faith in you.'

'I am glad the business turned out so well.'

'You brought home great bounty,' said Millfield. 'Master Quilley was delighted to get his horse back.'

'A happy accident.' Nicholas glanced across at the artist. 'What do you make of our limner?'

'Painters are always slightly mad.'

'Have you noticed nothing odd about him?'

'Several things but I put them down to his calling.'

'Look at his apparel,' said Nicholas. 'It is a very expensive suit for a man who claims that he has no money. Then there is the quality of his horse, not to mention those saddlebags of the finest leather with their gold monogram.

Master Quilley is not the pauper he pretends.'

'Then where does his wealth come from?'

'I wish I knew.'

'Haply, he has some rich patron.'

'One name suggests itself.'

'Who is that?'

'Sir Francis Walsingham.'

'Indeed?' said Millfield with astonishment. 'I find that hard to credit. Could Master Quilley really be in his service as an informer?'

'Who is better placed, Christopher? He visits the homes of the great on a privileged footing and sees things that no other visitor could observe. His calling is the ideal cover for a spy.'

'Do you have any proof of this?'

'None beyond my own suspicion. Except an item that I found in his saddlebag. See it for yourself.'

Christopher Millfield took the document that was handed to him and scanned through the names. He nodded in agreement as he returned it to Nicholas.

'You have just cause for that suspicion.'

'Do I?'

'Two of those names have already been ticked off by Walsingham. Three of the others are known to me from my time with the Admiral's Men. I dare swear that they were all prosecuted for recusancy.'

'What of Sir Clarence Marmion and the others?'

'We can but guess.'

'Birds of a feather flock together.'

'Your conclusion?'

'All of Master Quilley's employers are Catholics.'

'Could he be a servant of Rome himself?'

It was another possibility and they discussed it briefly before turning to other matters. Nicholas was glad that he had confided in his new friend. Millfield was now eyeing him with concern.

'How do you feel, Nick?'

'Much better.'

'Are you fully recovered from your ordeal?' said the other with anxiety. 'It heartened us greatly when you and Dick Honeydew returned but the pair of you did look more than a little bedraggled.'

'You should have seen us when we set out. We were caked in blood and filth with a stink on us you could have smelled a hundred yards off.' He wrinkled his nose at the memory. 'Dick and I stopped at a stream to clean ourselves up before coming back.'

'Both of you must be aching all over.'

'I will have to make some more of that ointment.'

'It has certainly helped me.'

'We will sleep well tonight, I think.'

Millfield smiled his agreement then looked across at Richard Honeydew. The boy still showed the effects of his incarceration but he was patently delighted to be back with the company and his face was animated.

'He is hopelessly in your debt, Nick.'

'I could not let them steal our best apprentice.'

'It goes deeper than that.'

'We are good friends.'

'You are like a father to the lad and risked your life for him. Have you ever had a child of your own?'

'I was never married, Christopher.'

'The two things do not always go together.'

Nicholas laughed evasively and changed the subject. He was enjoying his chat with the actor and finding new things to like about him all the time. When Millfield moved away, however, it became clear that not everyone shared the book holder's good opinion of him.

A worried Eleanor Budden bustled over.

'Do not listen to him, sir,' she begged.

'Master Millfield?'

'He is a very dangerous young man.'

'Why, mistress?'

'Because he does not believe in God.'

'Did he attest as much?'

'More or less, Master Bracewell.'

'I find that hard to accept.'

'Beware, sir!'

'Of what?'

'Atheism in our midst!'

Nicholas did not take the claim at all seriously and she did not pursue it since she wanted to enjoy their rare moment alone. Love made her eyes sparkle like gems.

'It was wonderful to see you back with us!'

'I share your delight, mistress.'

'I knew that God would not take you away from me.'

'My place is here with the company.'

'And mine is beside you.'

'We will get you to York with all due speed.'

'I have found the true path in you!'

Her ardour was quite unnerving and Nicholas glanced around for help. Being attacked by robbers or captured by rivals were nowhere near as frightening as being cornered by Eleanor Budden. If he was not circumspect, she would rob him of something he did not want to lose and hold him captive in a way that did not appeal. He fended her off with questions.

'How do you like the fellowship of actors?'

'Yours is the only company I seek, Master Bracewell.'

'Does nobody else interest you, mistress?'

'They pale beside you, sir.'

'What of Master Quilley? He is a famous artist. Have you and he had discourse yet?'

'Only when I interrupted him,' she said. 'He was angry when I came upon him playing with his cards.'

'Cards?'

'I have never seen the like before. They had strange pictures on them and he studied each one with great care. It was almost as if he looked for some kind of message.'

Nicholas Bracewell smiled in gratitude. Unwelcome as her attentions had been, he sensed that Eleanor Budden had unwittingly given him some valuable information.

His suspicion of Oliver Quilley deepened.

Days without his wife and nights without her precious bounty had wrought changes in Humphrey Budden. The house seemed empty, the children were fractious and his whole life was now hopelessly barren. Long discussions with Miles Melhuish were followed by even longer ones with the Dean. It was the latter who counselled action.

'You have sinned against your wife.'

'The memory of it is grievous unto me.'

'You must seek her forgiveness.'

'How may I do that?'

'Not here in Nottingham, that is certain.'

'Then where?'

'In York,' said the Dean sonorously. 'There is no better place for you to be cleansed and reconciled. Go to York, sir. Seek your estranged wife in that monument to Christian dedication. That is where your hope lies.'

'Will she take me back?'

'If you deserve it, Master Budden.'

'Should I travel with the children?'

'Alone, sir. This is a matter between two souls.' He lowered ecclesiastical lids. 'And two bodies.'

Humphrey Budden left for York the next day.

A bell had signalled the beginning of the Whitsuntide fair and pandemonium followed. Streets that were usually crowded were now overflowing. Shops and stalls that were usually busy were now completely besieged. York was aflame with life. Tinkers, travellers, pilgrims, country folk, merchants, knights and many more streamed in through the four gates. Minstrels, mummers, acrobats and jugglers competed for attention. The shrieking of children and the

259

yapping of dogs swelled a cacophony that was taken to deafening pitch by the constant peal of church bells. The city ran riot for three holy days.

Westfield's Men came in through Micklegate and made their way through the press to the Trip to Jerusalem, a name that had a special resonance for them. Lambert Pym gave them an exaggerated welcome and conducted them to their rooms with beard-scratching charm. Accommodation was also found for Oliver Quilley and Eleanor Budden. The exuberant Susan Becket appointed herself as Firethorn's bedfellow yet again. Jerusalem was a spacious metaphor.

Nicholas Bracewell was dispatched at once to the Lord Mayor to secure a licence for performance. When he came back with it in his hand, he found Firethorn poring over a letter from Sir Clarence Marmion that invited them to stage a play at his house. Here was good news indeed. York was proving to be a worthy shrine for pilgrimage. Not a moment was wasted. Playbills were printed and posted up, a stage was erected in the yard at the inn, and the first rehearsal was held. The hectic pace of it all made them think they were back at the Queen's Head.

A new drama by Edmund Hoode was to be given its first performance outside London. *Soldiers of the Cross* had a particular relevance to their venue because it dealt with a crusade and took Richard the Lionheart through a succession of epic battles. Westfield's Men had presented a crusader play before, a novice work by one Roger Bartholomew, an Oxford scholar with misguided aspirations about the theatre. Hoode's work had the mark of a true professional. It was well crafted, lit with fire and passion, and filled with soaring verse. In the play about Robin Hood, the same king had been but a minor character who slipped on near the end to knight the hero. *Soldiers of the Cross* made him central to the action and Firethorn's performance made him tower even more.

Nicholas Bracewell was industrious and watchful. He kept the rehearsal rolling along and noted any faults or omissions along the way. His stagekeepers were given a long list of jobs when it was all over. He worked well into the evening himself then adjourned to the taproom.

Oliver Quilley was sampling the Malmsey.

'Master Bracewell, let me buy you a drink, sir.'

'I cannot stay.'

'But I have not thanked you for finding my horse.'

'There was something else I found.'

Nicholas took out the list from the saddlebag and handed it over. The artist snatched it eagerly from him.

'I see that some names were ticked off, master.'

'Those commissions have been completed.'

'There is a question mark beside one person.'

'Is there?'

'Sir Clarence Marmion.'

'I cannot see it.'

Quilley glanced at the document then folded it up and put it away. An enigmatic smile kept Nicholas at bay. The book holder met his gaze.

'How did you know of Master Pomeroy's arrest?'

'Word travels fast.'

'Only by special messenger.'

'I have my contacts, sir.'

'So I believe.'

The artist gave nothing away. His unruffled calm was a challenge that Nicholas was unable to take up at that point. The book holder had a more pressing commitment and he excused himself. He would return to Oliver Quilley.

Night was taking its first gentle steps towards York as Nicholas shouldered his way through the crowds. Even in the turmoil of their arrival, he had found the time to enquire after other theatre companies. Banbury's Men had reached the city that same day. They were staying at the Three Swans in Fossgate. He went over Ouse Bridge and headed north, picking his way through clamorous streets that he half-remembered from an earlier visit some years before, and listening to the Yorkshire dialects that rang out on every side.

The first thing he saw when he turned into Fossgate was the Merchant Adventurers' Hall, a fine triple-aisled structure with a chapel projecting towards the River Foss. Incorporating brickwork and half-timbering, it was a long, high building that emphasised the prominent place that the Merchant Adventurers took among the fifty guilds of the city. Nicholas was reminded of something that his life in London made him forget. York, too, had its wealth.

The Three Swans was an establishment of medium size

constructed around an undulating yard. Banbury's Men were still rehearsing. Raised voices came from behind the main gates which had been locked to keep out the curious. He went into the inn and bought a tankard of ale, drifting across to a window to get a view of the yard. It was galleried at two levels and he estimated that about four hundred spectators could be crammed in on the morrow. Jerusalem, with its larger yard, had a definite advantage. That would please Lawrence Firethorn.

Light was dying visibly now but the players kept at their work, frantically trying to iron out the myriad problems caused by their damaged prompt book. Nicholas waited until nobody was looking then he slipped up a staircase and through a door. He was now standing on the gallery at the first level and able to see the last of the rehearsal. It was a pastoral romp of indifferent quality and they played it without attack or conviction. Through the gap in the curtains which had been put up in front of their tiring-house, he could see the book holder, holding his head well back from the stench of his text and turning the pages with care.

Giles Randolph took his customary leading role and the other sharers were ranged around him. But look as he might, Nicholas could not find the face he sought above all others. He was still straining his eyes against the gloom when a voice behind him made him turn.

'Have you come to see me, Nick? Here I am.'

The book holder found himself facing a drawn sword and the young man had every intention of using it if the need arose. Even after Richard Honeydew's warning, he was still dumbfounded. Here was the last person on earth that he had expected to meet. Nicholas had watched him being buried in a common grave in London.

It was Gabriel Hawkes.

Chapter Ten

The swordpoint pricked his throat and forced him back against one of the posts that supported the upper tier. Nicholas Bracewell was helpless. He could not move an inch. Behind and below him in the yard was a company of actors engaged in a rehearsal but he could not cry for help. The rapier would rip out his voice in an instant. All that he could do was to watch the man he had once liked and respected so much. There was an additional shock to accommodate. Dangling from his assailant's ear was the jewelled earring which had been thrown into the pit after his corpse. Nicholas gaped.

'You have come back from the dead, sir,' he said.

'It is but an illusion.'

'We saw Gabriel Hawkes being carted away with the other plague victims and tossed into his grave.'

'Your eyes did not deceive you, Nick.'

'Then how can you be here before me now?'

'Because I am not Gabriel,' said the young man. 'My name is Mark Scruton. The poor wretch who died was indeed Gabriel Hawkes. He was a kinsman of mine who had fallen on hard times and been swept into that hideous dwelling in Smorrall Lane. It suited me to take his name and his address while yet living in a sweeter lodging.'

'You were planted on Westfield's Men,' said Nicholas as the truth slowly dawned. 'That memory of yours was used against us. You studied from our prompt books and gave your findings to our rivals.'

'That was the bargain I struck.'

'To betray your fellows?'

'What future did they offer me?' said Scruton with contempt. 'To be a hired man at the beck and call of Master Firethorn? Fed on the scraps of parts that were left over? Employed or dismissed on a whim? There was no future for me, sir! I am a true actor!'

'Your art beguiled me,' admitted Nicholas.

'Banbury's Men held out real promise. In bringing your company low, I earned my right to be a sharer with them. That gives me the status I deserve.' He smiled with self-congratulation. 'Gabriel Hawkes had to vanish before your eyes so that he could reappear as Mark Scruton. My uncle fell sick with the plague but might have lingered a while and so delayed my plans. I helped him on his way to Heaven and spared him certain agony. You saw him taken from his foul bed and trundled off in his winding sheet.'

'Your earring was upon him.'

'It was my parting gift.' He flicked the jewel that now hung from his lobe. 'I have its twin, as you now see.'

Nicholas pieced it all together in his mind.

'You feigned illness in London to prepare us for the shock of your death,' he said. 'Then you travelled with Banbury's Men and advised them how best to damage our enterprise. You snatched Dick Honeydew away then worked with that ostler to steal our costumes.'

'You should not have found either, Nick.'

'It was my duty.'

'And your undoing. You know too much, my friend.'

'Enough to see you hanged for it.'

'Enough to get you killed.'

Scruton lowered the sword and thrust at his heart but Nicholas moved like lightning. Dodging a foot to one side, he let himself fall backwards over the balustrade and somersaulted through the air before landing on his feet in the yard. Blood was oozing from his left arm where the sword had grazed him but the wound was not deep. Pulling out his own rapier, he ran back into the building and up the stairs to do battle on more equal terms but Mark Scruton had not waited for him. Though the book holder searched high and low, he could not find the man anywhere on the premises.

Gabriel Hawkes had disappeared again.

Sir Clarence Marmion sat in his chair without moving a muscle. He was a dignified figure, slim, erect and quite serene, a trifle cold perhaps but carrying his authority lightly. He wore a black doublet, slashed with red and rising to a high neck that was trimmed with a lace ruff. Oliver Quilley scrutinised him with utmost care to find the mind's construction in the face but his subject was yielding little of his inner self. The artist made some preliminary lines on the vellum oval that lay before him on the table. His sitter did not flicker an eyelid. It was an hour before Quilley broke the silence.

'The question of an inscription, Sir Clarence . . .'

'Inscription?'

'Most people require a few words on their portrait to give it meaning or individuality. Sometimes it is a family motto or an expression of love to the intended recipient of the miniature. I have known subjects who called for couplets of verse or even maxims in Greek.'

'That will not be my wish, sir.'

'Then what is?'

'A Latin tag.'

'Speak and it will be penned in.'

'*Dat poena laudata fides.*'

Quilley noted the phrase then furrowed his brow.

'A strange request, Sir Clarence. "Loyalty, though praised, brings sufferings." There is some association here with Marmion Hall?'

'That is not for you to know, Master Quilley.'

'The artist must have insight into everything.'

'Practise your art without more words.'

He returned to his pose and Oliver Quilley worked

on until he had got all he needed from the first sitting. They were in the hall and the master of the house was seated against the far wall, his head framed by one of the gleaming oak panels. As the artist collected up his materials, he threw an admiring glance at the family portraits that hung all around them, noting with especial admiration that of the former Lady Marmion, stately mother of Sir Clarence. Dressed with controlled elegance, she was a gracious figure and prompted an outburst from Quilley.

'The lady looks so fine and dresses so well,' he said. 'Not like the women of the capital. What, sir! You cannot conceive of their monstrous fashions. Some wear doublets with pendant codpieces on the breast, full of jags and cuts, and sleeves of sundry colours. Their galli-gaskins are such as to bear out their bums and make their attire to fit plum around them. Their farthingales and diversely coloured nether stocks of silk, jersey and the like deform their bodies even more. I have met with some of these trulls in London, so disguised that it passed my skill to discern whether they were men or women!'

Coming from a man who minced about in flamboyant apparel himself, the attack had its comical side and Sir Clarence smiled inwardly. He then put a hand into his pocket and took out five gold coins.

'Here's payment for your work, Master Quilley.'

'Wait until I have finished, dear sir.'

'Take it on account.'

'If you insist,' said the other gratefully.

'A labourer is worthy of his hire.'

'An artist raises labour to a higher plane.'

'Did you do that for Master Anthony Rickwood?'

The question flustered Quilley but he soon recovered and answered with a noncommittal smirk, taking the money from his host and putting it quickly into his purse. Sir Clarence rang the small bell that stood on the table and a servant soon entered with a tray. It was the man who had earlier acted as a gaoler to the guest in the cellar. Instead of bearing instruments of torture, he was this time bringing two glasses of fine wine. He waited while the two of them took their first sip.

'You rode here alone, sir?' asked Sir Clarence.

'It was not a long journey,' said Quilley.

'Perils may still lurk.' He indicated a servant. 'Let my man here go back with you to York to ensure that no harm befalls you.'

'I will manage on my own, Sir Clarence. My horse will outrun any that bars my way. I have no fears.'

'You should, sir. These are dangerous times.'

'I will keep my wits about me.'

Sir Clarence excused himself for a moment and left the room with the servant. Quilley did not delay. He moved quickly towards the shelves of books that stood against the far wall. His choice was immediate. He took a small leather-bound volume with a handsome silver clasp on it. Slipping the book into the pouch alongside his artist's materials, he strolled casually across to the window to admire the view. He was still appraising the front garden when his host returned. Sir Clarence was in decisive mood.

'We shall have the second sitting tomorrow.'

'So soon?' said Quilley.

'I am anxious to press ahead with the portrait.'

'An artist may not be rushed, Sir Clarence.'

'Time is not on our side,' said the other. 'We have the visit from Westfield's Men tomorrow. Return with them and bring your belongings from the inn. You shall be a guest under my roof until your work is done.'

'That is most kind. Marmion Hall will offer me a softer lodging than the Trip to Jerusalem, and a safer one as well.' He gave a sly smile. 'The landlord tells me that one of his guests was recently carried off by officers. One Robert Rawlins.'

'I do not know the man.'

'It is just as well, Sir Clarence. He was a priest of the Church of Rome. Any friend of Master Rawlins will be dealt with most severely.'

'That does not concern me,' said the other. 'I am more interested in Westfield's Men. You travelled with them from Nottingham, you say?'

'An eventful journey in every way.'

'It gave you time to befriend them no doubt. Who is in the company, sir? I would know their names.'

'All of them?'

'Down to the meanest wight.'

Quilley reeled off the names and his host listened intently. The visitor was then thanked and shown out.

271

Delighted with his good fortune, he rode off at a canter in the direction of York. Coins jingled in his purse and his patron had hinted at further reward. Then there was the book that nestled in his pouch. He was so caught up with himself that he did not notice the other horseman.

Eleanor Budden knelt in prayer in York Minster and heard confusion. It had all been so simple in Nottingham. One voice had spoken to her with one clear message and she left husband, home and children to obey it. There was no further direction from above. As her knees bussed the hassock in obeisance to God, she waited for a sign that did not come. Her heart gave her one ruling, her head another and her soul a third. It was three days before she would be able to see the Archbishop himself and take his holy counsel. What should she do in the interim?

Had her trip to Jerusalem foundered in York?

She recalled the words of a sermon delivered by Miles Melhuish on the Sunday morning before she left. Keyed into her own situation, it had talked about the character of a true pilgrim and the nature of life itself as a form of pilgrimage. It dealt with the celestial origin of man and of his hope of returning to the realm from which he had been expelled after his fall from grace. The vicar's rotund phrases imprinted themselves on her anew and she was struck by his recital of the symbols of the pilgrim – the shell, the crook or staff, the well of the water-of-salvation, the road and the cloak.

The more she thought about it, the more inescapably

she was led back to Nicholas Bracewell. He had no visible shell or crook but he was both fisherman and shepherd to Westfield's Men, their main provider and their loving protector. She had met him in the River Trent, floating naked on the water-of-salvation. They had followed the road together and, in reclaiming the costume basket, he had found not one but several cloaks. It was all there. In her simple reasoning, the truth now revealed itself. To go on a pilgrimage was to enter a labyrinth in order to understand its mystery. The Centre was not in Jerusalem at all. It was here in York.

Nicholas Bracewell was her destination.

Excited by her discovery, she got to her feet and tripped down the aisle towards the Great West Door. It took her a long time to thread her way through the clogged streets with their happy fairtime atmosphere, but she eventually reached the inn and began the search for him. Nicholas had been given the luxury of a room of his own, albeit only a tiny attic space, and it was here that she cornered him an hour before the performance was due.

Her ardour was matched by his embarrassment.

'I must away, mistress,' he said.

'Hear me but speak first, sir.'

'We play before our audience this afternoon.'

'I ask but two minutes of your time.'

'Very well, then. What would you say?'

Eleanor Budden turned her blue eyes upon him and let them talk for her. In their passion and yearning and holy urgency, he saw images that caused him severe discomfort.

She was a beautiful and seductive presence but she was not for him. He carried Anne Hendrik in his heart and he did not turn aside for any other woman, particularly the estranged wife of a Nottingham lacemaker. Nicholas had great sympathy for her but it did not extend to what she so self-evidently had in mind.

'Let me come to you, master,' she begged.

'It is not appropriate.'

'You are my saviour.'

'I am unworthy of that role.'

'Do but let me warm myself at your flame.'

'You mistake me, mistress.'

'No, good sir. I worship you.'

It took him ten minutes to disentangle himself and he only did that by promising to have a further debate with her that evening. He went swiftly downstairs and tried to dismiss her from his mind. With the performance at hand, he would need all his concentration for that. As he passed a chamber that was shared by some of the hired men of the company, he heard something that made him stop in his tracks and forget all about the threat posed by Mistress Eleanor Budden. Lines of strident verse came through the door. It was the voice of Lawrence Firethorn in full flight as Richard the Lionheart, urging on his troops before their battle against Saladin, stiffening their resolve and making their blood surge.

Though he had heard the speech many times, Nicholas was still transported by it and by the devastating virtuosity with which it was delivered. When the door opened, however, it was not Firethorn who came out from the impromptu rehearsal of his lines.

It was Christopher Millfield.

York was a proud city with a mind of its own and it did not bestow its respect easily. More than one King of England had been turned away from its gates and the Earls of Northumberland, its hereditary overlords, had also met with indifference from time to time. A base for rebels during the Wars of the Roses, it had also been the focal point of the Pilgrimage of Grace, the uprising in 1536 which was directed largely against the dissolution of the monasteries and what were seen as the other dire results of the Reformation. The message of centuries was clear. York could not be taken for granted.

Yet it willingly capitulated to Westfield's Men. Ironically, they came with one of the only two medieval kings who had never visited the city. Richard I made up for that lapse now in the person of Lawrence Firethorn. He was inspirational. Fired by his example, the whole company responded with their best performance for months. *Soldiers of the Cross* flirted with magnificence. It was so enthralling that the hundreds of spectators who were jammed into the Trip to Jerusalem did not dare to blink lest they missed some of the action.

It was not only Richard the Lionheart who thrilled them. In the small but touching role of Berengaria, wife to the great crusader, Richard Honeydew found true pathos. Christopher Millfield was once more a melodic minstrel. Edmund Hoode had written himself a telling scene as a fearless knight who was impaled on an enemy spear and who delivered a lengthy death speech about the glories of the England for which he so readily died. The prominent mention of York itself, cunningly introduced at the last moment, set off a torrent of applause. *Soldiers of the Cross* gave them all this and more, not least some unexpected but quite uproarious comedic touches from Barnaby Gill as a deaf seneschal with a fondness for the dance.

It was the most sensational theatrical event to have come to York for a decade. There was magic in the air as Richard declaimed the closing lines of the drama:

> So in God's service we must find reward
> And satisfaction of our inward souls.
> There lies true gold, all else is but the dross;
> Onward, stout hearts, ye soldiers of the cross!

Prolonged exultation ensued. The city opened its heart to Westfield's Men and cheered them until its throat was hoarse. Struggling actors were treated as famous heroes. Memories of rejection were obliterated beneath joyous acceptance.

This was indeed Jerusalem.

Humphrey Budden heard the roar a mile off and wondered about its source. The closer he got to York, the more desperate he became to see his wife again and take her to him. Sustained by the hope of reconciliation, he had ridden from Nottingham at a reckless pace and was almost as foamed up as his mount. Contrition now ruled him. York was a holy city where all marital wounds might be healed. The sound that reached his ears seemed to have little to do with divine worship but it served its purpose in spurring him on through the final stage of his journey.

His horse flew in through Micklegate. A brief enquiry told him where the company performed and he clattered his way through the streets. When he got to the inn, people were coming out in a tidal wave of happiness and celebration. He tethered his horse, fought against the throng and tumbled into the yard, ending up in the arms of the surprised Nicholas Bracewell.

'Welcome, Master Budden. You come too late, sir.'

'Has Eleanor gone?'

'I spoke of the performance.'

'Where is my wife?'

'Retired to her chamber.'

'Take me to her, Master Bracewell.'

'With all my heart, sir.'

Second thoughts made him pause. Eleanor Budden might not be in a mood to welcome the husband she had so calmly abandoned in Nottingham. Her sights had been set on quite another target and the sweating Humphrey, for all his good intent, might not be able to divert her from it. Nicholas stood back to appraise the man. His height and build were ideal. The florid face could yet be redeemed.

'Come with me, Master Budden.'

'You'll bring me to my wife?'

'In time, sir. In time.'

Blissful congress was also on the mind of King Richard. Exhilarated by his own performance, Lawrence Firethorn was overjoyed with its tumultuous reception and even further delighted by the large bags of money handed over to him by the gatherers. *Soldiers of the Cross* had not merely been an artistic triumph. It had done excellent business. All that remained was for him to order celebration and ride in triumph through the night.

Dozens of beautiful young ladies crowded around him at the inn and offered him favours with fluttering lids. But he already had tenants in line for his bedchamber. Mistress Susan Becket would be first. Though the lady had succumbed wondrously to him at her own tavern, their romps had so far stopped agonisingly short of the ultimate joy. It was one long tale of *coitus interruptus* with the affairs of Westfield's Men coming between them like a naked sword to keep them chaste. All that was now over and he could take her to his heart's content.

But it was not enough. King Richard was lionhearted in love and wanted a dessert to sweeten the taste of the meal. Susan Becket was meat and drink between the sheets but it was Eleanor Budden who was strawberries and cream. His fantasies ran wild. In an ideal world, he would have both together in a shared ecstasy, each one submitting joyfully to his carnal appetites, holiness and whoredom blending into the very epitome of man's desire. Unable to achieve such delight, he settled for a compromise and called one of the boys to him.

'John Tallis!'

'Yes, master?'

'Bid Mistress Becket come unto my chamber.'

'Yes, sir.'

'Then bid the same of Mistress Budden. Tell her I am ready to read psalms to her now.'

John Tallis's lantern dropped open with a thud.

'Are they to come together, sir?'

'The one first and the other an hour later.'

Leaving the apprentice to get on with his work, he went off upstairs to prepare for a night of sensual abandon. He flung open the door of his bedchamber and gazed across at the fourposter which would accommodate his lechery. His laughter died in his throat.

The bed was occupied. Laid out on the coverlet was his second-best cloak. Scattered all over it were bills from his creditors. Defeat stared King Richard in the face. The hostile enemy stepped out from an alcove.

'Lawrence!'

Margery Firethorn had arrived that afternoon. She had not cooled down from the long ride and the steam was still rising from her. She was at her most bellicose.

'You betrayed me, sir!' she howled.

'That is not strictly true, my love . . .'

'Look!' she said, pointing to the bed. 'No sooner did you leave London than the vultures descended on me to pick my bones clean. Your debts have been my ruin, sir. I cannot pay them. Your creditors threaten distraint upon the house itself. We'll all be put out on the street.'

Firethorn recovered with commendable speed.

'Not so, my sweetness,' he said soothingly. 'And have you come all the way to York in your distress? It shall be remedied at once.' He tossed a purse on to the bed. 'There's gold for you, Margery. Enough to pay a hundred bills and still leave something over. By the gods, but it is a miracle to see you again. Come, let me kiss away your worries and ease your pains.'

Though softening, she kept him at arm's length.

'Why did you not write to me, sir?'

'But I did so!' he lied. 'Every day.'

'No letters came to Shoreditch.'

'Belike they passed you on the way.'

'We have been in a parlous state, sir.'

'I sent you love and money to hide my absence,' he said with ringing conviction. 'But how came you here?'

'On horseback.'

'Surely, not alone?'

'Lord Westfield gave me four companions,' she said. 'I turned to him in my plight and he was generous.'

'Too generous!' muttered Firethorn under his breath.

'And did you really send me money?'

'Nick Bracewell will vouch for it!'

Margery Firethorn relaxed. The one man she could trust in the company was the book holder. If he could support her husband's claim then she would be content. Her belligerence was wearing off now and Firethorn noted the fact. He moved in swiftly to seize the initiative.

'Your coming could not have been more timely.'

'Indeed, sir? Why?'

'Because I have a gift for you.'

'Another ring that I may sell if times are hard?'

'Be not so cruel to me, Margery.'

'I want no gifts that are not wholly mine.'

'Take this and see how your husband loves you.'

Margery looked down at the object he put into her hand and felt an upsurge of real joy. It was the work of Oliver Quilley, a masterful portrait in miniature of Lawrence Firethorn that caught his essence with uncanny skill. He had intended to give it to Eleanor Budden by way of blandishment but it now served a more urgent purpose. Margery was quite overcome. He whispered in her ear.

'Can you see the inscription?'

'Where, sir?'

'At the bottom there.'

She read it out with almost girlish breathlessness.

'*Amor omnia vincit.*'

'Love conquers all.'

'Oh, Lawrence!'

His lips sealed his hair-breadth escape. The embrace was interrupted by clumping footsteps on the stairs then Susan Becket sailed in with bold familiarity. Margery bridled at once but her husband was equal even to this emergency.

'Ah, hostess!' he said, snapping his fingers. 'Have a bottle

281

of your finest wine sent up for myself and my wife. Be quick about it, woman!' He killed two birds with one stone. 'And keep that psalm-singing hussy, Mistress Budden, away from me. I'll none of her religion tonight!'

Susan Becket backed out of the room in a daze.

Firethorn had been baulked twice but it would not happen a third time. As his desire surged, he swept Margery off her feet and threw her impulsively on the bed, mounting her at once and riding her hell for leather through a flurry of unpaid bills.

Mistress Eleanor Budden was resting in her chamber when John Tallis brought the request from his master. It was countermanded at once by a visit from Richard Honeydew.

'I have a message for you, mistress.'

'From Master Bracewell, I hope?'

'The same.'

'Well, sir?'

'He bids you call upon him in his room.'

'Heaven has heard my cry!'

'He'll entertain you there.'

The boy withdrew politely. Eleanor Budden began to pant in anticipation. Fulfilment of her dearest wish was now at hand. She loved Nicholas Bracewell and he had sent for her. God had directed them into each other's arms.

She climbed the steps to Jerusalem.

Tapping quietly on the door of his attic room, she opened it to let herself in. He was lying in bed. The curtains were drawn and the place was half-dark but she could see

Nicholas with a clarity that made her heart leap. A small candle burned beside his head, throwing its light on to the fair hair and the glistening beard. As he turned towards her, the sheet pulled away from him and she saw that he was naked.

All the fervour of her spirit prompted her. The pilgrimage ended here. Nicholas Bracewell was her chosen path. She ran towards it and flung herself upon him. He blew out the candle and they merged completely, kissing and twisting and thrusting away until their voices met on a pinnacle of total rapture. Eleanor Budden had never known such deep or divine satisfaction. The pent-up longings of her body and soul had been released in the mystery of the act of love. She was in such a state of languid intoxication that she did not mind when the beard of Nicholas Bracewell came away in her hand or when his wig was nudged awry. She did not even complain when his careful make-up rubbed off on her face. This was the acme of happiness. She was the bride of Christ.

Humphrey Budden was glad that he had come to York.

While the marital reunions were taking place, Nicholas Bracewell was sitting in the taproom with some of the other hired men and enjoying his supper. His attic room would be unavailable to him that night but he did not mind in the least. He could take credit for some skilful stage management which had enabled a wayward wife to find her spiritual goal and a discarded husband to reclaim his happiness. The book holder had more than enough to keep him occupied. *Soldiers of the Cross* had been an undoubted success but it was to be performed again on the morrow under vastly different conditions. He would have to ride over to Marmion Hall at first light to study the indoor playing area and make some preliminary decisions about the method of staging the play. As he half-listened to the idle conversation of his fellows, his mind was firmly fixed on the challenge of the next day.

Edmund Hoode came hurrying across to join him.

'Have you heard the good tidings, Nick?'

'Of what?'

'Banbury's Men.'

'They played at the Three Swans today.'

'They tried to, Nick, but with no success at all. It was some wretched comedy about country wenches and lusty lads. There's a fellow just come in who witnessed this travesty.' Hoode chuckled vengefully. 'He says that it was a downright catastrophe. Lines forgotten, cues missed and every accident that can befall a company in full sight of all. The audience shouted them off the stage. Not even Master Randolph could hold them.'

'This news is wholesome indeed.'

'*Soldiers of the Cross* has put them in the shade.'

'And rightly so, Edmund.'

'It is their just desert for daring to steal my plays. They have been roundly punished.' He gave a sigh. 'Though I would still love to know who played Sicinius. I'll call him a villain to his face if ever we meet.'

'Why did Banbury's Men fare so badly?'

'Because their play lacked quality.'

'There must have been another reason.'

'There was,' said Hoode. 'They missed a leading actor. One of their number dropped out of a crucial role and they could not repair the damage in time. His absence brought them down where they belong.'

Nicholas knew that the missing actor must be Mark Scruton. With his secret exposed, he dare not stay in York to be caught by the book holder. There was another result of his sudden departure. Scruton's wiles had endeared him to Banbury's Men but they would not tolerate his sudden defection. There would be no contract of employment for him, no elevation to the ranks of the sharers. If nothing else, he would not now climb to glory on the backs of Westfield's Men. Consolation could be taken. Nicholas believed they would never see him again.

As soon as he left his lodging, he knew that he was being trailed but he did not quicken his gait. That would have signalled his awareness of his shadow. Sauntering on through the streets of York, he turned down a dark lane at the same casual pace. When he reached the end, he went around the corner and stepped back into the first doorway. Pricking his ears, he could detect the stealthy approach of footsteps in his wake. He unsheathed his dagger and waited.

A stocky figure came around the corner and stood there in dismay when he saw that he had lost his quarry. He scratched his head and looked back down the lane from which he had just emerged. It was the last thing he would ever see. Someone came up silently behind him and put a hand over his mouth. Before he could move a muscle, his throat was cut with practised ease. The man collapsed to the ground in a pool of his own blood. His assailant stayed long enough to bend down and glance briefly at his victim. The Marmion coat of arms was on the dead man's sleeve. It was a timely warning.

Mark Scruton vanished quickly from the scene.

Oliver Quilley sat at the table in his room at the inn and examined the book that he had stolen from Marmion Hall. It was a missal, written in Latin and containing all the rites and ceremonies of the Roman Catholic Church. He was less interested in the contents than in the simple beauty of the volume, rubbing his hands covetously over the smooth leather and watching the silver clasp as it gleamed in the light of his candle. He opened the book to admire the artistry of its printing.

When he had enjoyed his prize long enough, he put it away in his pouch and took out a pack of large cards with bright pictures upon them. After shuffling them with some care, he began to deal them out in a prescribed sequence.

The last card on the table occasioned no surprise.

Oliver Quilley picked it up with a grim smile.

Mistress Susan Becket had a soft heart and it had been wounded by Firethorn's treatment of her. When she sought sympathy, she turned at once to Nicholas Bracewell who listened to her tale with patient understanding. Over a drink in the taproom, she poured out her woes and reached the point where her injuries could only be soothed by one balm. She leaned her head upon his shoulder.

'Take me to my chamber, sir.'

'You are not well, Mistress Becket?'

'Put me to bed and be my physician.'

'That is not possible,' said Nicholas evasively.

'Do not be misled by any false loyalty to Master Firethorn,' she purred. 'He has rejected me and I am free to choose whomsoever I wish.'

She turned her face to smile up to him and her head slipped off his shoulder. He steadied her and looked around. Salvation was standing on the other side of the taproom with obese readiness. Nicholas waved.

'Landlord!'

'Yes, sir?' Lambert Pym came waddling over.

'Mistress Becket needs help to reach her chamber.'

'I'll take her there myself,' he said with alacrity. 'Lean on me, mistress. We'll climb the steps together.'

She accepted the offer and took his podgy arm.

'Why, what strong muscles you have, Master Pym!'

'From a lifetime of shifting barrels.'

'I understand it well,' she said as she was helped up out of the settle. 'I have done my share of such labour. We are two of a kind, sir.'

'I knew it as soon as I beheld you.'

Lambert Pym's heavy-handed gallantry was exactly

what she needed and Nicholas was content. For the second time that night, he had guided an ardent woman into the arms of another man. Susan Becket leaned affectionately on the landlord as they ascended the stairs together. She would soon forget all about the indignity she suffered earlier. Like was calling to like. Both physically and spiritually, she had met her match in Lambert Pym.

'That was craftily done, Nick.'

'The lady is not for me.'

'I saw the reason why in Nottingham. Mistress Anne Hendrik is indeed a handsome woman and worthy of your steadfast behaviour.'

Christopher Millfield had watched it all from his table and come across to join his friend. Nicholas was pleased to have a moment alone with him. Since his meeting with Mark Scruton, he saw how groundless his earlier suspicions of Millfield had been. It was not the latter who had murdered Gabriel Hawkes at all. Remorse made Nicholas feel more warmth for his companion.

The actor was in a teasing mood.

'Which would be the greater ordeal?' he said.

'Ordeal?'

'Mistress Budden or Mistress Becket?'

'I have no curiosity in the matter.'

'One would crucify you and the other crush you.'

'Each has a more fit bedfellow.'

'I never took you for such a coward.'

They laughed together then Nicholas broached a subject he had been keeping to himself for some time.

'Do you know anything of the Tarot?' he said.

'Only that the cards are used as a method of divination. I have seen a pack once but that is all. Why do you ask?'

'I am wondering about Master Quilley.'

'A curious fellow in every particular.'

'According to Mistress Budden, he had a pack of cards with coloured pictures upon them. Could they not be the trump cards of the Tarot?'

'I cannot say, Nick.'

'Does he use them to foretell the future?'

One of the serving wenches came into the taproom and giggled when she saw Millfield. He acknowledged her with a friendly wave then shrugged an apology to Nicholas.

'I have some business to attend to, I fear.'

'One thing before you go,' said the other. 'Mistress Budden levelled an accusation against you.'

'Of what?'

'Atheism.'

Christopher Millfield let out a peel of laughter.

'The woman is absurd!' he said in mocking tones. 'If I were truly an atheist, I would have been arrested long ago. Yet I am still at liberty, as you see.' He went off towards the girl. 'Ask Mistress Budden to explain that.'

Nicholas waited until the couple left the room then he finished his drink. He was mystified. Something in the other's voice had alerted him to a danger but he had no idea what it was. After brooding on it for a while, he gave up and surrendered to a yawn. It was very late and he was tired. Finding himself alone in the taproom, he got up and made his way into the yard in search of a bed for the night. The Whitsuntide fair had filled all the loose boxes with horses but there was promise of some comfort in the hayloft. He climbed the ladder and dropped down on a soft and sweet-smelling bed. Before he could even slip off his shoes, he was asleep.

An hour passed then a noise brought him instantly awake. It was no more than a creak of a door but it took him to the open window. Down below in the yard, creeping silently towards the main gate, was a figure who was already known for his nocturnal wanderings. It was Christopher Millfield and he moved with purpose.

Something prompted Nicholas to follow him. He went swiftly down the ladder and out of the stables. Keeping low and well back, he trailed the other out into the street and over Ouse Bridge. His mind was a turmoil of speculation. Had he been too ready to accept Millfield's friendship? Could the man yet have some sinister intent? The night before the performance at Pomeroy Manor, the actor had gone for his first midnight jaunt. Not long after the performance by Westfield's Men, their host was arrested. Nicholas recalled the list he had found in Quilley's saddlebag. It was Millfield who knew that the names were all those of Roman Catholics.

As his mind raced on, his feet took him on a tortuous route through the streets of York. His quarry seemed to know exactly where he was going. They went up Blake Street and on into Lop Lane before Millfield stopped to knock gently on the door of a small, gabled house. He was admitted within seconds and candlelight soon lit the chamber above. The window was ajar and Nicholas could hear the faint murmur of voices. Whatever conspiracy was going on might be uncovered if he could only get a little closer.

Nicholas looked back to the corner of the street and saw an overhanging gable that was low enough to touch. He went straight back to it. Taking a firm grip, he hauled himself up and started to ascend the wall until he gained the roof. It did not take him long to work his way from house to house until he came to the window he sought. The voices were still too subdued but there was a chink in the curtain as he lowered himself down.

Embarrassment seized him as he peeped in. Here was no conspiracy of any political hue. Christopher Millfield was lying naked on the bed, kissing the young man in his arms with a passion that was its own explanation. Other factors fell into place. Nicholas recalled a flirtatious manner with women that evidently went no further and the interest shown in the actor by Barnaby Gill. He also remembered the speech he had overheard at the inn. It was not just Millfield's vanity that drove him on to learn the leading part in the play. Richard the Lionheart was a hero with whom he had some affinities. Though the world knew and admired him for his military feats, England's most popular monarch was not without flaw. Rumours about his male lovers were too numerous and too detailed to be wholly untrue.

Nicholas swung down from the gable and dropped

to the ground. Unnatural vice was a crime which bore a severe penalty, but he would never have enforced it. He felt slightly disappointed in Millfield but bore him no ill will. The man was entitled to his private pleasures, especially as he was so discreet about them. Nicholas had made an unwarranted intrusion. Chastened and not a little annoyed with himself, he trotted back in the direction of the inn. He needed sleep against the exertions of the morrow and should not be wasting his time in futile eavesdropping on a friend. As he went back over the bridge, he cursed himself for being so misled.

It was then that he spotted the body.

Caught in the moonlight, it was floating face down in the river shallows. He ran to the bank and waded into the water to take hold of the sodden corpse. As soon as he felt the weight of the small body and the quality of the doublet, he knew who the man was.

Master Oliver Quilley.

Nicholas dragged him to the bank and rolled him over on his back. Sightless eyes stared up at him. The handle of a dagger stuck obscenely out of his throat. A deathly pallor was already creeping over the face. But it was the man's right hand which caught the attention. It was wrapped around something as if trying to protect it at all costs. Nicholas had difficulty in prising the fingers apart and taking out the oval of vellum that was to have borne the portrait of Sir Clarence Marmion. Smudged lines could just be made out in the gloom. When Nicholas turned it over, however, he got the real shock.

Quilley had glued the vellum to a picture cut from a Tarot card. It showed a man who dangled from a rope that was tied to his foot. Nicholas recognised the image. It was the Hanged Man. Sometimes the card was called by another name.

The Traitor.

Chapter Eleven

Banbury's Men shuffled about disconsolately in the yard of the Three Swans and loaded up their waggon. After their disgrace the previous afternoon, they were quitting York for good. They had failed abysmally and would be given no further chance to vindicate their reputation. A dignified withdrawal was their only option and Giles Randolph had taken it. As he led his horse out of the stables, he was still seething with anger against the man who had let them down. Having helped to put them firmly in the ascendant, Scruton had brought them crashing down. There would be no position for him as a sharer with the company. Banbury's Men would manage without him from now on. Their future lay in improving their performances of their own plays.

Randolph surveyed his ragged band of players.

'Are we all ready, sirs?'

'Aye,' came the dispirited reply.

'Then let us ride out of this unholy city.'

He mounted his horse and rode towards the main gate. As he was about to go through it, the stately figure of an old man walked in. He wore an elegant black doublet with matching breeches and had a feathered hat swept down to hide half his face. The neat grey beard suggested age and distinction. He carried a cane and lifted it when he saw the horse bearing down on him.

Randolph reined in his mount to let the man pass.

'Good day to you, sir,' he said politely.

'Good day,' said the other. 'Where do you travel?'

'Anywhere to get away from this place.'

'Has York been so unwelcoming to you?'

'A foul prison!'

Giles Randolph urged his horse on and the procession went out through the gate. The old man waved them off as they passed but they paid little attention to him. He gave a wry smile and congratulated himself on the cunning of his disguise. If his fellow-actors did not recognise him, then he was safe from discovery.

Mark Scruton went off into the taproom.

Humphrey Budden and his wife rose early and went straight to York Minster to attend Matins. While still on their knees, they pledged themselves to each other once more and held hands as an act of commitment. Eleanor was a changed woman. The night with her husband had been a revelation. An ineluctable urge brought her to York in the service of God but it had somehow fastened her on to the

296

book holder of Westfield's Men. Whatever the origin of that intense and powerful feeling, it had left her. Jerusalem was no longer a distant target for a pilgrimage. She found it in the arms of her husband and longed for nothing more than to be back with her children in Nottingham.

'Master Bracewell!'

'Good morrow, Mistress Budden. And to you, sir.'

'We wish to thank you most sincerely,' said the husband, clasping him by the hand. 'We will never be able to repay you for your kindness.'

'Your happiness is payment enough, sir.'

They had arrived back at the inn to find Nicholas saddling up a horse in the yard. Eleanor was now a sober matron who hung on her husband's arm though the twinkle in her eye showed that a wistful memory still lingered. Nicholas was glad when the couple went off to collect up their belongings before returning home.

Lawrence Firethorn came hurrying into the yard.

'Nick, dear heart!'

'I am riding out to Marmion Hall.'

'Let me shower you with my gratitude first,' said the other with a bear-like embrace. 'Master Pym told me what happened last night. You lifted the burden of Susan Becket off my back when you played Cupid for her. I need not fear a meeting between her and Margery now.'

'How is Mistress Firethorn this morning?'

'Lying contentedly among my creditors.'

'I am glad that someone found happiness,' said Nicholas. 'My night was taken up with Master Quilley.'

'Poor wretch! It was a gruesome way to depart this life. Do they have any idea who might have murdered him?'

'None, sir. I am just relieved that they no longer think that I may be the culprit. The officers and the magistrate questioned me for hours.'

'I spoke up for you, Nick. My voice has weight.'

'Your help was much appreciated.'

Nicholas put a foot in the stirrup and mounted the horse. His mind was still playing with all the questions that the death of Oliver Quilley had opened up. He looked down at his employer and remembered something. Lawrence Firethorn was the finest actor in London and the nobility came in droves to watch him. He was well-acquainted with those at Court and party to much of their gossip.

'May I ask you a question, sir?'

'A hundred, if it pleases you.'

'What is your view of Mr Secretary Walsingham?'

'Pah!' exclaimed Firethorn. 'I spit upon him.'

'Why so?'

'Because he is linked to the name I detest most.'

'In what way, master?'

'Do you not know?'

'Why then would I ask?'

'Sir Francis Walsingham is now Secretary of State and our dear Queen has heaped every honour upon him that it is possible to have.' Firethorn curled his lip. 'But I remember how he began his great political career.'

'As a member of Parliament was it not?'

'Shall I tell you the town for which he sat?'

'I think I can guess.'

'Banbury!'

Marmion Hall that morning was in the grip of a deep sorrow. Sir Clarence put on a brave face in front of his family and his servants but they sensed what hung over them and it introduced a sombre air. The arrest of Robert Rawlins had been a devastating blow and they were still reeling from it. There was an additional setback for Sir Clarence. The man whom he had dispatched to York had been killed by his own intended victim. It was very alarming. The informer who had betrayed both of the accomplices was now closing in on Sir Clarence himself. Instant flight could be necessary. Preparations were made.

'Is everything in order?'

'Yes, Sir Clarence.'

'Keep a horse saddled and ready.'

'It is all in hand.'

'You will ride with me.'

'That will be an honour, Sir Clarence.'

The servant bowed humbly then moved off about his duties. His master hoped that the emergency would not arise but could not rule it out. After occupying Marmion Hall with such pride for so many generations, the family now faced a tragic possibility. The incumbent head of the house might be chased out of it like a rat.

There was one small compensation. Westfield's Men were visiting them that day and they might help to lift the veil of sadness, even to allow them a few hours of harmless pleasure. Sir Clarence knew of the company's work in London and had selected the play from their repertoire that would be most apposite. It was the same drama which had thrilled the spectators at the inn.

Soldiers of the Cross. It appealed to him because it sounded so many chords. He believed that he was engaged in another form of crusade.

Sir Clarence was in the hall to welcome Nicholas Bracewell when the latter arrived. The book holder was fatigued and explained what had kept him up most of the night. His host was dismayed.

'Master Quilley dead?'

'Murdered, sir.'

'Has the villain been apprehended?'

'Not yet, Sir Clarence.'

'This is bleak intelligence.'

'The fellow was amusing company.'

'That is what I found.'

'I believe that you commissioned him.'

'Master Quilley was to have painted my portrait. I wanted it quickly so that I could present it as a gift to my wife.' He looked up balefully at the oil painting of his father. 'I have not the time to wait for something of this order. Oliver Quilley was my only hope.'

'There are other limners for hire.'

'He came by special recommendation.'

Nicholas tried to pursue the subject but his host dismissed it with a wave of his hand, preferring instead to talk about the play and its mode of presentation. He was clearly knowledgeable about the theatre and had visited the playhouses during his occasional visits to London. It was a treat to discuss drama with him and it served to brighten his manner immeasurably. Nicholas soon decided that the stage would be erected at the far end of the hall. A panelled door opened into a room that could be used as the tiring-house. Curtains could be rigged up on a rail. Large windows let in a fair amount of light but it would need to be supplemented by candles and tapers.

While the book holder continued to work out the logistics of performance, Sir Clarence gave orders to his servants and rows of chairs were brought into the hall. Standees in abundance had watched the play at the inn but all the guests would be seated here. There would be far less sweat, swearing and jostling and a lot more refinement. At the personal invitation of Sir Clarence Marmion, all the gentry of the West Riding were coming that afternoon. It would be a select audience.

A large gilt armchair was brought in and placed at the end of the front row, directly beneath the portrait of the host's father. Evidently, it was Sir Clarence's own chair for he tried it out and glanced over at the stage. Nicholas could not understand why the master of the house did not occupy a prime position in the centre of the row. It seemed perverse to place himself at such an angle to the action of the play.

When all the arrangements were made, Nicholas was given refreshment then left alone to await the arrival of the company. He took the opportunity to stroll outside in

301

the sunshine and admire the magnificent formal gardens. One outcrop of rhododendrons claimed his attention. They were a hundred yards or more from the house and trained into a small circle. What intrigued him was the fact that the bushes were moving about as if blown by a minor gale and yet there was no breeze at all.

Shielded by an avenue of yews, Nicholas made his way towards the rhododendrons. They were still now but a noise told him what might have caused the movement. He was hoping to confirm his theory when a thickset man stepped out to block his way.

'This part of the garden is out of bounds, sir.'

'I was merely stretching my legs.'

'Stretch them in another direction.'

'I will.'

'Sir Clarence has given strict order.'

As he headed back towards the house, Nicholas asked himself why such privacy was maintained. Something else puzzled him as well. The man had the clothes and the bearing of a gardener yet he wore a dagger at his belt.

Why did he need to be armed?

Lawrence Firethorn arrived with his company to take possession of a new part of his empire. Having conquered York in such style, he was sure that he could score another victory at Marmion Hall. The complete change of performing conditions stimulated him and he took up the challenge at once, strutting about to get the feel of the stage and throwing his voice at the walls to test the acoustics. A rehearsal was called and everything was set up at speed. The company used the occasion to shake off some of the hangovers from the excesses of the previous night. Firethorn, by contrast, was brimming with energy. Hours of marital reunion had simply invigorated him.

Food and beer were provided by their host and they spent a pleasant hour in rest. The actor-manager stood aside with Edmund Hoode and Barnaby Gill.

'I like the feel of this place!' he said.

'We have not come here to grope it,' observed Gill drily. 'Save yourself for Margery.'

'I sense that something extraordinary will happen.'

'You will remember all your lines?'

'Take care, Barnaby. Do not try me, sir.'

'I wish I could share your optimism, Lawrence,' said Hoode gloomily. 'Marmion Hall feels oppressive to me. As for extraordinary events, one has already occurred.'

'Yes,' agreed Gill. 'We were paid yesterday.'

'I was talking about Master Quilley.'

'Do not remind us, Edmund,' sighed Firethorn. 'It was a tragedy of the first degree but it must not be allowed to blight our work. Master Quilley was but a traveller who rode along the way with us. His death is shocking but it does not directly affect us.'

'We cannot shrug it off like that, Lawrence.'

'We must. We are players, sir.'

Hoode argued for compassion but the others were too caught up in the performance that lay ahead to accord the dead man more than a token pity. When the playwright went on to suggest that the murder might somehow be linked to Westfield's Men, they ridiculed the idea at once. He was still trying to argue his case when Nicholas came up.

'It is time to prepare ourselves, gentlemen.'

'We are always prepared,' said Gill petulantly.

'Our audience is starting to arrive.'

'Then I must get into my costume,' decided Hoode.

He and Gill drifted off to the other side of the tiring-house but Nicholas detained his employer for a quiet word.

'We have a slight problem, sir.'

'Nothing that cannot be surmounted.'

'Christopher Millfield is nowhere to be found.'

'The man was right here but five minutes ago.'

'Ten,' corrected Nicholas. 'He is not here now.'

'Then he has gone outside to look upon the hedge.'

'Nobody was to leave the room unless they spoke to me first. Master Millfield ignored that ruling.'

'Then reprimand him, Nick.'

'I will when we can find him.'

'Send George Dart out on patrol.'

'I did that,' said Nicholas. 'He searched house and garden thoroughly but came back empty-handed. That is why we have a problem, sir. Master Millfield has disappeared.'

Mark Scruton waited in the shadow of a copse until he saw a dozen riders canter past on the road to Marmion Hall. He spurred his horse and came out from his cover. It did not take him long to attach himself to the rear of the other

304

guests. When they turned into the long drive that led up to the house, he could see other people being shown in by servants. There was enough commotion for him to mingle with the crowd. When a female rider turned to appraise him, he touched his hat graciously. A coach was trundling up behind them now and fresh hooves could be heard back in the distance.

Scruton dismounted and a servant took care of his horse. The actor walked with an upright gait, leaning on his cane for support. He was part of a crowd that swept in through the main door of the house. Waiting to greet them in the entrance hall was Sir Clarence Marmion and his wife, both attired in their finery for the occasion.

Giving them a false name and a confident smile, the old man with the grey beard withstood their scrutiny without a flicker of concern. Host and hostess bestowed a welcome on the next influx of guests.

The first test was over and he had come through it with perfect aplomb. Mark Scruton was in. It was now only a question of biding his time.

Christopher Millfield returned ten minutes before the play began and faced a tirade from Lawrence Firethorn and a stern reproach from Nicholas Bracewell. He apologised profusely and claimed that he had got lost in the garden but the book holder did not entirely believe him. With the performance at hand, however, Nicholas was in no position to press him on the matter. He did his rounds and made a final check before taking up his position behind the curtains. It enabled him to see most of the stage and a little of the audience. He was in time to watch Sir Clarence filing into his seat beside his wife and family. Directly behind the host was a distinguished old man in a black doublet and breeches. As the guest scratched his grey beard, Nicholas had a sense of knowing the man but he could not put a name to the face. Nor did he have any time for reflection. Audience and actors were ready. The book holder gave the signal to begin.

A trumpet sounded and the Prologue was spoken by Edmund Hoode in shining armour. Music played and the action commenced. It never ceased for a second. Westfield's Men adapted their style superbly to the conditions and to the spectators, working on both to get maximum return. Their audience was much quieter than at the inn but their concentration did not waver.

The seneschal made them laugh, Berengaria made them sigh, the impaled crusader made them weep and King Richard himself made them proud to be English and Christian. The performance by Lawrence Firethorn touched the heights and swept everyone away, including Sir Clarence himself who was patently enraptured. As the play moved into its final gripping climax, Nicholas stole a glance at their host and saw something that he had missed before. The old man who sat behind Sir Clarence was wearing a familiar earring. A brilliant disguise was spoiled by an actor's vanity.

Alarums and excursions brought the stage battle to a close and Firethorn delivered his address to the troops in his most compelling vein. He was calling them to arms in the service of the Lord when the main door of the hall opened and they poured in. At first, the audience thought that the intrusion was part of the play and they marvelled at the number of extras who had been dressed in uniform and armed, but they soon saw that the newcomers were the real thing.

Sir Clarence Marmion was ahead of them. Darting out of his seat, he clicked open the secret door in the oak panelling and dived through it. The old man went after him with astonishing sprightliness and got to the door before it closed. As he went through the aperture, he shut the door behind him. Nicholas observed it all and now understood why his host had taken the seat at the end of the row. He was right next to his escape route.

There was complete chaos in the hall as guests stood up to protest and soldiers pushed them roughly aside in their search. Firethorn finished his concluding speech but the play was already over. The real drama was now taking place elsewhere. Nicholas Bracewell was off at full pelt. Guided by instinct, he went out into the garden and sprinted along the avenue of yews. If the secret panel was a means of escape then there had to be an exit somewhere outside. He believed he knew where it was.

He reached the circle of rhododendron bushes and went through a gap in the foliage. What he had heard earlier was the whinny of a horse and he found two of them tethered to a post. Behind them lay a man in the Marmion livery with blood gushing from a wound in his chest. Nicholas stepped over the corpse to the thickest part of the bushes and pulled them back. A small door was revealed, cleverly set in a mound that was screened by foliage. He opened it and went in, finding himself in an underground passage that was lit at intervals by a few guttering candles. There was a pervading smell of damp and decay.

Abandoning all caution, Nicholas went blundering off down the tunnel at full speed. He felt certain that the explanation of all the mystery lay at the far end of the passage and he ran furiously towards the truth. His dash was far too reckless and he soon came to grief, tripping on some loose stones and pitching forward to strike his head on a small boulder. Dazed and hurt, he spat out a mouthful of earth then felt the blood that was running down his face from the gash in his temple. As he pulled himself slowly upright, he became aware of the danger he was in. Nicholas was completely unarmed.

It was not just Sir Clarence and Mark Scruton who posed a problem. Evidently, someone had entered the tunnel before him and the corpse in the rhododendrons bore ugly witness to the man's sense of purpose. Nicholas had to be more circumspect, especially as the passage ahead of him was in complete darkness. He crept along with the utmost care and caught the faint whiff of burning tallow. The candles in this section of the tunnel had just been extinguished. It put him even more on his guard.

Feeling his way along, he discovered how many spiders and insects had made their homes down there. When he felt something brush against his ankle, he stepped back in horror then heard the telltale patter behind him. It was a large rat. He was grateful that Richard Honeydew was not with him. Straining his eyes against the blackness, he inched his way along, finding the tunnel more and more oppressive. Its walls narrowed and his sense of being imprisoned became more acute. Something else troubled him and he lashed out with an arm.

'Who's there?' he called.

There was no answer but he knew he was not alone.

Sounds of a struggle came from up ahead and he heard Sir Clarence yell with rage. It forced him into a run that had him virtually bouncing off the walls as he hared along. Light surrounded a steel door ahead of him. He flung it open to find himself in a tiny chapel. Two men were locked in a desperate struggle.

Sir Clarence Marmion grappled with the old man who had pursued him and tore off his false beard. Mark Scruton tried to shake himself free and use his dagger. Before Nicholas could intercede, the actor seized the advantage. Getting a firm grip on his adversary, he threw him hard against the stone wall. Sir Clarence's head made contact with solid granite and he subsided to the floor with a groan, lapsing at once into unconsciousness. Mark Scruton stood over him then he swung around to confront the intruder. He began to circle Nicholas with his dagger at the ready.

'You have followed me once too often, Nick.'

'I had not thought to see you again.'

'It will be the last time.'

He made a pass with his weapon but the book holder

eluded its point with ease. The actor laughed.

'This was not your fight,' he said. 'It had nothing to do with you, Nick. You should have kept out.'

'Villainy must not go unchecked.'

'You know too much for your own good yet not nearly enough to understand the truth.'

'I know that you are Walsingham's man.'

'I was,' conceded the other. 'Until today, I was. It should have ended here at Marmion Hall. I gave them Rickwood. I gave them Pomeroy. This was to be my last employment as a spy. I would have been free to follow my real profession in the theatre.'

'You are no actor, sir,' said Nicholas with contempt.

'I was skilful enough to fool you,' reminded the other. 'What is spying but a form of acting? I was a master of my art.' His eyes narrowed. 'Then you came along and ruined my plans. Because you escaped me at the Three Swans, I had to run away from the company. They will never accept me as a sharer now.'

'Then I have done them a favour.'

Scruton jabbed with the dagger again but Nicholas was too nimble for him. The actor continued to circle his man and look for an opening. Nicholas stayed on the alert and tried to keep him talking.

'You betrayed your fellows,' he accused.

'It was needful.'

'But quite unforgivable.' He hazarded a guess. 'And you murdered Oliver Quilley.'

'I had to. He had told me all he could.'

'About what?'

'Marmion Hall. I used him as my eyes. He got in here and saw what I needed to know. When I had persuaded him to part with the information, I closed his eyes for good.' Scruton grinned. 'He was a scurvy painter and will not be missed.'

'You will be arraigned for his killing.'

'No, sir. I have friends in high places.'

Scruton made a sudden move and thrust hard with his dagger but Nicholas grabbed his wrist. They wrestled back against one of the pews and threshed about wildly for the best part of a minute. Nicholas managed to twist the weapon out of the other's hand and it fell to the floor with a clatter. Mark Scruton was enraged. With a fresh burst of energy, he flung the book holder back against the altar rail and got his hands on his throat. Nicholas was slowly being strangled.

So absorbed were they in their fight that they did not observe the figure who slipped in through the steel door nor did they see the gold crucifix being removed from the altar. Nicholas was in distress. A steel band was around his neck and it got tighter by the second. Scruton was a blurred object before his eyes. Making a last supreme effort, he grabbed his opponent by the arms and threw him violently away. Scruton went back a few yards. They were the last steps he would ever take. Before he could move in again, his skull was smashed open by one vicious blow from the crucifix and his brains spattered the white cloth of the altar. Having spent so much time betraying Roman Catholics, he had now been cut down by a symbol of their faith.

Christopher Millfield looked down at the corpse then threw the crucifix away. Banging sounds from above warned that the soldiers would soon find their way into the secret passage. Millfield did not seem perturbed. He flashed a smile at the panting Nicholas.

'You were right to suspect me.'

'Another of Walsingham's men?'

'Yes, Nick, but of a different order from this fool.' He kicked the dead body. 'Scruton had served his purpose as a spy. Such people have no further use. My job is to pay them off and send them on their way.'

'You have a brutal livelihood, sir.'

'It is well-paid and very well protected.'

Nicholas rubbed his throat and looked around at the scene of carnage. Mark Scruton lay dead, Sir Clarence Marmion was in a coma and the chapel had been wrecked by the force of the violence. He finally began to understand the steps which had led to this grim ending. Revulsion against Christopher Millfield stirred in his stomach but he had the grace to offer a grudging compliment.

'I should have listened to you, sir.'

'When?'

'When you told me you were the finer actor.'

Millfield was still beaming as soldiers rushed in.

It was a day of departures. Banbury's Men had already slunk away with their tails between their legs. Sir Clarence went off to London under armed guard. With her ruffled feathers now smoothed, Susan Becket returned to her own hostelry. Humphrey and Eleanor Budden went home to a new life in Nottingham. In the company of four liveried servants, Margery Firethorn rode back to Shoreditch to pay some bills and count the days until her husband's return. Mark Scruton joined Gabriel Hawkes in the grave. Christopher Millfield went off to terminate the careers of other spies on behalf of Walsingham.

Westfield's Men were to stay on for a few days in York. Their success at the inn brought in requests for further performances and they were to offer other delights from their repertoire. It was an immense comfort to know that their plays were once again their exclusive property. The man who had most cause to be pleased was instead subdued and withdrawn.

Nicholas Bracewell sought him out in the taproom.

'Be of good cheer, Edmund. Our troubles are over.'

'They leave much sadness in their wake.'

'We must strive to put it behind us.'

'I have done so,' said Hoode gloomily, 'but my mind is fixed on misery. I liked them both, you see, Christopher and young Gabriel, as I took him to be. I trusted them.'

'We were all taken in,' admitted Nicholas. 'Nobody more completely than me. I feel humbled by it all. I should have listened to Mistress Budden.'

'Did she throw light on these dark deeds?'

'She did, Edmund. That good lady warned me about Master Millfield. She told me that he was an atheist.'

'Was he so?'

'No Christian would use a crucifix to commit a murder. He is a godless man in every sense. And now I realise why he has escaped the law.'

'He hides behind Sir Francis Walsingham.'

'Indeed, sir.'

Hoode put a congratulatory hand on his friend's arm.

'Take heart, Nick,' he said. 'You can still be proud of your part in this business.'

'Can I?'

'You found that tunnel to the secret chapel.'

'I stumbled on it by accident. Master Millfield knew where to look and found it by design. That is why he disappeared after the rehearsal. He was conducting a search.'

Hoode sighed. 'Sir Clarence was a traitor and I am glad that he has been called to account but it grieves me that our company was used as a cloak for so much deception.'

'It has been rooted out now.'

'Let us hope so. I do not want another play of mine to be ruined by the arrival of soldiers. Which of those spies called them to Marmion Hall? Scruton or Millfield?'

'Neither, Edmund.'

'Then who, sir?'

'Master Oliver Quilley.'

'But how?'

'From beyond the grave,' said Nicholas. 'He was no spy but a disappointed artist who felt he was never paid his worth. He exacted further payment from the great houses where he worked by stealing things and selling them for gain. Master Quilley brought a book from Marmion Hall because its silver clasp promised a good price. They found it in his room. The book was a Roman Catholic missal.'

'And that led to the arrest of Sir Clarence.'

It was a last ironic twist to the whole affair. They shared a drink and Nicholas did his best to cheer his friend up but Hoode was still gripped by dejection. One question still tormented him.

'Sicinius . . .'

'Who, Edmund?'

'Sicinius.'

'Ah, your play.'

'I still do not know who stole my part, Nick.'

'Is it that important to you?'

'I would give anything to learn his name.'

'Then let me put you out of your pain,' said the book holder. 'I made enquiry about the performance by Banbury's Men of *Pompey the Great*.'

'Well? Well?'

'Your play was much admired in spite of their poor treatment of it.'

'And Sicinius? My Sicinius?'

'Gabriel Hawkes.'

'But he is dead.'

'Along with Mark Scruton.' He patted Hoode on the back. 'Be happy, sir. Do you not see what this means?'

'No.'

'You are the only man alive to have played Sicinius. The part is solely and wholly yours again.'

Edmund Hoode let out a whoop of joy.

315

'Thank you, Nick. This puts me in Heaven.'

'Close enough to it.'

'What?'

'Jerusalem.'

The playwright's smile widened into a broad grin.

A spiritual journey had finally come to an end.

If you enjoyed *The Trip to Jerusalem*, read on to find out about more books by Edward Marston . . .

To discover more great fiction and to place an order visit our website at **www.allisonandbusby.com** or call us on 020 7580 1080

ALSO BY EDWARD MARSTON

THE RAILWAY DETECTIVE SERIES

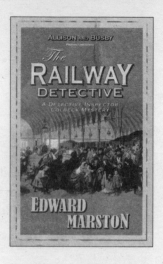

The Railway Detective
The Excursion Train
The Railway Viaduct
The Iron Horse
Murder on the Brighton Express
The Silver Locomotive Mystery
Railway to the Grave
Blood on the Line
The Stationmaster's Farewell

The Railway Detective Omnibus:
The Railway Detective - The Excursion Train - The Railway Viaduct

>o◇o<

'Historical crime writing of the first order . . .
compulsive reading'
Good Book Guide

THE RESTORATION SERIES

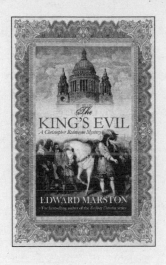

The King's Evil
The Amorous Nightingale
The Repentant Rake
The Frost Fair
The Parliament House
The Painted Lady

⊃o⋉oⵉ

'Marston continues to supply a superior brand
of historical mystery'
Books International